Which Life?
Land or Sea

Melina Douglas

Library and Archives Canada Cataloguing in Publication

Cataloguing data available through Library and Archives Canada

ISBN 978-1-55483-981-0

To my football buddies in Grade 8.
Thanks for all the good times.
Big shout out to Vanitia, Meghan,
Chelsea, Eric and Cole

*A percentage of the proceeds of each book will go to
One Village One World*

Table of Contents

CHAPTER 1

Silly Notions

"It's the bottom of the ninth. Two out and the bases are loaded! Last up to bat is the Bronx Bombers very own Felicity O'Connor and the crowd is going wild," blared the announcer above the roar of the crowd.

"This rookie has really been a spark plug this season, Bill."

"She sure has, Reggie. O'Connor has been with the Bombers for only a year now and has managed to turn this team around! Now they've come to win it all today at the World Series."

"A winning run would complete the list of incredible accomplishments this young woman has achieved this season."

"No doubt, she's the first woman *ever* to play in the major leagues. Looks like the manager took a risk and it paid off."

"That's right, Reggie. He got his gold at the end of the rainbow. Couldn't we all use a little bit of the luck he's been getting lately?"

An anxious hush falls over the crowd. This last batter could end the season. "O'Connor's outside the batter's box staring down Contreras."

"And here she comes, stepping up to the plate to break the five-five tie. Warming up the ball, ready to pitch is none other than Juan Contreras. The Sox paid handsomely for Contreras. They call him the King of Diamonds, Bill. And he's being paid like a king, signing a three-year deal for $64,000,000."

"I can see why. He has a wicked fastball topping 101 mph that has put many teams away for the season."

The field is nothing but a sea of green as I step up to the plate with my lucky bat. The dirt shifts beneath my feet as the sun beats down against my skin. I tune out the "Take Me Out to the Ball Game" music and the crowd's chatter. I can smell the hot dogs and popcorn wafting from the vendors above. This is it, my moment to shine. I feel the weight of every female baseball player in the world settle on my shoulders. I position myself in the batter's box, eager to hit the ball, eager to prove myself. I scan the outfield with a batter's eye spotting Sweeny, Smith and Anderson in the outfield with Terrero positioned at shortstop.

I remember my first home game on this field. My first at-bat in major league baseball was a pop fly. If that wasn't embarrassing enough, I smacked myself in the face with the bat and had a black eye for weeks. It seems like so long ago. No one laughs at me anymore, especially when I tomahawk the ball.

Konerko on first base could be an issue. I *have* to make sure the ball doesn't get anywhere near him. I wasn't about to make that mistake twice. Richard on second base has never dropped a ball under pressure. Slip one by him and I'm home free. Ozuna is a tricky one on third base. He's unpredictable. I let out a deep breath. I haven't been this nervous since I began practicing with the Bombers. My hands tighten their hold on the bat as I reposition myself and adjust my helmet. Sweat trickles down my back. Soon, all they will see is the back of my jersey, number 21 etched in their minds forever.

"Here comes the pitch."

The crowd is silent. All eyes are on Contreras as he winds up and delivers a textbook slider.

"Striiiiike one!"

"Tough break for O'Connor, Bill. What a whiff, she's going all out in this cracker box."

"Could the pressure finally be getting to her, Reggie? Contreras has been a thorn in her side since the Sox picked him up. Seems like bad blood between the two."

"O'Connor shakes it off and settles back into her unorthodox slouch. Juan has the ball in his mitt, his cannon of an arm at the ready, searching out home plate to throw the red and white leather."

The crowd is on the edge of their seats. Time seems to come to a standstill.

"And here comes the pitch. And it's..."

Beep. Beep. Beep. Beep.

Reluctantly, I woke up and rolled over with a groan, grabbed the alarm clock and threw it against the wall where it smashed into smithereens. "Damn," I thought. "That's the second one this week." I rolled over and buried myself deeper into the feather comforter and drifted back into Neverland.

I felt someone prod me awake. Unfortunately, I am not the nicest person in the morning. "Hey, sport! Time to get up, it's seven o'clock," Dad spouted cheerfully, his blue eyes twinkling and his ink black hair perfectly combed.

"Dad, has it *ever* occurred to you that not *everyone* takes an hour to get ready, unlike the freaks in the next room?" I growled.

"Aw, Felicity, don't be such a grump. Your sisters are harmless." He poked me in the shoulder, keeping his distance in case I attacked him. I noticed he was already dressed in his lawyer suit. "Come on kiddo, you have to get up!" He walked over and pulled back an avalanche of blankets. Dad "*tsk-tsked*" when he saw the clock, "So, another one bites the dust?"

"No, a little green leprechaun flew in and saved me the trouble," I said sarcastically.

He let out a long sigh. "Don't make me come back with a bucket of ice water."

I ignored the threat and reburied myself into my cocoon of blankets. "Dad, there has *got* to be more to life than going to school, coming home, doing homework, watching T.V. and then going to bed. You want to know what the greatest part of it is? You get to do it all over again the next day. Then, after school's done, it's replaced with work and then you die, Dad. YOU DIE! What a waste of a life. Don't you get sick of the same routine? There has to be more to life than this."

Dad sat down on the edge of my bed and listened to my rumblings. "I know, but that's life, Squirt. It can't be all fairy tales and dragons. You've mentioned this numerous times but, without an education, you will get nowhere. Honestly, Felicity. Without work, how do you expect to amount to anything in life? You have to grow up sometime and take responsibility."

"Taking parenting lessons from Mom, I see," I said bitterly, more of a statement than a question. I wasn't exactly thrilled to be lectured before noon. This was not one of my favourite subjects.

He chuckled, "Life will be what it will be but, at the moment, let's just concentrate on getting those grades up in school, eh? You will find that life will be a routine and that is something that cannot be helped, but it is only boring if you make it boring."

I muttered something unintelligible and agreed to get up as Dad closed the door on me. Passing the full-length mirror wearing nothing but my black and grey camouflage boxer shorts and a Habs hockey jersey, I headed into my en-suite bathroom. I loaded up on the toothpaste and began to brush my teeth with intensity. The problem with me was once I was awake I could never get back to sleep. People wonder why I'm so acidic in the morning.

My eyes strayed to my recently renovated bedroom, a place that still felt foreign to me. It had a bit too much pizzazz for my liking but once the interior decorator found out I liked fantasy, let's just say she went a little overboard. I spit out the toothpaste and washed my face with disgust. All this had happened a week ago and now I had a mythically enchanted forest in my bedroom. It no longer felt like it was mine.

I eyed the big mural covering the whole wall across from my bed, filled with unicorns galloping across a field as a red dragon soared in the sky above with two unicorns clutched in each claw and winged horses attacking the dragon with their hooves. Vines spiraled up the posts of my canopy bed.

My window was festooned with crystal sun catchers sending a kaleidoscope of rainbows bouncing off the other walls in the morning. Adjacent to that, a full-size hammock was in the corner surrounded by silk trees, fake flowers and vines hanging from the ceiling. Fairies and dragons popped up at random and a mini-waterfall sat in the corner with a few goldfish swimming in the bottom. At the flick of a switch, my ceiling became a starry sky. Not to mention the huge dolphin-shaped faucets spouting water into my bathtub, with the dolphin's mouth being the spout and the tail ends the handles. My computer and computer desk sat in one corner not far from the bathroom door where two big bookcases were filled with novels that I had collected over the years, along with knickknacks littering the shelves. I mused over the lack of décor in that area. *Heaven forbid that I neglected my studies.*

It was neat and creative, I had to admit, but it was going to take a little getting used to. The word overkill comes to mind when I looked at my room. I was thankful for the change, I suppose, but my parents didn't even ask me if I wanted this change. No, they did not and you want to know why? Because they are incredibly immature, that's why!

This wasn't about me and my so-called "pigpen" needing an upgrade. This was about my parent's personal vendetta against our neighbours, the Darnels. How did this little war begin? I have no clue. Maybe it started the first day the Darnels moved to Lakewood or the fact that the annual neighbourhood Valley Grove subdivision cookout was held in the Darnel's backyard. The neighborhood cookout for the past 12 years had been held at the O'Connor's. You do not break a 12-year tradition and expect to get away with it! It doesn't help that their home won "Best House of the Year" three years running and got on the cover of *Lakewood* magazine, something my Mom has made a lifelong ambition to do.

Both families try to make quite an impression during holiday seasons with each year more outlandish and competitive than the previous one. Even at Easter, it looks like a piñata exploded all over our front yard with spring colours. The lengths my parents and the Darnels go to are borderline crazy. Which brings me back to why my room has just been remodeled; the Darnels have a daughter, Alex, and she just had her room redone by a professional designer. Alex is an only child and goes to the best private Ivy League school. She asked Santa for a pony and woke up to one in her backyard. My sisters asked for a pony the same year and got a stuffed one. They both cried as they watched Alex ride her pony around the front yard. My sisters still harboured vengeful feelings. I don't think they will ever forgive her. In a nutshell, everything they do, we must do better. It's all one big competition, hence the new bedroom update.

Sometimes, it seems like my parents think the most important things in life are poise, elegance, vanity and their reputations. The sparks that fly between the Darnels and them only heighten their arrogance when victory is achieved and noticed by the community. My family's status has put me in a position where I am portrayed as someone I am not. Not to say I haven't gotten into my fair share of action where the Darnels are concerned. The feud can get contagious sometimes.

"Felicity!" Mom screamed at the bottom of the stairs.

"Coming!" I yelled, snapping back to the present. I still

wasn't dressed.

I yanked on a pair of hip hugger jeans, getting my feet stuck in the holes hanging about my knees (most of my jeans were filled with holes on account of my loathsome attitude towards shopping).

"Stupid jeans," I muttered, looking about the room. I found a black top and picked it up off the floor. I smelled it and figured it could handle one more day of use and threw it over my head. I ran to my mirror and thanked God for straight hair. I flattened my blonde hair with my hands, threw on my Bronx Bombers ball cap and snatched my black leather jacket off the chair. I grabbed my backpack and sighed regretfully as I took one last look at my bedroom before racing down the carpeted stairs to the kitchen.

CHAPTER 2

Family Business

I was hit full force by the sweet aroma of maple syrup and pancakes. I wasn't even down the stairs yet and my mouth was watering. I guess those are the perks of having a five-star cook in the family.

I stepped into the light blue kitchen. The window above the sink showed a pink sky as the family greeted me with the usual sleepy good mornings. My Mom, April, was busy in her immaculate kitchen. She was of medium height on the plump side with long curly black hair, big brown eyes with Obsessive Compulsive Disorder running through her blood. I didn't know how I was ever going to measure up to her. I can't even bake cookies without burning them.

I plopped down on the opposite side of the table while I watched the freaks eat their pancakes. My sister, Faith, was talking about how Ernie Johnson was strapped to a pole and left beside the railway tracks for initiation. It was the eighth time this year. The cops found him at the end of the day screaming for help after school. "I never thought grade nine would be this exciting; it's flying by. Hard to believe it's already May," interrupted my other sister, Anna Bell, much to my irritation as she spoke with a mouthful of food.

"Thank God," I mumbled. "I was beginning to think time had stopped moving. One more leech-sucking month…"

Faith rolled her eyes. "Did you ever get strapped to a pole when you went to school, Dad?"

I looked over at the end of the table where Dad was drinking his coffee and reading the newspaper. He peered over the paper and winked at us in a mysterious way, then went back to being engrossed in the cartoon section of the newspaper.

"What kind of things did they do to you, Dad?" Faith squealed, always looking for gossip. "Were you strapped to a pole? Did you get chased down and paddled? Were you forced to push pennies with your nose? Tell me, tell me!"

I felt my right eye twitch at Faith's high-pitched voice this early in the morning. My sisters were the spitting image of my Mom in her younger years. Long black hair, brown eyes, skinny, amazing cooks and they already had their lives planned out to a "T" with their future as interior designers. What they called creations I called abominations. Most days, I liked to pretend I was adopted.

Dad looked up at the girls. "Eat your pancakes," he grinned and went back to reading. I gratefully accepted my pancakes slathered in golden maple syrup and strawberries and a glass of orange juice from Mom. I wasted no time digging in.

Mom's pancakes were a major treat. Dad had been cooking our meals for the past few days because she'd had to work late. I shuddered at the memory: spaghetti, hot dogs, grilled cheese and soup. Not a single spice was added for flavour and there were no side dishes either. Also included in that lovely list would be microwave dinners. If my Dad had an ounce of creativity, he sure didn't show it in his cooking skills!

"Oh, Felicity. I almost think you missed me, the way you're wolfing down your breakfast. Do you think you were raised in a barn?" She chuckled as she began to meticulously rearrange everything on the table within reaching distance to her liking before she took a single bite of her pancakes. My mouth was too full of pancakes to respond.

Meanwhile, the twins prattled on with aimless chatter, filling the room with noise as Mom tried to silence them. As usual, the twins were engrossed in their own lives. I saw Mom pick up a wooden spoon - always within reaching distance - with a slight grin spreading across her face as she recognized my dread. I had been spanked numerous times by that death stick. I noticed the room had suddenly gone quiet as Mom sat with her arms crossed, spoon at the ready. Italians should *never* be ignored. "That's more like it. After school, you three are to come straight home."

My eyebrows scrunched together as I tried to recall what plans we had tonight. "Oh no, that's tonight!" I burst out. "I don't want to be stuck chained to a chair!"

"You don't have much of a choice." Dad spoke in a no-nonsense tone as he could see Mom beginning to fidget, which was a good sign that a fight was about to break out. "Used & Abused Animals are a very gratifying charity to support. Plus, there's going to be lots of food," he said, trying to bribe us.

"We've been to five charity functions already this year!

Not including, might I add, helping you with your Habitat for Humanity. I think I've been quite gratified enough for the year!"

"Watch that sass, missy," Dad warned.

"Felicity, I'll do your make-up and even pick out your clothes for you to wear tonight. That way you won't have to do any work," Anna Bell suggested, trying to help.

I glared at Anna Bell and said, "Don't encourage the ancients."

"I am not going through this again, Felicity. We clothe you, support you, feed you and keep a roof over your head. Your father and I don't ask for much." She began gathering the dirty dishes. "You're coming and that's final. No use arguing, because it won't change my mind."

I glared down at the table trying to contemplate who was making the biggest fool of themself in this argument. When I looked up, I noticed everyone except my Mom had left the kitchen and were busily putting on their shoes and coats. This was a regular occurrence. My mother and I don't always see eye-to-eye on most subjects. Not wanting to be left alone with the instigator, I took off without a word as Mom ignored me and began cleaning every inch of the counters with her disinfectant spray. I shut the door behind me without saying goodbye.

"Way to start off the morning," Anna Bell goaded. "Will you *ever* learn to keep your mouth shut?"

"All I know is you better be home *right* after school. You know how anal she is when it comes to punctuality. Guaranteed, she'll be by the front door with the death stick and timer in her hand just to irritate you. You better keep your lips zipped when that time comes. She'll just be waiting to get a rise out of you," Faith warned as we watched Dad drive away in his shiny, black Ford F-150 pickup truck.

"I'm not the only one who needs a lesson on keeping their lips zipped." I looked pointedly at her.

Anna Bell laughed as Faith fluffed me off promptly. They began an intense conversation over the difference between Gucci and Prada purses, as I tried to mask my irritation and followed behind.

As we passed our neighbour's house, we waved at Mr. Darnel. He was picking up the daily newspaper in his blue silk suit while carrying a cup of piping hot coffee in his hand and didn't return the greeting. With the Darnels, it's always a strained niceness. His brown hair was combed back and his black, beady eyes stared at us. He wore an expression of smugness. I *hated* seeing that look on his face.

"Why do you think he's looking at us like that?" I said to no one in particular, as he glanced at us once more. Looking at my confused face, he gave me a slight grin. This was not normal Darnel protocol.

"He smiled. Look, I saw it! He's *such* a lunatic," I said.

"He's just a big old fuss pot. You probably saw a grimace. He has *never* smiled," Anna Bell spouted, not believing a word I said.

"Oh yeah. How about the time he smiled when he saw someone run over a puppy or when the Davis' house caught on fire?" I replied saucily.

"Oh, come on, Felicity! Be realistic, he's not immune to feelings," Faith said with that serious tone she always used when it came to anything but gossip.

Sensing an argument was brewing, Anna Bell jumped in, changing the subject as usual to try and settle our quarrels. "Can you guys believe it? In just a few days, sexy Jesse is returning home from boarding school. He is *so* drool-worthy. Especially when he cuts the lawn in just his swim shorts." A muffled sigh escaped Anna Bell's mouth. "Heavenly."

"I heard he's staying for good. Remember, last summer he took quite a shine to you, Anna Bell," Faith said loyally.

"You really think so? Oh, and he's a senior, too!" Anna Bell squealed excitedly.

"Guys, something's different in the Darnel's backyard," I said distractedly, ignoring their twin bonding moment.

"Don't be ridiculous," Anna Bell said coming out of her daydreams and tossing her black hair behind her shoulder. "Alex just had her room redone. They shouldn't do anything major for at least three months. Anyway, who cares about the Darnels? Let's talk more about Jesse."

"Bell, look. Felicity's right. I can see it, too," Faith said uneasily, for once agreeing with me.

"Let's check it out," I said, never one to leave a mystery unsolved.

"Felicity," Faith hissed. "That's trespassing."

I turned around. "Faith, don't you *ever* get tired of telling people what to do *all* the time? Come on, don't be such a wimp, let's go." I saw Faith bite the bottom of her lip fighting back a smart remark. I snuck my way through the neighbours hideous puke green bushes and around to their big backyard.

A few seconds later, I heard two sets of footsteps following close behind me. "If we get caught, I'm blaming it all on you, Felicity," whispered Faith, venomously.

I ignored her threat and slowly peeked over the fence. All of a sudden, I knew why Mr. Darnel was so smug. Right smack dab in the middle of their backyard was an Olympic-sized swimming pool, complete with a three-tiered fountain bubbling in the centre of the pool and surrounded by the Garden of Eden. I daydreamed about all the midnight swims I was going to have when the family was asleep.

Faith and Anna Bell shoved each other, jockeying for position to get a better look. "Blimey, would you look at the *size* of that thing! Of course they get the *biggest* pool out there," Anna Bell said sarcastically.

"Must have been when we were gone last week to visit Grandpa Verney. Jeez, Mr. Darnel must have paid them double and worked them day and night to install this before we got home," Faith commented.

I whistled in admiration. "What a slave driver! He must be tickled pink by putting one over us."

"Run! Darnel's coming and he doesn't look happy to see us." Bell's eyes popped out in alarm. I wasn't afraid of Mr. Darnel, but the freaks were. We booted it out of the yard as fast as we could move our little legs and didn't stop until we were halfway to school.

"That was a close one," Bell said.

"Yeah, a little too close," Faith exclaimed, as she filled her lungs up with air.

"You gotta admit, it was kind of fun, Faith," I said triumphantly. If I could get Anna Bell to do it, Faith usually followed, but with a sour look on her face.

She looked me up and down. "Felicity O'Connor, all you need is a slingshot and I'll be calling you Dennis the Menace."

"I do believe that was *almost* a compliment." I grinned as we ran the rest of the way to school.

CHAPTER 3

A Banquet Fit for a Queen

I dragged myself into the crumbling three-story Lakewood High School, the hellhole I had been going to for three long years. I was followed closely by my sisters who were giggling like hyenas as they caught the eye of a few boys. Distance was quickly put between us as they were swept away in the crowd.

As I passed the principal's office and the drama department, two gold statues of the Lakewood Lions stood at opposite sides of the trophy case with their teeth bared as if daring anyone to challenge them. Lakewood High School hasn't won a championship, let alone a challenge, in so long that cobwebs and dust accumulated in the trophy case. The cafeteria/stage and gym were down a few stairs so I took a shortcut through the drama department coming out behind the curtains on the stage at the back of the cafeteria. I walked down a few steps, passing the lunch tables into a smaller area where all the food was kept, grabbed a chocolate milk, quickly paid for it and went out into the hallway that separated the cafeteria and the gym.

Out of the three levels in the high school, this area was always full of loitering students. A lot of people I found insufferable congregated near the water fountain/bench area, what I called the "Clone Zone." A group of 20 teenagers wearing expensive name brand clothes were sprawled all over the small area. I saw my sisters included in that group. Figures. Most teenagers categorized that group as preps and jocks. They could be stoners, geeks, freaks, sissies, drunks, goths, tramps, or gamblers. Call them what you want, it makes no difference to me what their social status is.

What gives all of them the right to think they are better than anyone else, that they're God's gift to the world? I hate that my sisters are associated with such a group. I know many students take the longer route around the Clone Zone just to avoid them. They all started to watch me as I climbed up the steps. It always gives me satisfaction when I pass them knowing that they will not make me stare at my feet as I go by, that their looks cannot phase or unnerve me like they do to most of the student population. I will never scurry past them even if they taunt or leer at me. I will always walk with my head held high. The reality of the situation is that there is safety in numbers. If you're alone, you're a potential target. (I *like* being a target if it means pissing them off. The fact that I'm not afraid to use my fists would be a good indication).

I reached the top step where a semi-muscular guy named Darryl, wearing an outrageously tight black t-shirt, stood in my way, not budging. I stood there for about five seconds waiting for him to move and, when nothing happened, I became impatient. A girl in grade ten stood beside me, and she was clearly trying to get by but her voice was no stronger than a mouse. I saw a small opening and barrelled through, stomping past him, breaking a space for the girl and me. I got death glares shot at me and smiled back politely as I headed to my locker, walking past lockers and down the long wheel-chair ramp crammed with people. My theory in life is that all girls are bitches and all guys are assholes but all of us are on different levels. Some in the Clone Zone weren't even half bad when you got them on their own. On the other hand, some just can't be helped.

My locker was located in the manufacturing hallway near all the shops for auto, woodworking and welding. I picked up my books for English and threw them into my backpack, setting off around the corner to find my best friend, Mandy Morrison.

I gave her a slightly amused greeting as I watched her shove her skateboard into her locker without much success. It was crammed full of her other friends' backpacks and skateboards. Her black hair had red and purple streaks and was styled in a spiky stylish look this morning.

"Hey, yourself. Don't just stand there. Help me shove this thing in! And grab my English book while you're at it." Mandy was wearing heavy black eye liner around her eyes today making the blue in them pop out wildly and she was dressed in her usual black clothing. A black choker was locked against her throat and thick multi-coloured bracelets clung to each wrist. I stared at her outfit; you wouldn't be able to tell from her punk look that she was a superb baseball player.

I rummaged through the bottom of her locker and after what seemed like forever I pulled out her textbook. "You know, this isn't in the greatest shape. The cover is hanging on by a thread." The warning bell rang and the travel music started to play.

"It's in perfect shape," she argued. "I've been saving up for a new baseball mitt so I'm not spending 90 dollars to replace a stupid textbook I never use."

"So, what are you going to do, hot glue it back together?"

She grinned back at me wickedly. "That's not exactly what I had in mind."

I thought it was best not to ask.

"Mr. Finklestein won't even know."

I gave Mandy an odd look. She is not what I would call the sanest person in the world. That is probably why we got along so well. She's the only person in school that I could actually tolerate. The final bell rang and we both sighed. "That's going to be another two detentions. You have a bad influence on me, Mandy."

"I'm not a bad influence, I'm just reshaping you." We both applied pressure to her locker to make sure it would actually lock. We tilted our heads to the side slightly. It looked like it would bust open at any moment and we didn't want to be around in case it did.

"They need to make bigger lockers," she observed.

We rounded the corner, choosing to take the longer route by the music room to grab our late slips at the office, instead of the wheelchair ramp. That's when I saw John Adamson (another infestation of suck ants that littered this school) chuck what looked like a mouldy sandwich at the face of Nicole, a little grade niner. My nose wrinkled at the smell confirming my prediction. John and his buddies began laughing like it was the funniest thing they had ever seen. My eyes narrowed as I saw the look on the blonde-haired girl's face.

Nicole wasn't all that attractive, due to acne covering her heart-shaped face, but she had great potential once it cleared up in a few years. My sisters had talked about her often. Her family didn't have a lot of money. She came from a family of six and that's why a lot of her clothes were hand-me-downs. Tears threatened to pour down her cheeks at any second. It broke my heart. "Felicity, I know what you're thinking, but don't do anything rash," Mandy advised.

"Rash?" I gritted my teeth. "I wouldn't dream of it," I said as I picked up a piece of the mouldy sandwich and headed towards John and his posse, who slowly stopped laughing as I approached. If I had caught him doing that to my sisters, he would have been a dead man. I am the only one allowed to torment my siblings. I stared him straight in the eye. "You forgot your sandwich." I smiled and pretended to hold it out to him. When he made no move to take it, I grabbed his shirt quick as lightning and mashed the sandwich into his face, gagging at the smell.

"Dude!" said one of John's friends, laughing. "You just *ate* my old tuna sandwich."

Bullies make my blood boil. Kids like Nicole have done nothing wrong. I hate most of the people in this school. I hate high school and how it's so categorized. How there are certain hallways for certain people. This school feels more like kindergarten, always needing to be supervised. Aren't we supposed to be mature by now? Why do people have to be so rude to each other? Is it a crime for people to live and breathe? Must they make a person's life a living hell when they have done nothing to deserve it? No wonder suicide is so high when it comes to teenagers.

"Ugh," Mandy plugged her nose. "You just made this whole hallway reek. That was awesome!"

I washed my hands in a nearby fountain, almost vomiting from the smell as I tried to wipe away my dirty deed. Adrenaline was running through my system. I really have to start controlling my anger. "I bet John won't be throwing any more sandwiches for a long time."

"You're just as crazy as your Mom. Uh oh, bad news bears! Here come the hall monitors."

Bert and Ernie were on duty. Both were a little chunky and took their hall monitor jobs a little too seriously. "Mandy, go to class. Felicity, you have to come with us," Bert said sternly.

Ernie gave me a small sympathy smile. "Next time, don't do it when we are a hallway away."

"Thanks for the advice." We turned in the opposite direction of my English class as I saw Mandy wish me good luck before taking off.

"Or you could not do it at all," Bert reprimanded, as I bit back a retort that would probably get me suspended.

We walked the rest of the way in silence. I didn't know much about Bert and Ernie, just that they had grown up and lived on the same street for 17 years. They were both graduating and going to the same college in September. They were an odd duo. One was really tall, the other considerably shorter. They sat me down on a hard white chair reserved for Principal Dunmore's guests. I sat there and picked at my hangnails, which soon started bleeding as boredom kicked in. I listened to the clock tick away under the watchful eye of Mrs. Haydon, the school secretary, as her fingers flew across the keyboard and she answered the phone.

Bert and Ernie found a straggler and sat her down beside me. She was dressed in skinny jeans and an off-the-shoulder shirt. I resisted the urge to strangle her after she began chomping on Double Trouble pink bubble gum, blowing enormous bubbles and snapping it.

A guy with a black Bob Marley shirt and shoulder length brown dreadlocks was sitting on the other side of me and was so tuned into texting on his cell phone that he didn't even notice his name being called into the office. I stared at the little device with a distasteful look on my face. *Cell phones! I didn't care how handy or convenient they were. Life still passed you by. Who wanted to be strapped down by something no bigger than your palm, where parents could get a hold of you at any time? Soon they'd be putting tracking devices in them!* I could hear an orchestra of vibrating sounds coming from the faculty's purses and pockets. *I was not going to turn into one of those zombies.* He snapped his head up after the third time his name was called and headed inside. His jeans rode low over his red boxer shorts displayed for the entire world to see.

Five minutes went by and I was surprised when Mrs. Haydon's voice interrupted my thoughts. "Felicity, you can go in now." *Wow, that was fast.* I took a deep breath and entered the office. *Showtime!*

Principal Dunmore's office was cramped. She had one tall bookcase, a filing cabinet and an oak desk. Certificates of all kinds were plastered on the wall behind her and the two chairs across from her desk were tiny due to the limited space. There were no windows in her office. I didn't know how anyone could work in this jail cell but somehow she managed. "Take a seat," she said.

After shuffling around the chair so I could sit, she took out my file and read it over. She does this every time, as if searching for an answer to her questions, so I sat and waited patiently for the verdict. If Mrs. Dunmore had a gavel she would use it. The rumours say she went to school to be a judge but something happened and she ended up being a principal instead. The justice scale on her desk only heightened my assumptions. She was a very petite woman with a few grey hairs mixed in with her brown that showed signs of her aging. She had a hard stare, brown calculating eyes, a no-tolerance policy and once she made a decision it was final. She and I had an understanding of righteousness in the world. I always had noble reasons for my actions.

"Why must you always stoop to their level, Felicity?" She closed the folder, her long, manicured, red nails tapping a slow and steady rhythm. Whenever she did this it was always a sign that she was thinking of a suitable punishment. "There are other ways to go about doing this. Why do you think we have hall monitors?"

"Yes, I know there are other ways, but what is detention going to do? Been there, done that, got the t-shirt. It accomplishes nothing but making parents angry. It helps stop the after-school bullying, but that's about it. Detention is a joke! What are school suspensions going to accomplish? It'll only make them brew over why they got into trouble in the first place and come back in full force. They probably *enjoy* not having to go to school. I know I do! It's like a vacation. At least with my method, they get a taste of their own medicine."

"But it also increases their hostility towards you. Next time they see you who knows what their actions will be? If you start things like the occasional swirly in the bathroom, even rubbing sandwiches in people's faces, you are contradicting your own beliefs. You, in turn, become the bully. I can't condone such behaviour; you make those very students want to exact revenge. I'm in charge of taking care of the students and their safety and how can I do that if you are purposely going to endanger yourself?"

"How could you possibly lump me in with *them?* I'm doing it for the greater good. I don't care if they want to be hostile towards me; at least they have a reason to. They just don't understand what it is they're doing wrong. Do you have *any* idea how frustrating that is?"

The principal sighed. "Felicity, I deal with these students on a day-to-day basis, along with the counsellors trying to help them. How can we help them if you keep setting them back? Some of them have family issues and that is why they lash out. Some of them are stressed with probation or with school, college applications and career choices. They have their reasons, even though it is hard to understand why they do what they do. Try walking in their footsteps for once. I don't know how many times I've had to ask you to go into counselling to try and solve this hatred you have towards some of the students."

"That is *no* excuse for them to hurt innocent people." I found myself angry with the principal today. This meeting was not going as I had planned. "Why are you taking their side?" I asked. I guess my luck at the principal's office had finally run out.

"I'm not taking anyone's side. John and his friends will be getting a suitable punishment once I am through with you. They will not be getting away with it." I could hear the hard edge in her voice and knew I had struck a nerve. "I will be calling your parents. You must be held accountable for your actions and you will be suspended for three days from school. I know you're better than this. I'm letting you off easy this time, but this is the last time. I'm going to have to start being stricter with you if you keep acting the way you do. I know you don't want counselling but I might just have to make it mandatory if I see you again in this office before school is finished. I will make sure Mandy picks up your homework. That is all. If you need your parents to pick you up, tell the secretary to give them a call. If not, I don't want to see you on this property until Thursday morning."

I shut the door, resisting the urge not to slam it. I still had to try and stay on her good side in case I ended up back in there, because I was *not* going to change. I ignored the urge to punch John in the face as I passed by him, next in line to see the principal. I had three days and that was nothing. He should get a week or, worse, be expelled. Expelled would suit me just fine. I shook my head. Three days off, and I'm still going to have to do homework. *Why did we go to school for eight gruesome hours only to come home and do more work? Didn't they torture their students enough for five days?* My parents are going to kill me. This was way worse than the time I crashed the car into the ditch. This involved my studies and, when it came to studies, my parents were insane about them.

After spending three hours playing Halo at my buddy's place and another three hours at the arcade, with my pocket 50 dollars lighter, I entered the driveway around 4:00 and heard a loud noise coming from the backyard. Forgetting about the little fiasco this morning, I ran inside the house, dropped my backpack at the foot of the stairs and looked out the backyard from the double doors in the kitchen. There was a huge hole in the centre of our yard and piles of dirt surrounding it.

"Mom, *please* tell me you're digging for buried treasure?"

"Well, I went to check things out at the Darnels. I thought it would be a very good idea to put a pool in. It's supposed to be the hottest summer yet!"

I stared at her numbly. "You do realize we had air conditioning put in last year because *last* year was the hottest summer."

"Summer's just starting and think of all the pool parties we can have. Trust me, you guys are going to love it! Not only does it have a fountain but it also has a slide, diving board, a hot tub connected to the pool, a waterfall and, best of all, the pool is heated."

"Great," I said slowly and with little enthusiasm. "That's just peachy. Sure, let's spend all this money on my bedroom and now on a pool when we could be feeding kids in Africa." I began to stomp up the stairs. Money controls this world, which is a rather sad and depressing thought. A thought my parents continually remind me of, telling me that I need a good job in order to prosper. I have a job, but my Mom doesn't think being a soccer referee qualifies as a suitable part-time job. They are happy with material things, but material things will run out eventually and then where will their happiness be?

"Once you're finished with your little theatrics, would you please hurry up and get changed. Your father and sisters are ready to go."

"Already? But I just got home."

"We want to be there early to help set up."

"At four-thirty?"

"Being early shows good form."

Pursing my lips, I began to feel my right eye twitch. I had had enough of my share of arguing for one day. "Fine." *Didn't the pressure of having to act perfect all the time in front of society stress them out? Lakewood isn't even that big. Why did they always feel the need to impress everyone?* "I'll be down in 15 minutes."

"It had better take you longer than that to get ready. Pick up your backpack," Mom said sternly.

"Sure thing." I gritted my teeth, leaving my backpack downstairs. "30 minutes." I *hated* dressing up but, from what I could tell, they hadn't received the phone call from school. So, it could have been worse.

The place where the charity function was held was outdoors at a very classy hall and patio garden just outside of Lakewood. Golden lights were strung on the rafters and in plants. The podium and tables were draped in gold and red. There were tables, centrepieces, silverware and chairs as far as the eye could see. Donation boxes were scattered throughout the area. Waiters in tuxedos held glasses of wine on silver trays. It was just like every charity event I had been to with my family.

Tom Darnel stood near the main entrance towering over everyone with his wiry frame. His short brown hair was slicked back to perfection and his eyes were so dark they matched his tuxedo. Tucked in beside him was his trophy wife, Amy. Even I had to admit Amy was dazzling, much to my mother's envy. She had hair the colour of spun gold. Amy had curves in all the right places from being a stay-at-home Mom. She found lots of time to stay in shape and the backless black dress proved it. How she ended up with Tom was something I couldn't fathom. I could already sense my parent's annoyance that they had beat us to the function.

"How nice to see you tonight, Tom and Amy. I see you brought your lovely daughter, Alex, with you," Mom pointed out. Mom was wearing a long, gorgeous purple dress that flowed and puffed out a bit to hide her weight.

"Yes. Well, she was just *so* concerned about the animals she insisted she come. She's also donating $1,000.00 of her own money," Tom praised. I let out an involuntary snort at the thought and Tom sneered at me. "If you check the newspaper tomorrow, she'll be in it." I looked at Alex in disgust. Her arrogant self was gussied up in a pink strapless dress, with more make-up than I knew what to do with, her brown hair forming long ringlets down her back. Natural ringlets that my sisters would kill for. She definitely got her looks from her mother's side. Just looking at her gave me a hankering to throw on my baseball cap and toss some dirt on myself. She was just too Barbie doll perfect tonight. I shuddered at the amount of time it must have taken her to get ready opposed to my meager ten minutes.

Dad coughed at the unpleasantness of it all. "Girls, why don't you go find us a table near the front and we'll meet you there in a few minutes?"

"Okay!" My sisters and I jumped to attention and bolted out of there as fast as we could.

"Felicity, you owe me big time." Bell looked at me with a mischievous grin, her blue dress nothing but sparkles.

"What are you talking about?" I asked, as we found a suitable table.

"The school called today when Dad was at work and Mom was in the shower." I saw Faith shook her head disapprovingly but was all ears regardless; she could never resist a good piece of scandal.

"Oh." I swallowed as my mouth went dry.

"You're just lucky it was me who picked it up and thank God for caller I.D. Your little stunt was news all over the school today, even though John tried to deny it ever happened. So I pretended to be Mom. I must say I put on quite the performance," she preened.

I don't think I could have loved my sister more than I did right then. "Bell!" I said, a little choked by surprise that she would do such a thing. "If you weren't my sister, I'd almost kiss you," I crowed.

"Anna Bell, that's bad!" Faith squealed, clearly pleased with her sister's little stunt. I looked up to the heavens and wondered why God created such a creature. *Why couldn't she get excited when I came up with my own schemes? Must be a twin thing.*

Bell shrugged her shoulders. "Spice of life."

"Hey, you're wearing my dress!" Faith's eyes went wide as I took off my coat. "What were you doing in my room?" People began to stare as she lowered her voice. "That's my favourite dress."

I grinned. "I know, but I have no dresses and this *is* a formal event. I couldn't just wear anything."

"You're the messiest eater in the world!" Faith was obviously horrified thinking of what might become of her red dress.

"She's wearing her ratty old sneakers with it, too," Bell observed. "That's so tacky. I don't know how Mom didn't catch that one."

I looked at her appalled. "These are my *lucky* sneakers, thank you very much. Never lost a game wearing them. Good thing the dress covers my feet. At least I won't have blisters at the end of the night."

Faith hissed, "You'll have more than just blisters. I can guarantee that!"

I found myself enjoying her pain. "You threaten me one more time and I'll start ripping it open with the butter knife."

"You wouldn't."

"Oh, I would."

Faith whimpered and then gave me such a scowl that even I could be proud of her.

Defusing the situation, Bell cut in, "Faith, it's going to be fine. It can be dry cleaned or sewed. Felicity wouldn't do it on purpose. Anyway, let's change the subject. Can you believe that in a few days we are going to have a pool? Jesse will have to come over and cool off sooner or later."

"Jesse already has a pool, dimwit." I just loved crushing

my sister's dreams.

"Oh. Well, then. I'll just have him over for supper sometime."

"You never give up, do you, Bell?"

"Not when it comes to Jesse," she sighed.

"Who cares about pools anyway? Beaches are way better. Like when we lived at the lake when we were younger. I'd much prefer that any day."

"Ew. Why?" they both said together in grossed out voices.

Faith looked around and whispered in my ear as if it was some big secret. "Fish pee in the water."

"And dead bodies are chucked in the lake," Bell said. Clearly, she had been watching too many crime shows.

"Don't forget the diseases."

"Sewage plants dump their crap into the water."

"Sharks."

"Mushy sand."

"Seaweed."

"Dead fish!"

"Pollution!"

I stared at them as they kept naming all the problems about beaches and soon I had to intervene. "FYI, freaks, this whole world is filled with diseases and dirt and a whole lot of germs and nastiness! Don't you remember all the good memories, swimming out really deep, treasure hunting, collecting seashells, playing with clay, trying to catch minnows with our bare hands, fishing, building sandcastles and playing with the neighbour kids, the Marley's, all summer long? You can't have forgotten about our sand ball wars. Those were the best! That's not something you can get with a pool." I looked at them for their reply.

"Nope, don't recall anything."

"Yuck, fishing."

Hopeless. Sometimes, I wondered if my sisters were brain dead. They only seemed to remember the meaningless things in life. Childhood memories are what shape you into the person you are. Something must have gone wrong with the twins. Dreadfully wrong.

"Can you believe those people?" said Mom, outraged as she took a seat beside me. "Tom Darnel said he saw you three spying on them from the neighbour's backyard."

"Ha, ha…really?" We laughed nervously.

"Do you believe them?" asked Faith hesitantly.

"Of course not! My family does not go around snooping. Tom is obviously going crazy. He's starting to hallucinate." Mom smiled happily at the thought, while she swirled her wine in a vindictive way. She caught us all staring at her. "Not that that means he's crazy."

Out of the corner of my eye I could see my two sisters let out a deep breath.

"Look, here comes the food!" Dad's expression was like a little kid in a candy store.

Now, I remember why I liked coming to these things. Looking at the whipped potatoes, the big, juicy, mouth-watering steaks smothered with fried mushrooms and onions, and the Caesar salad, I started salivating.

While we ate, an old, dandily dressed man stepped up to the podium. He had been running the animal shelter for at least 40 years. I thought he would disintegrate into dust in the next six minutes. I couldn't help but gawk at the man's elephant ears and big nose until Mom elbowed me in the stomach. In his scratchy voice, he told us about his experiences and how the animals managed to survive in many unsuitable households and blah, blah, blah, blah, blah. I was too focused on my food to listen.

It didn't take long for boredom to set in, as I looked about the room to see many avid listeners paying attention to him. They were all decked out in the latest fashions and made the area shimmer and shine. I spotted Alex at the next table across from me. I scowled. She just looked so fake. At least, I can admit that I'm not here for the animals but by my mother's conscription.

I still had some potatoes left on my plate when my mind started to wander and I came up with an evil plan. I thought back to that gleeful day at McDonald's when I was six years old when Mandy and I had shot spitballs at a monstrous woman. We hid in the PlayPlace for an hour after she finished reaming out my parents. I was grounded from my Game Boy for two whole months. I wondered what the consequences would be this time? How would Alex react? The thought was too tempting not to try it out. No one was watching. I felt someone's eyes on me as I turned back to my table and Faith was staring at me. "What?" I mouthed.

She wiggled around back in her seat to listen to the drone of the old man's voice. I scooped up some mashed potatoes with my plastic spoon, turned around and took aim, closing my right eye.

Alex was wearing that beautiful pink dress. She had told me today that the finest designer in Italy had created it just for her. Over the years, I've been able to fine-tune my lie detector, and at that statement it went sky high. As if she even *knew* anybody in Italy.

I let my missile fire away. Not only did it miss its target, it hit a bald guy sitting right in front of Alex. The man stared at Alex with disapproval and wiped off the guck. I loaded up once again and fired, purposely aiming for the old bald guy, hitting him right in the ear. I quickly turned around as Alex turned red with embarrassment. I loaded up the last of my firepower and turned around. Alex had a spoon in her hand now, also loaded with potatoes. This was going to get ugly. I let loose the third shot that landed - *splat* - right on the bald guy's head. He turned around and caught Alex in the act with spoon in hand. I gave her a smile, turned around and pretended to be interested in the speech.

"Well, I never!" came the man's booming voice as he stood up, knocking his chair over and causing a big scene.

"But, it wasn't me!" Alex's voice was frantic. Faith's green eyes turned to me as the guilty culprit, but she pursed her lips and didn't say a word. Faith may be a prude at times but, when it came to family, she was definitely one I wanted in my corner.

"Then, what's this?" said the man. He held up the spoon.

The speaker stopped his ramblings. "Is everything all right over there?"

Tom interjected. "Yes, yes quite all right. She just hit her plate and some food spilled on Dave. We're so lucky Dave is such an honourable and courteous man."

At such praise in front of everyone, Dave picked up his chair and sat down, grumbling to his wife. The speech continued as I turned around, upset that nothing more had come of my little mischief. Mr. Darnel was looking at me with satisfaction, having debauched my plans. He raised his glass to me in cheers. He may have been happy, but Alex was far from it. But I knew she wouldn't do anything. Not in public anyway.

Dessert came on platters in an array of colours. There were so many decisions. I contemplated the choices for at least five minutes. I saw the waitress hop from foot to foot with impatience so I quickly picked a few things. A shish kabob of chocolate strawberries, chocolate cake and two raspberry tarts decorated my plate.

"Felicity, you're only allowed one," Mom scolded.

"I'm stuck here on my Friday night, Mom. I'm going to eat whatever I want, when I want and how I want it. Besides, it's just going to get thrown out if I don't eat it. There is no rule, it's not written on the pamphlet to take *one* dessert." As soon as I had taken all I wanted, the waitress whisked herself away. "See, she didn't care."

My Mom fussed with her dress. "That's not the point. It's not the proper thing to do."

"This world ran out of etiquette a long time ago, so why bother to bring it back?"

"Because, we don't want the whole world to turn into a bunch of savages," Dad cut in, giving me a little chuck under the chin. "This is the best place we have eaten all year."

"Attention, attention… attention everyone," said a woman with rosy, flushed cheeks. "It's now time for the auction. If everyone wants to head into the building on your right, that is where the bidding will take place and, if you want to make a donation on your way, please feel free." Bodies began moving from their seats to head into the grey building, as I sat at the table clearly not finished eating my desserts.

"And that is why you just take one," Faith informed me quietly. I harrumphed and took my sweet time watching the waiters and waitresses whisk away the plates, hoping they would give me time to eat the rest of my desserts. I was the last one sitting at the table enjoying the quiet as everyone else was in the auction building. All the din had died down and the crickets began chirping. I could hear the auctioneer start his speed talking as a dog was sold for $200. A few more animals were sold for absurd amounts. Just as I finished my last bite, Bell and Faith ran up to me holding two cats. Both big, white puffballs like the cats from the toilet paper commercials.

"They're sisters!" Faith said as she nuzzled one with blue eyes.

"Aren't they adorable?" Bell chimed. I stared at them helplessly. My room remodelled, a pool and now pets. *Was I the only one in the family who worried about finances?*

Faith took my look to mean something entirely different. "Oh, don't worry. Mom and Dad aren't going to leave you hanging out to dry. They're getting you a dog! I know how much you've always wanted one."

Excitement bubbled up inside, but I quickly squashed it. I ran into the building to persuade them not to spend any more money.

"Here we have a Shiatsu, only three years old." The lady pointed to the white and brown dog. It was such an ugly little thing.

Dad's voice entered my hearing. "$100!" he bellowed at the top of his lungs. I recoiled at the thought of owning something so hideous and small. He should know me better than that.

Tom Darnel replied. "$150!"

"$200!"

"$300!" A tiny man stood up and quickly shrunk away as my Dad and Mr. Darnel turned in his direction with a look of irritation. To everyone in the room it was obvious that the bidding was only between them and no one should interfere. They battled it out for a little while longer until Tom finally won and paid the steep price of $450.

The lady was clearly pleased as the next animal was brought out to be auctioned. "Now we have a puppy, he's a black Lab and is only six months old," said the woman.

"$300!" Dad jumped back up, determined that I should have something. No one else objected and the pup was mine. I would have settled for an older dog. But, oh no, only the best for me from my parents.

I went up and collected the puppy, its green eyes starry bright and tail wagging. I couldn't help but thank my parents a million times. I tried not to think about the fact that maybe, just maybe, the only reason we had these animals was because of the Darnel's snide little comments tonight that had leaked into my parents' minds.

In the end, when all the animals were auctioned off, we went home. My parents discussed how the Darnels behaviour was absurd, laughing over Alex's disgraceful display. Then we were drilled on the proper care of our pets and how it was supposed to teach us responsibility.

I fell asleep with my newest companion, who I'd instantly named Tucker. Today had turned out ten times better than I had expected.

CHAPTER 4

Curiouser and Curiouser

"Oh, man. Nice hit! That one's outta the park," gasped Tara, looking out at the baseball diamond as the ball I'd just belted flew into a large clump of trees with dense underbrush. The rest of my teammates who were just arriving stopped to watch the scene.

I grinned cockily, "Dang straight it is!"

"Dude, we only brought four baseballs. That's our best one." Mandy looked at me pointedly, then back at the small forest where the ball had disappeared and then back at me.

I opted for the more diplomatic response of the two by letting out a sigh and grumbling, "Fine. *I'll* go get it." Once Mandy and I got into an argument, we wouldn't stop until our voices became hoarse.

I headed to the back of the baseball field kicking up dust. Long dead grass littered the ground, beer bottles occupied the fence line, condom wrappers decorated the ground and Wendy's fast food polluted the air. My friends looked far away in the distance. *This place was a wasteland.* I couldn't believe it was the only baseball diamond we had in town.

"Home sweet home," I muttered sarcastically.

I approached the clump of trees. *How was I expected to find a single baseball in this mess?* Trees and shrubs lined the area so thickly I could barely see five feet in front of me. I gritted my teeth. *If I didn't find this baseball, I'd never hear the end of it and, if I did, I still wouldn't hear the end of it.* Fighting my way through the thicket, cobwebs stuck to me like glue, burdock clung to my clothes like lice, rose bushes pricked me at every turn, sticks from neighbouring trees scratched my skin, and my arms and legs were bleeding.

I was just about ready to yell every kind of curse word I knew until I noticed the trees were thinning. I stomped my way over towards the trees, realizing how pointless this mission was. I wished I had a chainsaw to destroy the whole area. When I finally broke through, I came to a small circular valley of grass. A huge oak tree stood alone in the middle of the barren area. My eyes narrowed at the tiny white ball as if I could blame everything on it.

Heading towards the tree, the sun shone down on it, creating a circle of light as dust particles flitted around in the air. All around the perimeter flowers blossomed, but not a petal touched the inner circle. I picked up the baseball and noticed there was a large puddle beneath the tree. It hadn't rained in Lakewood in more than a week and the ground around me was completely dry.

It was a perfectly circular puddle, like a shimmering jewel in the sunlight. The water was crystal clear and as blue as Caribbean waters. My eyes widened as I peered in. The puddle seemed bottomless. It just kept going and going. I dipped my hands in, expecting it to be cold, only to find it lukewarm.

It felt like silk against my skin. *Strangest puddle I'd ever seen! How had this little piece of paradise gone unnoticed for so long? Someone obviously knew about it. Look how trimmed the grass was.*

I turned to admire the oak tree. It was daunting, but perfect for climbing. Odd, no twigs or leaves littered the ground. Out of the corner of my eye I saw something shimmer in the puddle. I whipped my head back around and peered into it a second time. There was nothing there, but I knew I had seen something. It disappeared as fast as a shooting star. *Could it be gold?* I checked again and no shimmer showed any evidence of it ever being there. I laughed at the notion; something about this place gave me the willies. I couldn't hear any birds or insects. The place was just too serene for it to even exist in this world. It was unnatural.

My gaze slipped back to the puddle. What if there really *was* gold down there? I dismissed the thought. The water was too deep to even reach the bottom. I could hear my name being called faintly from somewhere off to my left. Suddenly, I felt a strong sense of protectiveness for the area. I wanted to keep it my little secret, a place I could escape to.

When I emerged from the thicket I was greeted by a bemused Mandy looking me over from head-to-toe. "It's about time you stopped playing George of the Jungle. Practice is almost over."

"My line of talent doesn't need practice," I gloated, as we raced back to see the others.

My teammates and I went out for our usual sacred ritual after practice: Godfather's Pizza. Entering the small building, all of us crowded into the three booths off to the side as Tracey went to collect our pre-ordered, four large pizzas. A symphony of voices filled the pizza place.

Mandy sat across from me and asked, "So, what are you doing tonight?"

I smirked. "Oh, so you're actually asking me for once, are you? Letting me make my own decisions, that's very…" My voice trailed off, as heaven was set in front of me: Meat Lovers pizza, my favourite! Faster than a speeding bullet, the pizza box was opened as steam wafted in front of me with the most enticing scent. Everyone else in the room ceased to exist.

"God, you're disgusting when you eat sometimes!" Mandy eyed me and my half-eaten pizza disdainfully. "Anyway, there's this party tonight and I was kind of hoping you would come with me."

"Where's it at?" I slowed my eating down to keep Mandy from yelling at me.

Mandy was silent as she picked at a piece of pepperoni and popped it in her mouth. "Alex's house."

"I'm busy." I took a swig of water.

Crestfallen, Mandy stared at the table. "I was afraid you'd say that."

"Then, why bother asking? You know what would be brilliant with this pizza right now? An ice cold beer," I said, attempting to change the subject.

"It's just that it's a pool party and all these guys from Alex's school are going to be there. Come on, Felicity. You're my wing woman! You *know* I always need that extra little push to get past my shyness."

"You don't need those spoiled rotten private school guys." I grabbed a second slice of pizza, hoping this would be the end of the conversation.

"It's the concept. I need practice at flirting. You and I both know it." Her eyes pleaded with me.

I stared at my water in front of me. I felt like I was in a sea of discontentment. *Someone always wanted something from me.* "Don't you have any hot skateboarder friends you can ask?"

"No!" She gave me a horror-struck look. "You will *not* believe what I put up with around them. Belching contests are the worst. Sometimes they don't shower for days!"

I let out a sound between a hiss and a grunt. In the tiniest voice I said, "I'll see what I can do," gritting my teeth.

She jumped up and looked like she was going to hug me, only to realize that was *soooo* not our thing. She sat back down, slightly embarrassed. "Thanks."

"Maybe I can cause some mayhem," I said, trying to think optimistically. Suddenly, I felt the urge to flee the building before Mandy could sucker me into anything else.

Jessica stood on top of a chair. "Alright, before everyone leaves…" She directed her gaze at me, stopping me in my tracks. "We have been challenged on Sunday by the Lancelot Stallions. I ask you, do the Lakewood Lions accept?"

I grinned devilishly as everyone on the team cheered. We despised the Stallions. They'd cheated in every game, taking away our hard-earned victories. Payback was long overdue and this time we were stronger.

"That's what I thought," smiled Jessica. "Be at Lakewood Park, four o'clock on Sunday. It's time to take back what we deserve!" This was followed by another cheer as the room buzzed with excitement.

Night had set in as I opened the front door and flipped my navy hoodie up over my head. The sound of Alex's party next door was in full swing, filling the neighbourhood with energetic music, boisterous voices and lights blazing from all windows. No cops patrolled the area. *How handsomely had the Darnels paid the cops for their silence this time?* The party sounded like fun - loud music, drinking booze, forgetting that I was stuck in this godforsaken town. Then, I thought of the last party where I had to deal with someone barfing on me, along with the depressed drunks and the wicked hangover. The prospect of hot guys and Mandy's desperate plea was almost enough to lure me in. *Almost.* It was pretty slim pickings when it came to Lakewood.

"Felicity," came the high-pitched whine of Faith with Anna Bell hot on her trail. I cursed myself, wishing I had left earlier. "I hear you have a game on Sunday against the Stallions?"

"You heard right," I said stiffly, realizing my parents were headed my way. If my sisters knew about my game with the Stallions, naturally, all of Lakewood knew.

"Justin Peltoski said that his brother's girlfriend told him that Brianna was going to break one of your legs so you couldn't play in the game," Bell said breathlessly.

I grinned at the threat. They were scared. "Well, you can tell Justin Peltoski that he can shove it up his…"

"Hey, noooow," Dad cut in. "Why don't you put your good behaviour to use and help your Mom with the supper dishes?"

Ignoring the comment, Faith pointed out smartly, "I bet most of the town will show up for the game."

My Mom's eyes widened to saucers while I continued to roll my eyes skyward. "Girls, you must be on your best behaviour at the game. Everyone will be watching. Remember the town picnic last year with that wardrobe malfunction?" She shuddered at the memory, staring directly at the three us. "The Johnson's always bring it up when I see them."

"Your Mom's right. No need to embarrass us in front of everyone," agreed Dad.

"You hear that, he thinks *we* embarrass *them*. Shouldn't it be the other way around? Besides, I was only trying to fix that loose thread on Stacey's shirt," Anna Bell smirked.

"Yeah! And that skirt was so short you could pretty much see everything anyways," Faith joined in.

Mom's eyes narrowed and they quickly shut up.

"Yeah, we're real animals," I mumbled. I can't remember how many fun events we had missed because they thought I would do something stupid to tarnish the family name.

"And where do you think you're going tonight, missy?" Mom looked at me questioningly.

"Nowhere."

"That's not what it looks like."

"It's a Saturday night," I explained.

"It's already ten o'clock. You had better not be going to Alex's party."

"Can't you just trust me?" I looked to Dad for some backup, but he had mysteriously disappeared. *Perfect.*

"No, it's not that I don't trust you. I just think that tonight you should stay home. There are ruffians about. Your sisters aren't going out tonight." She spoke as if that would make a difference. "Why not spend some quality time with them? Plus, you have Tucker who needs taking care of. You have responsibilities that can't be neglected, Felicity."

I felt my eye begin to twitch. *Did she just skip her whole teenage life? I had spent more than enough time with the twins last night, and I had played with Tucker most of the day before baseball practice.* "Fine." I trudged up the stairs. I knew long ago that it was pointless to argue with her. Her word was law around here.

Walking into my room, I switched on my television to the baseball game and turned the volume up high. Everyone knew when I was watching baseball. You stay out of my way with aimless chitchat. Tucker's tail wagged at my appearance as he held a sock in his mouth and I realized I had locked him in my room accidentally.

"Sorry, boy. You can't come with me tonight. Not this time." I left my bedroom door open a crack so Tucker could come and go at his leisure and crept out onto my balcony. I scaled the small ledge, cautiously passing the twins' window as I saw the two of them chattering (constantly) while doing each other's manicures and pedicures, totally oblivious to anything around them. A small pang of envy gripped me, wishing I was as close to them as they were with each other. As I see it, the twins are angels in my parents' eyes and are slowly trying to morph me into one of them. I always get great satisfaction from disobeying mother's orders. Mom has always been the enforcer; Dad, on the other hand, is just the follower. He never had much of a backbone. All jokes and no teeth. *Why be someone I wasn't? I refused to go through life like my family, always wondering what people thought. When I had something to prove, I'd do it without considering the consequences. If that didn't please some people, so be it.* Pushing those thoughts away, I reached the maple tree on the other side of my house and began my descent until I was at a reasonable jumping distance. I landed on the ground causing barely a stir and took off running towards the baseball field and my new secret place.

I felt my way through the thicket of bushes and trees. It was creepy at night when all the tree's branches looked like arms ready to grab me and my flashlight moved around erratically. Crickets chirped everywhere in the vicinity. I tripped over a stone as I landed in the circle, flashlight sprawling off to the side. I got up and began to brush away the dirt. The full moon's rays were cast directly on the old tree. It was breathtaking. I half expected fairies to jump out and start dancing under it. There may be no such things as fairies, but there were fireflies. It screamed of the unnatural. So much beauty in a world full of malice. *This place was so unreal!*

I grabbed my flashlight, walked towards the tree and sat down beside it, trying to block out the day's events and not think about how mad Mandy was going to be. This place was peaceful. It was exactly what I needed for my hectic lifestyle. Feeling parched, I cupped my hands into the water and was surprised to find that it was still warm. When I put it to my mouth to have a drink, I spit it out immediately. *Saltwater! This place made no sense.*

My heart started pounding as I noticed a slight glow illuminating the bottom of the puddle. *Had to be gold! If I could get my hands on it then I could really leave Lakewood behind.* I reached my whole arm in to touch the glow but the bottom was endless, almost causing me to fall in. My eyes widened as I wrenched my dripping arm out of the water. *Magic!* Exhilaration bubbled inside of me at the thought. How can a puddle be limitless? I grinned to myself. The whole world is just one big storybook after another.

Well, I never was one for procrastination. I looked around to see if anyone was watching. Nobody was and I began taking off my clothes. *Let's see how deep this thing really was.* I jumped into the puddle and plunged into darkness.

CHAPTER 5

A Whole New World

When I opened my eyes, the only lights I saw were the rays of moonlight shining down through the puddle. Everywhere else was pitch black. *This place felt like a black hole. This wasn't an ordinary puddle.* I could feel empty space surrounding me.

My body began to tingle all over as tiny bubbles swirled, encircling my body. I felt a tug, like the slight pull of an undertow, dragging me down deeper into the water. A shiver shot down my spine causing my body to jerk as I cringed in pain. The second time my body went into spasms, I began to panic. I was sinking deeper into the abyss, away from the puddle opening and my only access to air and home. My lungs began to burn as I used up the last of my oxygen. *I didn't have much time!* I started to pump my arms and legs as hard as I could, trying to swim up to the entrance, but the undertow's current began to pull me more forcefully, causing the water to churn. *I'd never make it.* My lungs squeezed my insides as I said a silent prayer. *If I survived this, I would destroy that puddle. No wonder no one had ever said anything about it. They probably never had the chance.* I tried not to think about how many deaths this puddle might have caused.

I could see the undertow was beginning to spout, spiralling in a more tubular fashion as it picked up speed. *I had to get out of here.* I looked helplessly towards the puddle, no more than a small spot of light. In a last ditch effort, I summoned my final bit of strength and hurled myself out of the spiralling water and into the darkness. The tugging sensation went away instantly. I felt my heart rate increase as my body screamed for air. Bubbles still swirled around my body tickling my feet and pressing lightly against my body. A chill raced through me. *I was going to die.*

I swam towards the puddle, desperately trying to reach The Surface as the lack of air forced my mouth open. My vision began to flicker as I became disoriented and water began to pour in, choking me. The bubbles that spiralled around my body shot up instantly into the water above me and spiralled down straight into my throat, forcing my mouth to open wider and turning my insides numb. *So, this is what dying felt like.* After a few moments, the bubbly feeling disappeared inside my body and around my legs. I realized the bubbles were what was allowing me to breathe. *Could be worse. At least I still had my thoughts and feelings.* I had always thought there was a heaven. Looks like you just become a ghost haunting the place where you died. I looked around hoping I had company but no other ghosts roamed the darkness. *This was what I was going to be stuck looking at for all eternity!* I was unamused as I watched what had been an undertow transform into a vortex with the water churning in a powerful spiral. *Whew! Dodged a bullet there.* I squinted my eyes into the darkness and noticed something glowing. A surge of relief washed over me. *Finally, some progress. Must be God's tunnel of light. I knew he wouldn't forget me.*

As I got closer, I struggled to swim, as though my legs were stuck together. I felt something slippery and smooth brush against my hand. I yelped, wondering what kind of creatures hid in the dark. I looked down, hoping it wouldn't be a barracuda or some kind of hungry, man-eating fish. It was a large tail attached to my skin. My eyes widened as my brain connected the dots. *It was my tail! I had a tail. I was a mermaid.* If the tail wasn't attached to me, I wouldn't believe it!

Confusion and excitement filled me as I approached what seemed to be a gigantic shimmering clear dome. It reminded me of a giant soap bubble. *Odd place for heaven to be. No pearly gates, no clouds, no long lost relatives.* Inside this unique sphere, the main source of light was coming from a gold castle encrusted with white diamonds. *Swanky place.* It sat on a small hill above a large city. Tearing my gaze away from its immense size, my eyes followed a winding road from the castle down below. My eyes widened to the size of coconuts. *Oh my God! It was an underwater city.*

At the one end of the city was a black cruise ship. White sand layered the ocean floor and dark sand served as public passageways. Colorful coral and anemones were everywhere. Houses were made of coral, stone, seaweed, jewels, shells, stained glass, clay, barnacles, wood and silver. There was even one made from whalebones in the shape of a whale. Each of them was unique. They were all different shapes and sizes.

The city was strangely deserted. Red siren lights located all over the city flashed on and off. There were more red lights to the left side of the sunken ship. I began to see the problem. The last traces of the moonlight from Lakewood shone down on the area where all the hubbub was coming from. A vortex spiralling up to the puddle was spinning out of control. Dots in the distance showed figures trying to control it. A tall chain link fence surrounded the vortex to keep people out of the area. I swallowed. *I hoped none of this had anything to do with me.*

I squinted, with only the castle's glow to help me see. Below my waist, my tail was the colour of forest green. It was so different from any colour I had seen on land. Diamonds were on various parts of my tail and each scale was tipped with gold. The caudal fins were a lighter green with pinstripes of silver running through them. I looked at the rest of my body. Everything seemed to be in the right place except for the fact that my upper torso was naked! The bubbles that had changed my legs to a tail had decided to make a few adjustments of their own. I saw a murky reflection of my face in the dome's reflection as my fingers touched my face and hair. My blonde hair was now twice its usual length, wavy and streaked with gold. My skin was a few shades darker, giving me a tanned look. My bitten nails were now long and were literally white diamonds! My belly button was pierced with a dolphin ring and encircled by a tribal sun tattoo. A stud pierced my nose, an orange starfish occupied both earlobes, small aqua diamonds were attached to my temples and a tattoo of a swirling purple design was etched on my lower back. *What I wouldn't have given to have had a mirror right then.*

I probably wouldn't have recognized myself. If mother could have only seen me! The thought of her horrified look just made me embrace my new freakish self in a more positive way.

Thinking of my Mom made me curious about home, wondering if they had noticed my absence. I stared at the vortex, which was causing most of the commotion in the city, contemplating what I should do. It was going to be next to impossible to get back to the puddle with the vortex blocking the entrance. It would suck me right back down to this underwater city the moment I stuck my tail in the turbulent waters. *Too dangerous. I'd just have to wait it out. Besides there was no way I was leaving until I got a chance to do a bit of exploring. No one back home was going to believe me!*

Sidewalk lights were glowing in the city as night began to set in more firmly. I scrutinized the dome carefully, running my hand along its surface. It had a thin layering and was slick exactly like a soap bubble. The dome was repelling the darkness away from the city and keeping clear blue water inside. I wondered if the dome would burst as I pushed myself through it, leaving the security of darkness. It didn't pop, but it began to vibrate where I had punctured a hole signalling my entry. *Uh oh! Not good.* While the dome re-knitted itself back together, I swam down to the bottom as fast as I could, trying to get as far away from that area as possible. Ducking behind a building, I grabbed two bluish purple seashells and strapped them to my breasts with seaweed, scaring a few small seahorses out of the pink and white coral they were occupying.

Seconds later, strong mermen warriors flew past me with

swords drawn and riding hippocampi. I gawked at the sight. It was like something out of a painting. The half-horse, half-fish creatures were beautiful. They resembled a breed called quarter horses. The one in the lead was stunning, the largest and blackest. Bubbles sprayed from his nostrils as he let out a whinny. Somewhere in the middle of his stomach, scales started to form. Where his back legs should have been was a large glimmering silver tail. I had never seen horses with tails before but they sure moved a heck of a lot faster than regular horses. The rest of the hippocampi swam by, all with different shades of colours: paints, bays, browns, reds and whites. Most of the tails matched each horse's original colour but there were a few mismatched tails.

The warriors disappeared around the corner, headed in the direction from which I had just come. Shaking my head at the reality of it, I headed in the direction of the vortex to see if I could get some answers.

CHAPTER 6

Jeremy Sea

Swimming into the city, the place looked deserted. A few panic stricken merpeople had managed to get themselves stuck in an alleyway. I swam by merpeople looking out their windows with worry, fear plastered on their faces. The red lights continued to flash as sirens began ringing all over the city, urging everyone to get to a safe place. Silver fish cut through the water like tiny silver daggers.

I continued on, entering the heart of the city and began to see even more merpeople. They were all swimming frantically away from the moonlit vortex, trying to get to their homes. A beautiful albino mermaid swam past me, her skin and scales as white as snow, almost as if she was a ghost, her top was made of pearl and diamond in a tube top fashion. She was such a rare sight that it was hard not to stare at her beauty. *I wondered if any of the merpeople had tried to come to Lakewood? How many of them were actually merpeople and not human?* While I was contemplating this, I noticed someone in front of me barring my way with an annoyed look on his face.

I scrutinized the merman, hoping he didn't see me as an imposter. He was much taller than me, a muscular six-foot-three, head-to-caudal fin. Shaggy blonde bangs of hair brushed his forehead, a three-inch scar over his left eyebrow. A shark tooth necklace lay across his chest tied with a black string. He looked to be about my age. His sea green eyes bore down on me with lips pursed in disapproval. No jewels of any sort adorned his tail and his scales were the same forest green as mine. Merpeople's tails and fins were various shades of green with the mermen having plain tails and the mer-women's tails being flashier, adorned with jewels and dia-monds.

"Alright, we don't need any heroics today, missy," his deep stern voice said as his arms attempted to block me from going any farther. "It's a sure way to get yourself killed."

I stopped abruptly. *Missy?* My first encounter with a non-human and he calls me MISSY! The chain link fence that contained the swirling vortex had been thrown open as the mermen attempted to keep it under control so it wouldn't de-stroy anything around it until it ran its course.

"Sir!" I spoke harshly. Instantly, I realized I didn't want to draw attention to myself and lowered my voice. "I don't know what you're talking about." This wasn't my world any-more. I didn't know their customs.

He looked at me curiously. "A girl with that kind of de-termined swimming is something only the warriors of this water share. Why are you not hiding? Do you not heed the warnings?"

The cheek of this man. I was no child. He was the same friggin' age as me! "I could say the same for you!"

He raised an eyebrow in surprise at my brashness. "What is your purpose for being out of doors?"

I let out a big gush of bubbles. *This was getting us nowhere. Who did he think he was? The police?* "I confess, I have never seen this place before and I wanted to get a glimpse of it," I said.

He laughed, lowering his guard. "Of all times, you come at the worst. You tourists are all the same. Tell me, do you *want* to get yourself killed or just laugh in the face of death? There is a human about! We are in code red! It is not a time for sightseeing. As we speak, they are readying a poisonous toxin to be released into the water to put the human into a permanent sleep so we can capture and kill it. Do you not see the bubbledomes over merpeople's houses? You should head back to Poseidon's hotel. Take Jellyfish Alley. You're not safe out here."

So they were after me. Suddenly, dread overtook me. The thought of a poisonous toxin putting me to sleep when I had just discovered this magnificent place was out of the question. I had almost died once; I was not about to feel that panic in my heart twice in one day. "I'm not a tourist, I just moved here a month ago," I lied. "And what about you, why aren't you hiding?"

A look of irritation crossed his face. "Boy, you sure are a stubborn one, aren't you?"

"I'm no coward," I spoke indignantly. "Let me help!" I flicked my tail in defiance.

"This ain't no drill, sweetheart." His green eyes glittered back at me.

"I'M. NOT. MOVING." I gritted my teeth, knowing I

should just swim away, but I had never been able to back down from a challenge.

Glancing behind him, the merman realized he was getting glances from the other warriors who had been working on the vortex, grabbing strings of churning water and pulling, trying to slow down the vortex' rhythm. "Come on!" he grunted as he took hold of my elbow and dragged me away from the area. "You're going to make me the laughing stock of the ocean." He began grumbling to himself, towing me along with ease as if I was no heavier than a feather. "Don't you understand the most dangerous thing in the world has just happened? This is the second case of a human entering our world."

Wrenching my arm out of his grasp, I stared at him icily. "Who do you think you are? I'm not as dim as you think! I can take care of myself."

Grabbing my shoulders painfully, he turned me around. "Enough with the theatrics. You see those green, splotchy clouds?"

"Yeah," I said quietly.

"Those ain't clouds." He took my hand and pulled me around a corner close to the main street of the city where shops and businesses lined the road. "Whereabouts do you live?"

I hesitated, then thought up a lie. "On the far side of the city."

The merman cursed under his breath. "You'll never make it in time. Come on!"

"How did all this start?" I asked, slightly out of breath and feeling like my arm was being wrenched out of its socket by his strong arms. No one loitered in the streets. All the homes had bubbledomes around them protecting them from the toxin.

"Does it look like we have time for questions?" He gestured wildly towards the city as a plume of green began to sweep through. "*Any* merperson found outside who's been drugged by this poison will be killed! Merperson or not, we don't take *any* chances, not since the last time." Distress showed clearly on his face.

"What about the animals?" I asked. I saw a few sea creatures scurry out of our path and hoped they wouldn't die because of my arrival.

We barrelled into a small subdivision as houses blurred before my eyes. "It'll make them drowsy, but that's all. It's not meant to harm animals."

"But, what about you and the other soldiers?" I asked.

"See this mask that's strapped to me? It protects me but, without it, I'd be just as vulnerable as every other merperson."

I had no time to admire the scenery as the man stuck his hand on the centre of a door. The sensor scanned his hand and clicked open as he threw me inside, sending me flying into a potted plant.

Heart pumping from the swim, my tail throbbing from all the powerful strokes, I stared at my "rescuer" with contempt. Despite his roughness, however, I had never laid eyes on anyone more handsome.

He stayed by the door, quickly pressing buttons and brushing his blonde bangs out of his face irritability, as I stared out the window. A translucent sheen descended around the house as dark green smoke began to batter the shield without success. It plunged the city into total darkness, snuffing out streetlights.

Meanwhile, I glanced around the small living room. An electric blue glow fish provided the light. The house was made of white coral with odd shapes extending from the walls. It was rough and looked uncomfortable. A far cry from what I was used to at home. White sand covered the floor. A huge harp sat in the corner for entertaining and four rocks covered with some type of moss for padding sat in the middle of the room to serve as furniture. One door led into an adjacent room on the left and another door was across the room on the right.

"Sit down!" he commanded, pointing at the rock that served as a chair while he paced back and forth. I stayed as quiet as a mouse; all my retorts were shoved to the back of my throat. He was angry. "How am I supposed to fix everything with the underworld in an uproar? All because of you."

"Me?" I squeaked, suddenly becoming shy around him, a feeling I was not accustomed to. Felicity O'Connor *never* does shy.

"Yes, you. Now I'm trapped." He flung down his gas mask. "I can't go out and look for this human if I'm stuck in the bubbledome. This was going to prove to the King that I am a worthy warrior!"

"Well, you didn't have to 'save' me." I crossed my arms over my chest.

"You didn't give me much choice!" he growled. "To have someone's death on my conscience is not something I take lightly, even if it is someone like *you!*"

"And what…exactly is *that* supposed to mean?" I stood up, staring him dead in the eye. "Insulting me is ill-advised," I warned, with my fists clenched.

He stopped his pacing. His chest was heaving, his muscles tense, as we looked at each other with anger until a smile crept onto his lips and he laughed, breaking the tension. "You are like no merwoman I have ever met."

I eyed him warily, wondering if this was some kind of trick, then began to laugh, as well, the night's stress rolling off my shoulders.

Between bouts of laughter, he said, "I honestly thought we were going to end up in an all-out brawl. I dare not hit a mermaid. Can I at least know the name of the mermaid who has caused me so much trouble this evening?"

I paused, trying to think of a name. "Crystal." I paused again to think of a last name. I spotted the harp and on the bottom it said Clearwater Inc. "Crystal Clearwater."

"Alright, Crystal, nice to finally put a name to your face. I'm Jeremy Sea. Why haven't I seen you in school before?"

"Like I said earlier, I just moved here about a month ago." I swam towards the window so he couldn't see my face. "What are you trying to fix? One mere merman cannot fix everything that happens in the world."

"If one makes the mess, only he should be the one to clean it up."

"You want to tell me about it?"

He looked around the room as if searching for unwanted ears listening in on our conversation. Letting out a deep breath, he said, "I do not know what the future will hold from this day forward but I shall take the blame should anyone else be implicated. It is my fault for the code red. My friends and I are to blame for all of this."

"I'm sure it's not *all* your fault," I said quietly, knowing it was actually all *my* fault.

"I let the King's daughter cross the Forbidden Area today." He looked at me as though I should reprimand him. He stayed silent for a while, as I remained motionless. Obviously, I did not grasp the enormity of the situation. "Do you not judge me?"

"You did not ask me to judge, but to listen." I said hoping it was a good answer because I had no clue what he was talking about.

He took my arm, brought me to a long rock couch and sat down beside me, eager to tell his tale, as I tried to ignore how limited the space was between us. "A code red has only been issued once in our history books, thousands of years ago. A human was caught and killed. Times were hard for a while, constant fear, round-the-clock surveillance, in case the human had spoken of Atlantis to other humans."

Jeremy continued to talk. "Today, one of my friends decided to swim across the Forbidden Area. Her name is Shell Reef. She's the King's daughter. We didn't think it was going to be a big deal. The whole school had done it except for Shell. When she went to swim across the area, we had a direct hit from the human's sun. That's why we're not supposed to swim across it. The sun hit Shell's tail right as she was at the centre of the Forbidden Area. Usually, we can get away with it. We have green tails so they don't show much reflection. But, since Shell is royalty, she has a gold tail and you can guess how much it shone when the light hit her. *Like one big game of risk.*

Because of that, a human must have caught a glimpse of it and found the entrance to Atlantis. Nobody knows what happened except my friends, Shell and me. We have many ways to disguise the entrance from the human world, but I guess it wasn't good enough. I hope they catch the human, but it's going to be hard. Once they're in the water, they automatically turn into one of us."

"Why?" I asked feigning a frightened face.

"Nobody knows or understands why. Something in the water, we think. That's why we have to be very cautious. They don't have all the things that we possess, so at least that's one way to catch them. I just can't believe it managed to escape the vortex trap. It *should* have worked," Jeremy muttered to himself. "As soon as a human jumps in the Forbidden Area, it should be sucked right towards us. I helped build that vortex myself and I know it should have worked. Although, it has been a hundred years since it's been used. Shouldn't have mattered, though."

I swallowed hard, interrupting him. "What will they do once they catch the human?" *I didn't think I wanted to know the answer.*

His voice became serious and his face was set in a grim expression. "I think the King will order his men to have the human killed. He will show no mercy. It seems like the only logical answer. If we don't, then the human will go home and tell everyone in his world about us - and our world will be destroyed. A single man can change our future forever and destroy us. They just can't be trusted." *Or a single woman.*

Jeremy continued on, as I began yawning, the day's

events finally catching up with me. "Could you imagine walking on two legs and not living in water? But being able to survive in both. They sound like a ridiculous species! But, they sure are powerful. Why else would the gods have favoured them with so many differences from us?"

"You fear what you do not know," I mumbled sleepily, as I felt myself nodding off. For the moment, I was safe.

CHAPTER 7

Home As I Know It

I woke up to light streaming through the window. I wiped the sleep from my eyes, stared at my tail and grinned excitedly. Forgetting caution, I flung open the front door to see the glittering city for the first time during the day. I drank in the scene before me. Everything was blue, bright and shiny. The dome that surrounded the city was still operational and kept the blackness at bay. It was strange. Even though darkness surrounded the city, somehow Atlantis still had regular sunlight throughout the city, just like Lakewood's day and night. The bubbledomes were off the houses as schools of fish swam in and around buildings, their scales gleaming. Hippocampi whickered happily, merpeople flocked the streets, and sea organisms littered the area, showing shocks of vibrant colour. Delight and happiness bubbled inside me at such a sight.

"'Bout time your lazy tail got up!" Jeremy said, as he came up behind me and nudged me playfully on the shoulder. "You coming to school today or what, Superstar? I could show you around, give you a tour. Your choice."

I smiled slightly at the nickname he gave me. I saw a few mermaids and mermen waving at Jeremy as he waved back, each one with its own distinctive colours. I felt more and more of an imposter every second. "No, it's okay. I'll catch up with you later." If I wanted to keep my true identity hidden, I really needed to master a poker face but, with everything so beyond belief, it was going to be tricky. Jeremy wasn't exactly stupid.

"Alright, suit yourself. Stay out of trouble, don't make me have to come save you again!" he joked warmly, as he swam away to join his chums, leaving me alone with my thoughts. He turned back to wave goodbye and I blushed slightly, not realizing I had been staring at him the whole time.

I swam towards the heart of the city. It wasn't just the merpeople who were busy, but the plants, too. Different kinds of coral were disbursed throughout the city sending vibrant flashes of bright colours and creating homes and food for many of the fish that swam around the area. I passed by a house made completely of fire coral. Sea urchins were everywhere. Another house made of seashells had a garden of red sea fans eating small fish and plants.

I passed a small, wooden building and on it the sign read "ReLocation." I looked in the window. Merpeople sat at coral desks and were writing on kelp paper, putting notes up on the message boards, crossing off houses, writing "Taken" on them and then signing their names. *Good a place to start as any, I guessed. Looked to be the same procedure as back home.* I pushed on the door and swam in.

Ding!

All talking and motion ceased as everyone stared at me, their eyes bugging out of their heads. They leapt out of their chairs and swam to me as fast as their tails would move them, swarming me. *Ugh...realtors.* ReLocation became a zoo of chaos. *Buncha freakin' loonies!*

They were jumping all over, throwing their cards at me and asking to show or build me a house. I already had at least six paper cuts from their crappy cards. I closed my eyes and grabbed for the first person on my right.

Once the vultures finally realized they had lost their prey, they sulked back to their desks. After the crowd left, I saw who I had a death grip on: a medium sized merman with black slick hair and a huge keg belly. His nametag read: "Mark Aqua." "Hi, Mark. I'm Crystal Clearwater." I held out my hand for him to shake. *Even with that keg belly of his, he still managed to look good for an older guy. Must be a merpeople thing. At least, this way everyone was treated equally. I was beginning to like this place more and more.*

He shook my hand with a firm grip. "Come on over and step into my office." He led me to a tiny cubicle with walls made of shell shards. "So, you're looking for a house, are you?" He tsked as his head gestured towards the group not far from him and took a seat across from me. "It's despicable the way my co-workers will do anything to get paid extra sand dollars. But thanks to the King's new law to abolish poverty, the merpopulation doesn't have to pay a single sand dollar for property. So, what's your pleasure? Where do you wish to live or relocate to?"

"I want to relocate." I paused, realizing I hadn't even considered the payment part of it. Handy that new law just came out, almost like it was meant to be. They sure made it pretty darn easy for a human to live here. Despite being intrigued, my stomach felt uneasy. Hope this place wasn't being monitored. "I was living close to the Forbidden Area but, after last night, I would feel safer if I moved away from there. But, um, not too far away from the school." I added quickly. "I have given my old place to the neighbours kids for them to live in since they were in need of a home and mine suited them perfectly."

"Reasonable enough," he said, as he searched through his hundreds of diagrams of kelp paper. "Hmm…I have the perfect lot for you. We can build your new house from one of my own designs." He began rummaging through his desk and lifted out a different stack of kelp paper. He showed me a series of designs. "Mergirls *love* this design," he boasted, showing me a home of hot pink coral with pale pink jewels encrusted around the door and windows. Purple urchins hung all over and bright blue flowers flowed over one side of the wall. I shook my head immediately. *I hated pink.* Some of his co-workers were getting ready to pounce, wanting to steal away Mark's customer.

"I'll take that one." I pointed randomly to a design I had looked at previously. It was smaller than the rest but it would fit my needs perfectly.

"Excellent. Now, all I need for you to do is stick your hand into this." He pulled out a slab of gooey, nasty looking stuff, giving his fellow employees a sharp, toothy grin.

I stuck my hand into the soft, grey clay, not questioning why. I didn't need to draw any more attention to myself. I felt the stuff harden immediately around the bottom of my hand. When it solidified, I took my hand out.

"Great, now come with me and we'll go see your new house." He rolled up the diagram, grabbed the hand imprint and swam towards the back of the building in what could only be called a cocky strut.

We stepped outside to the back part of the building. Mark whistled and, in seconds, there was a red crab the size of a car in front of us. I tried to hide my amazement. *Holy! How many steroids was this thing taking?* It was the height of half my tail and as long as a car. On top of its shell sat two huge comfortable seats. Once we sat down, he took off as fast as his six legs could scurry towards our destination. I called it the 'taxicrab.' "Not the fastest mode of transportation, but it is the most reliable," Mark commented.

An abnormally large water snake swam beside us, its tongue flicking in and out lazily. The snake had three set of gills cut on each side of its body. It was slightly higher than the taxicrab and along its body there were seats, all of which were full of teenage merpeople talking loudly to one another. It reminded me slightly of a school bus. I hated snakes in Lakewood and my opinion on the matter stayed the same here.

We stopped for a red glow fish light as the traffic piled up behind us. I saw Poseidon's Hotel from a block away. It was daunting and massive, one of the nicest buildings I had seen so far. It towered fifty stories high and was a dark blue and black. A huge statue of Poseidon, the size of the hotel, was wrapped around the building, as though he was protecting it. Bubbles shot from the roof at certain times like confetti, then fell like snowflakes to the ground.

A huge Humpback whale cruised down the street as merpeople scrambled to get out of the way. I couldn't take my eyes off it. It was the largest mammal I had ever seen. *Sea-World didn't even compare to this place. I wished my mouth would stop popping open every time I saw something new!* The light changed and the crab moved on. I watched the whale until it punctured through the dome and was swallowed up into the darkness that surrounded Atlantis. A Sperm Whale followed shortly after, with two harpoons embedded in his skin and a few nasty scars lining his body, his echolocation creating a pleasant melody in the water.

Mark chuckled quietly as the crab continued on. "The first whale was Rhinestone and that's Moby Dick. They transport all sorts of merpeople from place to place. No one trusts the darkness anymore. These are dangerous times. Not many merpeople get the chance to see both of em' at once. Pretty darn intimidating, if you ask me. Moby's kind of famous around here. Doesn't come around a lot but he's a busy whale. I wouldn't want to get on his bad side, though. There are rumours that he swallowed a whole ship of them humans. Good riddance to them! Rubbed one human the wrong way, that human still hunts for him desperately."

"How could he swallow humans? Isn't the Forbidden Area the only place where humans come from?"

"There is one other, a place called The Surface, but few merpeople have ventured there. You have to pass the Seaweed Desert before you reach The Surface and, even then, it's difficult with all the different wildlife lurking around. Old Moby and Rhinestone, though, they're so big no one bothers them. Tourists ride on them to see The Surface. I've heard the tales, and it's said to be quite astounding. Never did it myself. Much too afraid. Lucky for us, the humans can only breathe underwater with their magic devices for so long."

"Have you heard anything from last night about the human?"

"Not a peep. They're keeping it all very hush hush. Your guess is as good as mine. We'll be hearing 'bout this human invasion for years. Most excitement we've had in a long time, not since the last code red. I just hope it isn't in connection to the last one. Gives me the willies just thinking about it." He let out a sigh. "The market isn't as good as it was a thousand years ago when sea land sold for thousands of sand dollars, before all this darkness surrounded Atlantis. We raised herds of hippocampi a few miles away from Atlantis and grew our food in sand. We had so much land back then the population increased along with the house sales. We didn't have to have our food shipped in like nowadays, risking our strongest and bravest creatures to venture into the darkness with our supplies. Sand stretched throughout the land as far as the eye could see with no dome covering the city. Those were the good ol' days. Now we are all jammed inside this dome like a bunch of sardines." Before I could ask another question, the crab came to an abrupt halt. "We're here!" he grinned as we got off and looked at the empty lot four blocks from the school.

Mark set the kelp paper design of the house in the middle of the property and the slab of clay with my hand imprint on top of it. A solid shape of some kind began to push its way out of the design. The paper and clay were soon swallowed up as it grew and expanded. It created a ruby red crystal house. It came with a deck, a bunch of flowers and an underwater tree in the front yard filled with yellow star-shaped flowers. Huge mansions surrounded my new home. It was like comparing a human to an ant. I felt as though the rest of the houses could swallow me whole. "It's beautiful. Just what I always wanted." *If only houses could be made that fast on land...*

"Really?" Mark's eyes shined with happiness and I automatically saw dollar signs. Apparently, even though the houses were free, the King still paid these sales sharks a pretty good commission. Greed is everywhere. There really is no escaping it. "I guess I can leave you and get back to work. I have loads of designs that I must sell." Daylight reflected off a tiny bald spot on the centre of his head as he left to harass another customer.

I stared at the building in front of me and I felt giddiness bubble to the surface. This place was mine: my house, my territory, *mine.* I put my hand on the centre of the door, the way I had seen Jeremy do it, in hopes that the scanner would work.

The door scanned my hand and opened into a room with four huge white pillars on all four corners of the living room walls. My home glowed red with the colour of the jewels. Tall windows in the living room gave me a view of the backyard. I could see a patio and a stable type of barn. *What the heck did I put in that?*

Ignoring that part of the house for the moment, I turned in a circle and let my guard down to relax and enjoy Atlantis. My place was pretty bare and I wondered where I was going to get the sand dollars to furnish it properly. The left side of my wall had a wooden lattice filled with a variety of huge, colourful flowers. My bedroom jutted out on the left side of the living room. I swam through the seaweed curtain that created a small barrier between the two rooms. My bed was a huge clamshell, polished and shiny. It was open and the bottom was covered in sheets and mossy pillows. The inside was pale pink and the outside was pearl white. A big viewing mirror was in the corner. Red curtains fluttered from the currents of the windows. A dresser was off to one side, a black coral desk on the other. *Not too shabby. I liked that it wasn't cluttered like my room back home.* It seemed like merpeople didn't need a lot of things to be happy.

I took a deep breath as I approached the mirror. I stared at the creature before me, hardly recognizing myself. I began to touch my face, watching the mirror's reflection to make sure this wasn't some kind of spell. My eyes freaked me out. They were the colour of blue crystal. I'm pretty sure *none* of the other merpeople had eyes like mine. I dashed out of the room not wanting to think about it too much. *I hoped this didn't single me out as a human!*

A small kitchen on the right side of the living room had nothing but stone countertops, a few cupboards to store food and a small window. It was quaint. It reminded me of Jeremy's house.

I stared at all the rocks for furniture knowing that the only thing comfortable would be the bed. *I wished I had human furniture.*

Content that I was no longer homeless, I went in search of the school. The school turned out to be the gigantic cruise ship; it must have been one of the fancy ones when it was operational. Barnacles and starfish hugged the hull of the ship. Grey stones spelled out: *Atlantis School of Fins, Home of the Atlantis Snails.* I looked over to see a massive statue of a snail in the front entrance. On the side of the ship written in gold was its former name: Odyssey.

The Forbidden Area across the road had sunlight from Lakewood shining down onto the chain link fence. I realized I was never too far away from home. It was guarded by soldiers but the Forbidden Area was no longer a vortex of swirling water and, instead, was calm. *How could something as tiny as a puddle in Lakewood be so vast and hold so many lives?*

I swam into the school, trying to ignore all the splendour: marble floors, glass staircases, statues, chandeliers, pillars and glass figurines were all still gleaming from the ship's former glory.

I saw a sign that said 'Main Office,' which looked like some sort of ice-cream parlour before the merpeople renovated it to their liking. I peered into the little area. Seashells were ringing off the hook. Kelp paper was scattered in all directions and messenger fish were waiting at attention. Merpeople were bustling around trying to look important and sending shrimps on quests for detentions and late fees on books.

I kept swimming, wanting no part in these activities, perfectly at ease to snoop. Each classroom I looked in on had sandboards attached to the walls for teachers to write notes on, as students sat straight on stones looking interested. They had no desks and no paper, as if all they had to do was listen. A few merpeople were writing notes down. I snorted; no way could school ever be that interesting. This was not like my school, not even close. These students actually *wanted* to come and learn. I passed hallway after hallway, getting lost in the school as the teachers spoke passionately to their classes. I passed by a window on the third floor and saw mer-people outside playing some sort of game.

"It's called Turtle Hurl." A voice smooth and sleek whispered into my ear. His breath brushed against my hair giving me goose bumps.

I jumped in surprise. "Oh!" I turned around quickly to see the Prince of Atlantis within an inch of my face. "I didn't see you there." His tail was bathed in gold from the daylight streaming through the window. He was a tall dark-haired beauty but his name wasn't Jeremy. I didn't even know what his name was. That fact would probably have me singled out as a human. *Since when did royalty hang around with the public and go to public schools, not private ones?*

He flashed me a grin and I quickly returned to the game. It reminded me vaguely of football but with a turtle. It was much more of a challenge because the turtle had a mind of its own. It would go one way and then suddenly veer off in the opposite direction. It was a full contact sport. The girls in the class actually *played*. I'm talking, every single girl played. None were off to the sidelines flirting with a boy or hugging the sidelines. Not one! From what I could see, the girls were kicking butt. That's what I love about sports - the ability to tune everything out, to release your anger, to run and never have to stop. Gym was such a nice escape.

"You must be the new girl, Crystal?" The Prince joined me to watch the game in progress.

"How did you know I was the new girl?"

"I can tell. I don't usually have to go and talk to mermaids. They usually come to me," he smirked.

"Oh really, is that so?" I spoke, slightly irritated by his smugness.

"So, what's a cute thing like you doing here all by yourself?"

I resisted the urge to roll my eyes at his feeble attempt at flirting. "Avoiding mermen like you, I suppose." I smiled, thinking of how much Mandy would love to see all the good looking guys here.

"Ah, shoot. Come on now, you don't really mean that. You hardly know me. With a name like Sebastian, you can't go wrong." He grinned as his tail hit mine playfully. "You seem to know Jeremy, though." He winked at me, trying to gauge my reaction.

"I don't know what you mean." I tried to keep my emotions in check, not sure what he was getting at. "I met him for the first time yesterday."

"Once, evidently, was enough. He's telling everyone how he saved your life during the code red, said he found you near the Forbidden Area."

"He didn't save my life!"

"I didn't think you were the kind of girl who needed saving."

"I'm not. But I suppose he *did* save me from the toxic poison your *Dad* put in the water."

A foghorn blared and I yelped, the noise ringing in my ears. "You're awfully jumpy today. It's just the lunch bell. Then again, I tend to have that effect on merwomen." Students came swimming out of all the doors. They began to swallow us up. "Come on, let's go get something to eat. I'm starving! I'll introduce you to everyone." Without waiting for my reply, he grabbed my hand.

The cafeteria was a wide-open space with three levels in an oval formation. Mahogany wood lined the floors and archways surrounded the entrances, as vines of flowers wrapped around the tables and banisters. Human tables and chairs were placed everywhere, still in pristine condition. This whole ship was in excellent condition. It showed no signs of why it had sunk; no moss anywhere, no gaping holes. The ship had just been renovated to meet their needs for classrooms and offices. *If they despised humans so much why would they want to learn in something humans had created?*

I couldn't help notice all the envious glances the mermaids shot my way as I swam with the Prince. The realization that I was with royalty hadn't quite set in yet. "This isn't even half the school," Sebastian informed me, as he grabbed two trays from the food court, filled both of them up, then threw down some sand dollars to the cafeteria worker. We swam up to the 3rd floor and he plopped a tray in front of me.

I stared at it in disgust. "What is that?" I poked the little circles in front of me.

"Lobster and salmon stuffed in seaweed wraps. It's one of the best meals they serve here. Just eat it; it's not going to bite."

I nibbled timidly on one and found it to be passable, as my stomach growled. I realized I hadn't eaten anything in more than a day. I stared down at the clustered groups. From my vantage point, I could see everything that was going on, even the long table that used to be the captain's table. I scanned the cafeteria for Jeremy but there was no point because all I could see were tails shimmering like crazy. The sight was really pretty to see from so high up. This school was something I wasn't used to. *What did you do when all the students were beautiful?* I felt oddly out of place, not because of the lack of human feet, but because of the atmosphere. No one can be discriminated against when everyone looks amazing. I'm not going to lie, I didn't hate the feeling; fewer people for me to have to beat up on.

Three mermaids swam over to our table with curiosity clearly on their faces as the Prince waved them over. "Crystal, this is Coral, Rainbow and Star."

Rainbow was a head taller than the other two and obviously the leader. She had long red hair with red streamers woven into it, a pale face and fiery green eyes. Her tail also supported streaks of reflective red in a corkscrew design. Her chest was barely covered by two small pink starfish as her hair cascaded around her chest, making it look like she wore nothing at all. She stood out among most of the mermaids I had seen all day, a fact I think she already knew. "So, you're the new girl," came her voice as she sat close to Sebastian and looked me up and down.

I stared at her, realizing some things about high school never change. I put on my brightest smile to show her that her presence didn't faze me. "Yup, that's me."

"Look at her eyes!" Star squeaked with excitement. Star had medium length black hair that sprouted out in all directions, silver eyes and glitter dusting her arms. Her skin was tanned and her tail was plain with no jewels, just sea green with steel blue sparkles. She was wearing two big brown snail shells with gold edging around the ridges of each shell on her chest.

Sebastian flashed a grin that made the three girls sigh dreamily. "Yeah, they've been like that *all* day."

I didn't have the slightest clue what they were talking about. I did enjoy the scowl Rainbow gave Sebastian though. "What are you talking about?" I asked.

"Your eyes! They've crystallized. They only do that when you're at your happiest," Star explained.

"Yeah, because she met me," Sebastian joked, as he stuffed a wrap into his mouth.

"What's the real reason?" Star interjected.

I stared over the table as I tried to think up a lie. Coral, who was the smallest of the three, not to mention the quietest, hadn't uttered a single word. Her shoulder length straight brown hair hung around her face hiding her full lips. She had strings of pearls woven into her hair, turning it into a sort of cap on her head. She had a small nose and big violet eyes. Her tail was dark green with an electric purple and blue design wrapping all around it with a lot of swirls. She was pretty in an unusual way. She smiled at me encouragingly.

"Oh, I don't know," I spoke casually. "Must have been when I met Sebastian. I've never met royalty before."

Sebastian smiled. "Well, I am kind of a big deal," he boasted jokingly.

"Is that your natural tail? It's gorgeous," Star asked me, as her hand traced some of my scales. I noticed how sensitive the feeling was, as goose bumps lined my arms.

"Star!" Sebastian swatted her on the arm. "That's rude."

"Obviously, it has a bunch of add-ons." Rainbow looked at my tail sceptically.

"Nope, it's not a fake. Everything is smooth, no bumps to suggest add-ons. It's so hard to tell sometimes and mermaids lie all the time about that stuff," Star sighed. "I wish I was born with a tail like that, instead of this one."

"You have a very nice looking tail, Star. Very shiny." I smiled at her, hoping to cheer her up.

"I look like I have the scales of a fish!" she squealed.

"But a very nice fish." Sebastian laughed.

"Where did you come from anyway?" Rainbow interrupted, clearly not impressed with the conversation.

I hesitated, unsure of how to answer and wondering if their underwater countries were different from mine. "New Zealand, in a really small town you've probably never heard of." I couldn't stare them directly in the eyes. I didn't want to see their calculating glances.

"We don't get many new people here on account of the Forbidden Area and the darkness. A lot of hot tourists, though," Star pouted miserably. "Not that it matters to you. Seems to me you've already caught Jeremy's attention." I blushed slightly, cursing myself for such an obvious gesture.

"Here comes her royal highness now," Sebastian mused. Shell Reef swam nearby, glanced briefly at our table, gave a brief nod to her brother and went to sit at the table across from us. Sebastian's sister was shimmering with gold all over. She was exquisite to behold. She had blonde hair and tanned skin with a necklace of silver jewels around her throat and bracelets layered on her arms, along with a gold armband in the shape of a dolphin. A gold and red glossy bikini-style top was on her chest with gold beads attached that hung down to her belly. A small silver circlet was placed on her head. She was blinding to watch.

"She's probably looking for you." Rainbow examined her nails. "You might want to run for cover."

"She won't touch Crystal while I'm here." Sebastian didn't take his eyes off his sister.

The gesture still didn't make me feel safe. "Why?"

"She's Jeremy's girlfriend." Star summed it up for me as Coral gave me a sympathetic glance.

"His girlfriend?" I choked on some lobster. "He told me they were just good friends."

"Friends? They're meant to be together. They're the best dolphin riders in the school," Rainbow explained with a hint of jealousy.

Sebastian burst out laughing. "Ah, that's all jellyfish fodder! Shell is meant for no one - except for every merguy in the school whose interest is chasing tail."

Star's voice lowered. "She's the one who caused the code red. Everyone knows it, but no one is going to do anything about it because the King would probably chop off Shell's tail, he'd be so angry." She held her tail tenderly as if the very thought was going to make it fall off.

My eyes widened. "He can do that?"

"He's the King. He can do whatever the heck he wants," Rainbow replied saucily. All three of the girls nodded their heads like triplets. It was hard for me to sit at the same table as these people. Popular and interested in gossip; it went against all that I live for.

"Odd, she didn't come say hello." Rainbow bit the bottom

of her lip.

"That's fine by me." Sebastian finished his meal and put his elbows on the table. Rainbow ignored the comment and took off to join Shell without saying goodbye.

"Don't mind Rainbow. She's always like that because she hasn't given away her pearl yet, and Shell obviously has," Star drawled.

The two girls grinned while I sat there confused. Luckily, the foghorn sounded, ending their secret joke as everyone swam to class.

I found myself following Coral for the rest of the day. I was happy for the silence after lunch. I had thought merpeople's personalities would be different. Then again, I had only been talking to brainless teenagers. Meradults, however, might not find my ignorance quite as appealing. All around me I could hear students buzzing about the human invasion.

I sat behind Coral in all her classes trying to see if I wanted to subject myself to school. There was a class called Human Ed that all merpeople had to attend. Mrs. Sushi drilled me on my experience during the code red, much to my humiliation. The class was worth going to because I had, in turn, learned something about Coral in the process. She is a *big* history buff.

At the end of the day, I managed to get her to open up and talk to me. "So you like history?" I asked off-handedly, as I held her locker door open.

Her violet eyes widened to saucers. "Please! Promise me you won't say a word to the others. It's totally not cool."

Her tone of voice surprised me. It wasn't what I had expected at all. It was light and sweet, one of the nicest voices

I'd heard so far. "My lips are sealed."

She let her taut body relax. "Was I that obvious?"

"Well, when you put up your hand on every question about the Forbidden Area's history, I put two and two together."

"Drat it all! I've lived here my whole life. I can't help it if that hippo of a teacher can't get his facts straight. It just sets me in a rage. *Clearly,* the Forbidden Area was created by Thanatos, who is the embodiment of death and was wishing his evil upon us. Humans couldn't have created something as technical as that. Thanks to the Sea God, Poseidon, he gave us the skills to create the vortex to catch humans and keep us from harm, along with this cruise ship to help us learn and see how they live. We can study them and see what makes them tick. The code red may be Shell's fault but it is by Thanatos' doing! 'Course, everyone here must blame it on the humans because it's the *only* plausible answer. History says the Forbidden Area existed from the moment darkness engulfed the city, which is too far back for me to remember. Others say it just showed up one day, which is total nonsense. Atlantis fears the Forbidden Area, yet cherishes it, for we are of a very curious nature and appreciate unusual things no matter how terrifying.

"Humans are weak and too stupid to be able to find Atlantis. Don't even get me started on the wars! Never once has Poseidon come to our aid when we fought jellyfish, sharks, eels or whales! He can't help us directly. He can only guide us. That's what all the gods are like. It's in all the books. They cannot interfere with the world, but only help it along by influencing others. That is why Poseidon has so much more of an advantage than Thanatos does, because it is better to embrace life than death."

I stared at her in shock. I had not expected such passion. Noting my reaction, she blushed profusely. "Why do you never share your views with the others? Why are you so quiet all the time?" I asked.

"Because my ideas and thoughts are too big for them and if I brought it up they would give me the same look you did. Besides, not many merpeople care to talk about that stuff anymore. I happen to find it interesting. Just like the myths of wild merpeople roaming the seaweed forest. I believe they exist, just that..."

I heard a sharp, brisk voice yell my name and it echoed down the halls: "Clearwater, come here for a minute." Mrs. Flounder, the gym teacher, was a few tail swims away. She had the longest mermaid tail I had seen so far. She was also the clumsiest in tight areas because of it, but get her in open water and I bet there would be no way anyone could catch her.

"Don't tell a soul," Coral whispered and took off towards the opposite end of the hallway, embarrassment clearly on her face.

"Jeremy tells me you've got a good shot at becoming a dolphin rider," said Mrs. Flounder, who was an older merwomen. To a human, she would look to be in her late thirties.

"I do?"

"Sure you do, dearie. I hold Jeremy in the highest regard." I cringed at the little endearment. I hated it when people call me dear. It's one of my biggest pet peeves, right next to chewing with your mouth open and pinching people's cheeks.

"Our school has won the state championship for many years and we don't intend to stop. Jeremy thinks you would be a great asset to the team if you can pass. We have practices after school almost every day - and we expect you to be there. Plus, since you're new, it wouldn't hurt you to do some extra practice at home either."

"Well, I could give it a shot, I guess."

"Since you have never done any dolphin riding before, I will give you an instructor to show you how to ride in a few easy steps. If you pass the test, in no time you'll be riding the hurricanes and whirlpools." I gulped. *Did she just say hurricanes and whirlpools?* I did some inventive cursing. *What had I just gotten myself into?*

CHAPTER 8

Terminated

I sat down by the entrance of the school watching all the merpeople leave in droves as school ended. Now that all the hubbub had died down, I truly realized how alone I was. It was hard for me to live in a world I knew nothing about. Worst of all, I couldn't tell anyone my secret because that would mean my death. My conscience weighed heavily on me. I wanted someone to know my secret so they could help me understand this place without having them run screaming to the King.

I watched two merteens tossing a blue and pink jellyfish back and forth to one another. With each catch they'd move farther apart from each other and make another toss. There was something important that I needed to remember, but for the life of me I couldn't figure out what it was. I watched them some more, racking my brain hoping to find some solution to the unease I was feeling.

One of the mermen dropped the jellyfish. It unfolded and tried to escape as the two mermen went on a merry chase. The jellyfish's stealth surprised me, but one of the mermen laughed as he held it up in his hands victoriously, then they started the game all over again. I smiled, as it reminded me of when I was a kid and I'd play catch with water balloons.

My eyes widened. *Catch! Baseball, the game! Ugh, it had probably already started. I'd never missed a game!*

I swam hard and fast, as far away from civilization and the castle's view as possible, which was pretty much to the other end of Atlantis. Seaweed of every kind and length sprouted up, some even reaching close to the dome's ceiling. This must be the seaweed forest. It extended out past the dome and into the darkness, but how far it went into the darkness I could not tell. I eyed the area suspiciously, thinking about what kind of wild savage merpeople might be lurking in that jungle.

I looked up and there was the shimmering dome above me. *This was a huge risk. If I did this, I might never get the chance to see this place again.* I stared out at the magical city and watched it shimmer, as light slowly began to fade with night setting in. *If it was any other team than the Stallions. Anyway, Atlantis wasn't going anywhere.* With that notion firmly in my mind, I shot up into the air and lifted both arms up over my head. As I passed through the dome, the impact rippled over the dome's surface and stung me as I cried out. That had never happened the last time. I felt my left side start to go numb.

I had to act fast before I lost feeling in my whole body. The darkness around the dome engulfed me, making me invisible to those inside. I spotted the puddle entrance from the last rays of sunlight shining down from Lakewood and swam towards it. As I closed in on the opening of the puddle, a large shape lurked nearby, off to my right. I shuddered and swam faster, trying not to think of the monstrous whales I had seen earlier that could eat twenty of me in one big gulp. I squinted, attempting to make out its form, and all I could see was two red eyes. Fear skirted about in my stomach. I was close enough to the puddle's entrance that I could see the oak tree on the other side.

I knew as soon as I entered the puddle area the vortex would start up again and try to suck me back down. My whole left side was numb and it was creeping over to my right side. If my whole body went numb, I would be immobilized and fall into the city, unable to move. They were sure to have guards out searching for me. With one last burst of energy I swam into the rays of dim sunlight, gripped the puddle entrance and, using my right hand, felt for grass on the other side and hauled myself out, all before the vortex could pull me back down. One last lame kick of my numbing tail and I was out, breathing in the fresh air as I rolled myself onto land, my fingernails digging into the cool soil.

I sat there coughing and shaking as my tail melted from my body and my pale legs were laid out in front of me. Gems fell off my skin, turning to liquid and soaking into the ground. My long hair shrank to its original length and was pin straight again. All my tattoos began to slowly retract into my body until there was no sign of them. All signs of numbness were gone as I flexed my muscles. *Incredible!* A cool breeze alerted me to my nakedness as I found my clothes off to the side, right where I had left them. They felt rough and course against my body. Everything felt so restrictive. *Ugh. So itchy!* I was happy to be back to the real me. All the colours in Lakewood looked faded and dull in comparison to Atlantis. A cheer erupted from the crowd at the baseball diamond, snapping me back to the present. *I only hoped I wasn't too late...*

A huge crowd occupied the stands. A few benches that were shoddily put together had cracked and split in half due to all the weight. A crowd like this was unheard of. Many spectators were sitting on lawn chairs or blankets. A few others were in the parking lot, tailgating, drinking beer and shouting encouragement or jeering. The city must have cleaned up the baseball diamond because no trash littered the ground. There were new bases, re-chalked lines and batter boxes. The grass was all cut and trimmed for the occasion.

I rounded the corner to our dugout and could tell it was hopeless. I was too late. It was the ninth inning and the Stallions were ahead by six. I cursed myself for missing the biggest game of the year. I didn't want to face my team. My humiliation was intensified as the Stallions struck out my teammate, Amanda, to end the game. They yelled out in savage triumph and victory as the whole team ran up to congratulate each other. *That should have been us.* I watched my team walk back to the dugout with signs of defeat written all over their faces and in their body language. Everyone tried to cheer each other up, as I remained silent in the corner.

"Well, look who decided to grace us with her presence," Jessica said sarcastically. "Glad you could *finally* make it." I forgot how cruel Jessica could be when she lost at sports.

"Hey, lay off!" Mandy came to my defence, dirt plastered on her right side indicating she managed a good slide during the game. "She isn't the whole team, we failed together. We can't rely on Felicity all the time. We did our best, Jess."

"Alright, ladies. That's enough." Our coach, Brad, walked up. "Go on now, time to shake hands in a very *sportsmanlike* manner." He eyed everyone on the team. All of them grumbled as they filed out and headed onto the field. I stayed where I was since I wasn't in uniform and hadn't played in the game. I always found this part a bit silly. You should shake hands *before* the game when you don't hate certain players. It's a danger zone out there with players swearing, giving dirty looks, and some ending up with bruises from secret pinches and hard pokes. Usually, our team wasn't so vile at the end of games, but the Stallions brought out the worst in us.

After all the handshakes were done, as I walked up to Mandy to get some of the details of the game, I heard three players from the Stallions giggling and whispering, "It's a shame that cow over there didn't get a home run earlier. They could have won the game," one of them said.

Much to my surprise, I realized they were talking about Mandy. I looked at her and saw her blush with embarrassment. *No one insulted my best friend.* Fury raged through my body as I ran towards the girl and tackled her. Verbal abuse was never really my strong suit. Her face kissed the dirt as I mumbled into her ear, "You know, I really think this look is quite an improvement on you. We don't have to see so much of your face." Hands wrapped around my hair and I felt a violent tug as I was dragged off her and punched in the gut. The air was knocked right out of me as pain shot through my body. Fortunately for me, this wasn't my first rodeo. I knocked her legs out from under her as we grappled on the ground.

This caused a chain reaction from both teams and soon a huge brawl had started. With adrenaline pumping, I grabbed the girl I was on the ground with and landed a punch on her cheek. Jessica was a maniac, letting out all her pent-up frustrations from the game as she tossed a Stallion into the crowd, which caused all of us to tumble over. Everywhere you looked there were legs, arms and ponytails. I heard the coaches frantically try and pull the players off one another. I felt someone yank me roughly by the collar. Fist raised, I was ready to land a punch, only to stare into the eyes of my father. *Yikes!*

"In the truck. Now!" Dad said, with his vein almost popping out of his neck. I had never seen him so angry. Needless to say, it was a silent ride home with my sisters in the back giving me worried looks and my parents in the front turning an unhealthy shade of purple.

As soon as we drove into the driveway, other vehicles started pulling up along the street for this big bash my parents were throwing following the baseball game. I silently thanked everyone for their punctuality as my parents became distracted, forcing them to entertain their guests.

My sisters and I hopped out of the truck and booked it upstairs. They wanted to change and I wanted to get as far away from my parents as possible. The less they saw of me the better. I changed into my Corona bikini and took a look in the mirror to assess the damage. *Yikes!* I had some pretty nice war wounds. I had a cut on my lip, my left cheek was red, there were a few scratches on my face, my right eye was puffy and several blackish blue marks occupied my arms. All in all, not too shabby.

I heard my sisters' voices echoing from inside their room, arguing over which bikini top would match which bottom and saying they both wanted to wear the same top. I stood by the doorway watching the argument with fascination. "Felicity! Who should have the pink bikini top?" Bell asked. "Good God, Faith. Look at Felicity's wounds! All those welts and bruises."

I ignored the comment. "Who bought it?"

"I did," they said in unison. They glared at each other.

"It's just, I know for a fact that Jesse is going to be here and I want to look smoking hot, and I can only achieve that in this bikini top!"

"Well, I want to look like a goddess for Bobby so I *need* this bikini top!" Faith screamed.

"It's mine."

"No, it's mine!" The freaks began shouting as they tugged at the top.

I sighed, headed to their walk-in closet and began a tedious search, knowing full well that if they both bought one then there must be a second top around here somewhere. The best thing about the twins is they always have two of everything. I found it squished in a corner. "Hey guys, I found another one. See, problem solved."

They hugged each other and apologized for being silly. I sat on the bed watching them, a strange look on my face. I shook my head, unable to understand what goes on inside their brains.

"BELL!" Faith said, infuriated. "We *cannot* wear the *same* bathing suit out to the party. We may have the same clothes but we don't wear them at the same time. We are *not* in kindergarten anymore!"

"Well, looks like you're changing because this one isn't leaving my body."

"No!" Faith sighed. "Fine. You want to play it that way then I'm going to wear mine, too. I'm not changing."

"YOU CAN'T DO THAT!" Bell said, panicking. "We'll look like total dorks."

"I'm not changing."

"Neither am I."

"Fine."

"Fine." They both glared at each other with their arms crossed.

"Then we'll sit here until we can think of something else, because this will not do."

I left them to their bickering. I was way out of their league when it came to that kind of arguing. The last time I decided to help them, Bell didn't speak to me for a week.

I went downstairs where the party was in full swing. I headed out to the new patio with the new pool and smelled the BBQ. My stomach growled as I went searching for a hot-dog. That was one thing Atlantis lacked: amazing food.

Mandy came running up to me with two hot dogs and passed one over to me. "Hey! Did your parents fry you yet? Don't be upset about the game, Felicity. It wasn't your fault. You weren't even there."

"That was the biggest crowd we've ever had. What if there were scouts in the audience? That could have been my chance to prove myself, you know."

"Felicity, this is Lakewood...not some big city. There will

be plenty of other chances. Trust me, you're too good not to get noticed, and if you get that scholarship for college next year, then you'll be good to go. You've got more of a chance of getting out of here than anyone on the team."

"I hope so. It all rests on that scholarship." I looked around the backyard and spotted Alex surrounded by five guys who were her errand boys. "Ugh, why does she have to be here?"

"Honey, there you are. Your mother and I have been look-ing for you everywhere," Dad said with open arms as I gri-maced at his fake-sounding voice.

"Oh gee…sorry Dad."

"Your Mom and I just need help carrying out the hors d'oeuvres. Mandy, why don't you go and change into your swimsuit. Felicity will join you shortly," Dad said, as he put his hand on my shoulder.

"Yeah, no problem, Mr. O."

"Let's continue to the study. Your mother is there waiting for you. We would like to get this over with so we can *all* enjoy the party," he whispered in my ear as he guided me into the house.

We walked into the study. They sat me down on the brown leather chair (also known as the punishment chair when we were little). The fireplace and bookcases made the study seem small and my parents' proximity didn't help much either. I could see the computer's screensaver flick back and forth as it flashed different pictures of the family, which gave me something to focus on other than my parents' faces.

"Do you know why we pulled you out of the party?" Mom asked.

"Possibly."

She let out a sigh. "Possibly isn't going to cut it. Your father and I are very upset with you. You completely humiliated us, for one thing. We felt like idiots watching *your* baseball game when you weren't even there. Let alone how pointless this party is, since it was meant for you."

"Oh no, you don't! You can't pin this party on me. I never asked for it." *Hadn't they even noticed I'd been gone for two days?* "You sure it's not because the Darnels had a party a few days ago?"

"That's not the point, right, Dekker?" My Mom stared at my Dad who had been standing there silently.

He coughed a little, "Right," as I rolled my eyes. All this had to do with my mother's influence over him.

"You have seriously disappointed us," Mom cut in. "The O'Connells do not fight."

I held a laugh. "That's rich. Stop with the delusional fantasies." I felt all the tension and rebellion stir in me and directed it towards my mother. When I was in Atlantis, I noticed how calm and happy I was. Atlantis is *nothing* like this place. It's better. "We fight all the time - with the Darnels, with each other, and with society. The whole world is one big argument waiting to happen!"

"Felicity, don't speak to your mother like that!" Dad piped up.

"Honestly, Felicity. When are you going to grow up and take responsibility for your actions?" Mom asked.

"Maybe I'm not ready to grow up! I'm not ready to be responsible. I don't know what I want to do or who I'm supposed to be. How can I choose to do anything if you keep breathing down my neck all the time? It just pushes me further away. I just want to have fun and enjoy life, not think about school, homework, or the future. Did I ever once deny that I started that fight? My sisters *never* have to deal with this."

"That's because your sisters never argue or fight." Dad spoke quietly, which infuriated me more.

"Sooner or later, you two are going to run out of things to blame me for and then what are you going to do? It must be a *real* burden to actually have to care about the black sheep of the family."

"Felicity!" Mom said, astonished.

"Well, it's true, isn't it?" I fumed.

Mom became really quiet. "Is that how you truly feel? We love you Felicity, but sometimes your sisters are much more sensible and don't rush into things. They use their heads where you use your heart. You're just a lot more to handle. Try and put yourself in our shoes for once."

"Are we done here?" I asked, sitting rigidly in my chair.

"Yes," my mother's weak reply came and I headed out of the room feeling guilty about what I had said. I had obviously hurt my Mom more then I had intended to. *Good, maybe that would knock some sense into her.*

I walked into the backyard, the picture of innocence, as though the conversation had never taken place. I did a cannon ball, splashed into the pool and soaked Alex and her boy toys. This created a lot of squeals and screams. The loudest squeal came from Alex, which made me smile.

I dove down to the bottom of the pool, allowing the water to ease my sorrows. *Was I really a bad daughter? I guess I shouldn't have said those things to them. It was a little harsh, but it was hard to get them to listen to me in any other way.*

I surfaced and, to my surprise, I was at the other end of the pool. Since Atlantis, I noticed I could hold my breath a lot longer. Then, I felt someone bump into me. I turned around to apologize and scowled. *Could my day get any worse?* Karl Biggums, the quarterback of Lakewood High's football team. He was the slime of the earth and had been invited here by my sisters. He's as arrogant as they come!

I went to public school with him and haven't been able to shake him since. He was as good looking then as he is now. He's tall and has brown hair with blonde highlights. And he's a superb athlete. So, it wasn't a surprise that all the girls in public school had a crush on him, me included. He knew more about girls and sexual innuendos than I thought was normal for a kid in public school. It was like he had hit puberty way too early and didn't have time to experience childhood. At the time, I didn't understand the stuff he was saying, which made me the butt of more than a few jokes in grade five.

I was really shy back then, couldn't even speak to a boy and struggled in school. I always had my nose in a book and wasn't much to look at. Needless to say, I wasn't high on the popularity list. I tried to ignore who I was and imagine I was someone else. I wanted to be liked. I wanted to be accepted, but rarely got the chance.

My first encounter in public school with him wasn't a good one. I never said a word to him, never spoken to him once since he had came to public school. I had just arrived at school one day when he came up and started screaming in my face. I was so scared my mouth went dry and I couldn't speak. I didn't have a clue what he was talking about. Someone had hacked into my MSN at the school library and sent him a very sexual e-mail. It was the only time Karl had ever talked to me. It made me afraid to show my interest for anyone in case they reacted the same way, which didn't help my shy factor one iota.

The second encounter wasn't any better back in grade eight. It was a class party and music was playing. My friends and I were talking in a circle when he came over to talk to us. He began pointing to some of the girls saying who he would dance with. My feelings bubbled to the surface. I wanted to know if he would point at me, just to see if I would be worthy enough for at least a dance. By that point, I knew I didn't have any shot of actually being with him but it gave me hope that if someone like him would at least dance with me, I couldn't be all that bad. My self-esteem was so shot by grade eight that I didn't think I was worthy of anything. When the moment came, he skipped over me like I wasn't there.

I made a vow that I would no longer change myself for others, that I would be true to myself and not change a thing about me no matter what anyone said. It was the worst, but best, thing that ever happened to me. The day Karl skipped over me, he made me a stronger person. A fact I hated to admit.

"Sorry, Felicity." Karl's reply snapped me back to the present. "This place is packed."

"That's okay," I said crisply, wanting to get away from him. He was a lot nicer now than in public school, so I've been trying to forgive him. Childhood may be fun, but children can be so cruel. The worst part about all this is that he doesn't even realize what he did to me back in public school.

"One heck of a party your parents throw. You're lucky your parents are so cool."

I almost choked in disgust. "We're talking about the same parents right, as in those two over there?" I pointed out my mother sipping wine and my Dad drinking a beer.

Just then, Alex swam up to us in her tiny silver bikini. "Aren't you going to introduce me to your friend?"

"Huh, I *thought* I saw an annoying tick floating around somewhere. Oh, here you are!" I smirked as she gave me a look of scorn.

"I'm Alex." She lifted her hand for a handshake, puffing out her chest like she could make her boobs any bigger.

"Karl," he said, introducing himself. Her chest puffing had the intended effect, as Karl couldn't help but stare.

"You two have fun now…" I swam off, realizing there were too many people around here who I wasn't a fan of. While no one was looking, I got out of the pool, grabbed my towel and walked through the side gate to freedom, bikini and all. *I know exactly where I want to be and it sure as hell isn't in this world.* Just as I was about to make my getaway, someone grabbed my hand. I stared up into blue eyes. "Hey, Jesse."

"Felicity, what are you doing?"

"I'm running away."

"Well, that sounds logical," he grinned. "And why are you running away?"

"My parents."

"Oh, I see. Do you want to talk about it?"

"Not particularly."

"Well, my bedroom window is always open for you if you need me."

"Thanks for the gesture. Just like old times, huh."

"Yup."

Jesse had always been there for me when Mandy was gone or my sisters didn't understand. Late at night, we would always prank call the Darnels, drink beer together, and reminisce. He was my other best buddy in secret. We didn't announce it to the world, but we were always there for each other.

"Jesse," came Bell's melodic voice. "Come on back to the party. I have to show you something upstairs." Bell noticed our tête-à-tête and gave me the evil eye. It looked like her bathing suit situation was solved. She wasn't wearing a pink bathing suit, but a red one, instead. She must have really wanted to impress Jesse.

Jesse walked towards her and turned back to talk to me. "Let me know how that works out for you." He left to be ensnared in the claws of Anna Bell.

I smiled. It would work out. I was going to live in Atlantis. *That* was where my real home was. *That* was where I was meant to be.

CHAPTER 9

Home Sweet Home

Heart pumping and lungs aching, I pushed any thoughts of my past and my family out of my mind. A stitch in my side began to form but I pressed on, my pace quickening once I reached the baseball field. I kicked viciously at the purple Stallion's banner that was left behind from earlier. My feet couldn't carry me to the puddle fast enough, as I gave one last burst of speed for good measure. I hardly felt the scratches as I crawled through the bramble and bushes. In no time, chest heaving, I was out of the thicket and running to the puddle. I gave a cry of glee and dove in, bathing suit and all.

I hurled myself out of the vortex' pull and into the darkness. As I let the transformation occur, my spine spasmed and water and bubbles wrapped around me in a silky embrace. Bubbles shot down my throat, turning my insides numb and allowing me to breathe underwater. I crowed in delight as I felt my powerful tail swishing strongly underneath me.

My happiness burst like a bubble when I noticed all the red eyes that encircled me. There were at least six pairs. I swallowed as all my feelings turned to dread. I had forgotten about these guys. Only their eyes shone in the darkness, making it difficult to see what kind of creatures they were. Atlantis wasn't very far away. I could see the gleam of the castle from here. As if on cue, they swam towards me. I rocketed up, forcing some of the red-eyed creatures to collide with one another. Then, I spiralled downward in a zigzag formation towards the city. I felt the water stir on my left and nosedived quickly. I heard the snapping of teeth where my body had been. I reeled from surprise, veering under a creature.

I felt another presence tensing, ready to spring, as I did a quick summersault and felt the creature's teeth chomp down a hair's breath away from my head. Terrified, I found a whole new meaning to the word speed as I left a blaze of bubbles in my wake, dodging the unknown creatures here and there until I burst into the dome.

I fell as a net wrapped around me, sending me to the ground with a thud. Panting hard and struggling to free myself, I felt the rocking of the waves and heard the swishing of 20 mertails heading in my direction. This must be another one of their traps to get rid of humans. *Clever.* I was searching desperately for something sharp when I spotted the skeleton of a fish. The bones would be sharp enough to do the trick. I rolled, avoiding a stingray that had made its home in the sand, and stared at the piercing barb on the end of its tail.

I was running out of time. I began to move the skeleton back and forth against parts of the net. As the threads began to fray, I was able to poke an arm through it. Grabbing the fish bone, I ripped an opening for my other arm, then began to cut the net where my tail was trapped. With my tail free, I untangled the rest of my body. I grabbed the net off the sea floor and dove into a large patch of floating seaweed that was rooted into the seabed, knowing this hiding place wouldn't last long. It wouldn't be hard to spot the trail I had left in the sand. Giving myself time to catch my breath, I could hear voices not too far off. As I peeped cautiously out of the seaweed, I saw I was near the castle.

A big crowd was standing in front of the fortress. It looked to be the whole city. Up on the hill by the impressive statue of the sea god, Poseidon, stood four figures, all clad in gold with crowns adorning their heads. I swam cautiously the long way around the patch of seaweed, listening for noises as I followed the patch up towards the big crowd. I brushed myself off using my hands, trying to clean as much dirt and seaweed from my body as possible. I could see the King's guards searching the crowd and the area I had just come from. I craned my neck to get a better look and saw Sebastian and Shell standing there proudly. Their expressions were too far away for me to see.

"They will attack at any moment!" the King thundered, as I realized I had probably missed half of his speech. "The human seems to be invulnerable to our traps. The great white and hammerhead sharks have teamed up and are getting ready to attack. They yearn for merpeople meat and are using the human as an excuse. *Anyone* who leaves the protection of the dome and enters the darkness will do so at his or her own risk. That is where the sharks will lurk. They will never give up. When you hear the sirens, it will be time to fight! They said if we give up the human they will do us no harm. Under no circumstance is anyone allowed to throw a merperson out of the dome if they suspect that merperson is the human. You come to me first - or there will be severe consequences." He stared menacingly at the crowd.

"Battle is imminent. When the alarm sounds, every able-bodied merman is to meet at this location." He and his wife stepped onto a huge pinkish white shell with seahorses attached like a chariot and sat down. "Stay alert and be ready," he said, flicking the reins and heading across the city at a fast pace. The crowd began to murmur uneasily. Some mermaids burst into tears as they clutched their husbands and others cursed the human.

Star, Rainbow and Coral stood a few feet away as they waved to me and made their way through the crowd. "The King can be so dreary when battle lust gets into his heart," Rainbow said nonchalantly. "We've defeated the sharks before. This time won't be any different."

"You wouldn't say that if you had to fight," Coral said quietly. "This will cost hundreds of mermen's lives. History always repeats itself. We can't win all the time."

"Come on, Coral. Have a little more faith in our men and this city," Star joined in. "Even if you don't, this is not the time or place to speak of such things. Can't you see the fear on the mermen's faces? Positive thoughts are better than negative ones."

"I do have faith. I was only trying to be logical," Coral stammered, as her face turned red with embarrassment.

Rainbow tossed back her long red hair, ignoring Coral as she turned her attention to me and changed the subject. "Mrs. Flounder says you're trying out for dolphin riding."

"I guess so," I shrugged, suddenly feeling sick.

Rainbow laughed. "*Please*, you can't be serious. You, a dolphin rider, hah! The very thought." She waved her hand around as if to ward off such a ridiculous notion.

Before I could interject, I heard Star butt in and couldn't help but grin. "Just because *you* didn't make the team doesn't mean *she* can't."

Rainbow scowled. "Fine, then. If she's so great, let's have her prove it!" Rainbow swam off alone in the direction of the school, leaving the three of us behind.

Star laughed uncontrollably. "This is so much fun! I've never seen her squirm before. She's not usually this rude to merpeople. I don't know what you did, but you're taking her out of her comfort zone. Come on, let's go!" Star grabbed my hand as we followed Rainbow. I opened and shut my mouth. We were on the brink of war and all they cared about was dolphin riding.

At the back of the school there was scarcely anyone at practice. The track was empty except for a few dolphins roaming around. A mermaid with a gold tail was on the track riding her dolphin through hoops and loops with unfathomable precision.

"That's Shell Reef. I don't think you've met her yet," came a voice from behind me and I jumped in surprise. I could see in his eyes that the news about the upcoming war had him worried. "Whoa!" Jeremy cupped my face in his hands, tracing some of my scratches. "Are you alright? What happened to you?"

"I fell into a nasty batch of coral." I jerked my head away so he couldn't see the marks that were left from the baseball game.

He looked at me puzzled. "Alright, if you don't want to tell me, I won't press you. You can't honestly expect me to *believe* that excuse, but we all have our secrets. I don't like seeing you like this."

"It's nothing," I spoke quickly, changing the topic. "Where is everyone?"

"With the latest announcement, everyone wants to spend time with their families. Mrs. Flounder told me to look after practice. Shell's just letting off some steam. She represented the Snails last night at a Dolphin Rider competition and came out on top of everyone."

"How did you do?" I asked, genuinely interested, but with my eyes still glued to Shell. She had some kind of strap hooked from her tail fin to the dorsal fin of her dolphin. It looked like she was surfing.

"I came in third. I wasn't expecting a Zip Storm, but I came out alright, I suppose. Pretty good for my first time going into one of those babies!" The comment didn't have as much pep in it as it should have.

"Are you scared?" I turned to face him.

His smiled faltered. "Don't have time to worry about being scared. I have to protect the merpeople, even a Superstar like you." His tail knocked mine playfully. "Come on, let's go see if you're dolphin worthy." I glanced up the sand hill to see three figures sitting on top of it, one with a sour look and crossed arms. Competitiveness bubbled to the surface. I wanted to show Rainbow that I wasn't some clownfish to be toiled with. I followed Jeremy, more than ready to prove myself and get Rainbow off my case.

Jeremy rambled on: "It is very rare for a merperson to share a bond with a wild dolphin. Sometimes, the wild dolphins like you but, in most cases, they don't. So, try not to be discouraged if you do not get bonded." He pointed to a large group of dolphins clustered around some kind of feeding bin. "Now, go and swim up to them, but not too close to where they feed, and see if one will come up to you. My dolphin, Sunrise, took about an hour, so be prepared to wait." At the mention of her name, a dolphin swam up to Jeremy and nuzzled him on the cheek, as they spoke to each other in echolocation.

I have never seen a dolphin this close before. The thought that I could actually have one after today made me eager to give it a shot. "Sure thing, boss."

I did as Jeremy instructed and stood waiting for them to turn around. These were not your normal sea dolphins. Their gills were right behind their dorsal fins, allowing them to breathe underwater forever. A few minutes went by as I was continually ignored for food. I pictured Rainbow's smug smirk. I looked down at Jeremy for reassurance and saw Shell had come to watch my progress, her hand entwined with Jeremy's. *Ugh, how was I ever going to compete with a princess?* Losing patience, I swam to the ocean floor, picked up a rock and hurled it into the fray of dolphins who all leaped back in alarm as they focused on me.

"Oh, this one's got a temper."

"Impatience is not a valuable trait."

"I won't be seen with a rider looking like that."

"Nothing but skin and bones on that one. It would put my family to shame."

I looked around oddly for the source of the comments and realized that it wasn't a merperson talking to me but the dolphins. I could understand them.

"An unusual breed."

"Not very smart, is she?"

My face blushed with embarrassment as one dolphin in particular caught my attention. He had a scar from the tip of his tail to halfway up his underbelly. Noticing that he was being watched, he showed off by doing a back flip.

"That one is a male," I heard Jeremy yell down to me. "He's definitely got some spirit in him. Pretty young, too."

Suddenly, all the dolphins' chatter turned to echolocation so that I could no longer understand their nasty comments. "I don't understand, Jeremy. I can't hear them anymore."

"That's good! It means one of them has picked you. Now, you have your own echolocation that only the two of you can speak and understand. An unbreakable bond. Wild dolphins are born riderless, so their thoughts roam free while a merperson is in the process of being chosen. Once picked, all their thoughts can no longer be heard. After that, only that team of dolphin and merperson can share each other's thoughts."

When I looked away from Jeremy, the young dolphin was floating in front of me. *"Dude, I'd much rather hang out with you than with all these dried up tuna heads. You got some nerve huckin' that rock at us. We coulda bludgeoned you to death. You've got pep and guts, two things I really admire. My name's Tidalwave, at your service."*

I stroked the dolphin's grey skin. It felt like rubber. "Crystal," I introduced myself. I surprised myself with dolphin language and laughed. "His name's Tidalwave," I yelled down to Jeremy, as he gave me the thumbs up.

"That's enough for your first day. I don't want to overwhelm you," Jeremy replied. "Besides, practice is over. It was just a short one. Come back tomorrow at the same time and place, if the sirens have not gone off."

Coral and Star greeted me excitedly as they rubbed Tidalwave's underbelly. Rainbow had an annoyed look on her face. Jeremy spoke to Shell, then swam up to us. "If you're not busy, Crystal, I was just wondering if you wanted to come to the Sea Shell Spa. By the looks of things, we all need our tails washed. They're starting to look pretty gross. The Spa was put in for Shell by her Dad, so it doesn't cost anything."

"I wouldn't want to intrude," I spoke honestly.

"Of course you wouldn't be intruding! It's good for you; bring your friends. It'll help take our minds off the oncoming battle. Could be tomorrow, could be two weeks from now for all we know."

I looked over at Shell. She was watching us. She flicked her hair and gave me a look that meant quite the opposite of what Jeremy was saying. "Sure, sounds like fun." *Liar, liar pants on fire.*

"Great, see you at five o'clock," he said and swam away with Sunrise at his side.

"Oh, my god! The most popular merguy at school just invited us to the spa!" Star piped happily. I noticed all their eyes crystallized like mine, showing them at their happiest. "Besides Sebastian, of course." She looked fleetingly at Rainbow.

Rainbow's frown was replaced with a smug look. "Looks

like we should go and get ready then! Come on, girls. Oh, Crystal, we'll meet you at your house around 4:30, since I doubt you've ever been to this place."

"Perfect," I said, as they swam away chatting.

I jumped as a voice echoed beside me. I forgot all about the fact that I had Tidalwave as my companion now. *"That one sure is a fireball, isn't she?"*

"Yes, she most certainly is. I don't even know why I'm doing this. Spas and I just don't mix."

"I think you and I both know why..."

I sighed. "Is it really that obvious? Oh, what's the point? I don't have a chance. He has a girlfriend, a princess no less, and do I really want a guy that all the girls go crazy for?"

"You can't help what the heart wants. I can't wait for you to start riding me. Our first hurricane is going to be amazing. I've never competed before, but in one course they had hurricane after hurricane. The field was nothing but hurricanes. A lot of merpeople couldn't keep their seafood down, if you get my meaning."

"Whoa, slow down there slugger, one thing at a time."

"Alright, point taken. At least you can show me where my new home is going to be. Here, grab my dorsal fin and give me directions." I grabbed hold of his fin with both hands. *"Hold on,"* he cautioned, as we sliced through the water.

At 4:45, I stared out the window impatiently, waiting for the girls to show up. They took fashionably late to a whole new level. I was excited to do my first merperson excursion, to see what it was they did for fun around here. By the time five o'clock rolled around, I had pretty much given up hope. The three shrimp I had dispatched reported they weren't at home. I didn't have the slightest clue where the Sea Shell Spa was and Tidalwave wasn't back yet, so I couldn't bum a ride from him. He was too busy getting his shelter in the backyard ready, so I figured maybe I shouldn't go out. Tidalwave had warned me about a water tornado coming in later that night. Disappointment clouded my face. I wanted to hear Jeremy's laugh again. I wanted to get to know the real Star and not just her ditzy side. I wanted to learn more about the history of this place from Coral and attempt to find out why Rainbow was so angry with me. *This was the perfect opportunity and I was missing it.*

I had a brief flashback to my public school days when Mandy wasn't really a part of my life. We had grown up in Lakewood but she went to a Catholic School so I didn't get to see her very often. I wasn't without friends, because everyone in grade 8 generally got along. Up to that point, I had considered Brandy to be my best friend throughout public school. We lived on the same street and hung out all the time. That slowly changed when a new girl came to school. Within a month, they were best friends. Turns out, Brandy had never considered me a best friend, just a friend. She was always the centre of attention at school - outgoing, pretty and smart. The total opposite of me, so I was happy to just be around her. I was a fool. My parents had tried to warn me time and time again that she was self-centred and never treated me right, but when you want to fit in so desperately you don't always understand what your parents are trying to say. I finally realized that *true* friends wouldn't interrupt you when you were talking, *true* friends wouldn't push you out of a circle, and *true* friends wouldn't ignore you as though you weren't there.

And that's what I felt like… invisible.

One day, my attention turned to football because the "cool" group was yammering on about grown up things on the tarmac at school. I was sick of listening to them. We were kids, not adults. I walked to the back of the field and hung out with some of my other friends. It was the smartest thing I had ever done. We started playing football day in and day out. They treated me like a person. They shaped me into the person I am today. It was *them* I had to thank. Because of *them,* I was in the best physical shape of my life and I worked off all of my energy and rage during football. It was fun. When I played, I would completely forget everything and anything that existed and concentrate on football. With sports, there was always a certain amount of respect. I even managed to talk to some of the guys because all you do is concentrate on the game not the gender. I was happy. I vowed I would never revert back to that stage in my life. I had healed and was better for it.

After waiting until 5:15, I threw my hands up in frustration. I realized this group of girls in the sea world was different from the ones back home - but maybe they weren't as perfect as I thought. After giving it a few more minutes, I decided it was probably an honest mistake and went to check things out myself. I headed out the door in search of the spa. The main strip was a bit past the school where the market was, so I might as well head in that direction. The water I swam through was cold and thick as soup. I gnawed on my bottom lip as I swam farther away from my house. No one was out and about tonight. The water tornado warning must have kept everyone inside. Some of the houses even had their bubbledomes up for extra protection.

How could they have forgotten me? I came up to the main strip to see all the stores closed. The place looked like a ghost town. No sea creatures roamed the area and the hair on the back of my neck prickled uneasily. Maybe I should have turned around and gone home. There was no sense in getting lost. I looked around and noticed that I had passed the spa a few shops back. It had a lit up sign and its façade was created from different shards of glass with two pillars hugging the doorway. I grinned triumphantly. Everything seemed to work out for me down here. Why couldn't it be like this in Lake-wood?

I entered through the doorway to receive an irritated look from the receptionist, as she sat up and informed me rather rudely that the spa was just closing.

"What do you mean closing? My friends are in here."

"They are the last customers for the day, I'm afraid." She swam towards me, opened the door and motioned with her hand for me to leave.

"Can I at least go and see them? I could care less about the treatment. I don't even know where they're going afterwards and, if you haven't noticed, it's kind of creepy out there."

"Yes, well, we can't all have our own way now, can we? I want to be home with my family, but Shell is royalty and if she wants a spa treatment I'm stuck here making sure her needs are met. It's policy. You aren't allowed back there," she stated bitterly.

"Can you at least ask them where they are going or how much longer they're going to be?"

"No," she said rudely.

"Fine! I didn't want to come here in the first place. It's not like I traveled halfway across town to get here. It's not as if I'm asking you to swim across the world. I just want you to ask them one small question. It isn't that big a task, but I guess for you it *must* be!" I swam out the door wanting to punch something.

"I thought that was your voice yelling. Stirring up all sorts of trouble are you?" Sebastian was leaning against the purple glass outside the spa, which illuminated his sculpted body to a dark purple.

I smiled weakly, embarrassed that he had to witness my temper tantrum. "Hi."

"Don't worry about Gillie, she's just upset about her husband having to fight in the war. She always gets a little cranky when it's past closing time and she has to deal with an abandoned teenager."

"I'm *not* abandoned."

"Sure looks like it to me."

I swam toward a rock formation in front of the spa, refusing to look at him and accept the fact. "Well, I'm used to it. I can take care of myself," I stated firmly, showing no emotion. On the inside, though, I felt my heart ache. I was hoping for a fresh new start down here, for merpeople to actually *want* to be around me. I had been on my best behaviour for everyone, locking away my sarcastic thoughts and comments. *Why did it have to be such a struggle for me to make friends? Was it because I got annoyed by people easily?*

Sebastian joined me at the rock formation, put his arm around me and grinned. "Well, you got me, why else do you think I stayed and waited for you? The problem, Crystal, is that those three have been close for so long Rainbow thinks you're trying to wedge yourself in and take over. Rainbow's a real nice mermaid. She just feels threatened."

"That's ridiculous. It's not like I did it intentionally!" I said, exasperated.

"She doesn't like you stealing the spotlight."

"Well, what am I supposed to do, disappear? Be somebody I'm not? I didn't come here looking for enemies. Why do girls always have to make things so bloody complicated? It's a miracle that you merguys can manage dating mermaids at all."

He laughed lightly. "We can't. We just try and keep them happy. Come on, I better take you home. This weather doesn't look too promising." He put his fingers to his mouth and gave a shrill whistle.

"What about the others in the spa?"

"Well, Gillie didn't tell you the truth. They left about 20 minutes ago. Sometimes, at the end of her shift, if she's feeling particularly wicked, she likes to send merpeople on wild goose chases. She probably left out the back door five minutes ago."

"Oh, brilliant!"

"I should get back home, too. I have to help father with battle tactics. He's going to have my tail for being out so late."

A grey hippo rounded the corner in a playful mood, gills running down the centre of its chest. Sebastian rubbed his hands along his smooth neck. "Easy, Snogglepuss, we've got company." The hippo perked his ears up at the mention of his name and snorted in reply.

"Snogglepuss?" I said, slightly amused.

"I was like five years old, okay. Give me a break." He smiled good-naturedly and hopped on, grabbed the hippo's neck and held the other hand out to me. "Hop on." I eyed it warily. I had never been on a hippo before. They were dangerous on land. I could only imagine how dangerous they were in the water. I noticed Snogglepuss wasn't exactly the cleanest creature, either, as I brushed some dirt and seaweed off his back. "Is Crystal a little scared?" he taunted.

"No! I'm scared of nothing." I cringed as the hippo yawned, opening his cavern of a mouth. I swallowed slightly and grabbed his arm and hopped on, holding his waist as we rode side saddle down the empty street.

"Some days, merteens come to Main Street and have speed races on all kinds of animals. I'll take you to one sometime. By the way, you might want to hold on a little tighter."

"Hip! Hip!" He motioned to the hippo as Snogglepuss grunted and started to move, jumping off a rock and doing a barrel roll before landing safely on the ground and taking off like a rocket.

After Sebastian and Snogglepuss dropped me off, I saw Tidalwave's tail sticking out the door of his shelter in the backyard. "Well, look what we've got here..." I kicked his tail lightly.

"Hey now, careful. That's some valuable merchandise." His tail disappeared and out poked a slim head. *"That water current is really starting to pick up."*

"Are you going to be safe enough out here?" I asked, concerned. I didn't want to lose him when I had just got him.

"*Pfft, this is nothing compared to out in the wild.*"

I glanced at the scar on his belly. "Can I ask you a personal question?" He didn't reply so I just took it as a yes. "How did you get that scar on your belly?"

He was silent and I could see in his intelligent eyes that he was deciding whether or not to tell me what happened. "*I don't really remember much about the incident. It happened when I was just a calf. My whole family was swimming along near The Surface and I wanted to see what that big thing in the water was. It was loud and made my ears hurt. It poured some nasty stuff into the sea and sky. Mom yelled at me not to go any closer, but I couldn't help it, I wanted to see. So I swam closer, and it was a big ship. Mom followed me and was caught in a net. She tried to push me away, but I was scared and just wanted to be with her. I jumped into the net, as well. She fought, but she couldn't escape. The net was raised out of the water, and the humans grabbed her and slit her throat. I don't know why they did it. I begged them to stop but they wouldn't listen.*

"*They came for me next. I was so little. The one man picked me up and tossed me around by the tail then took his knife and began to cut my belly from my tail up to my nose. They were all laughing. When I kicked out with my tail, the man gasped and slipped and I dove back into the sea. I had lost my family by then. They had all swam away in fear.*

"*I ended up swimming with a pod of humpback whales until I found some of my own kind. I've never been back to The Surface since. It took me years to figure out what type of humans they were. They're called fishermen, scorned by every sea creature alive. Fish are meant to stay in the water,*" he said passionately.

"Before all this darkness surrounded Atlantis, we used to have farmland as far as the eye could see, where all sorts of plants and animals could be raised. Humans ruined that, too. As soon as the Forbidden Area came, so did the darkness. No one has been able to get rid of it."

"That's horrible!" I exclaimed. My stomach twisted nauseously. *He must have loathed humans and here he was bonded to one! If he ever found out my secret, he'd kill me on the spot. I wanted to tell him some humans were fighting for sea animals to live and not for them to become extinct. A lot of humans cared. He'd just met some of the bad ones.*

Tidalwave's eyes searched mine and, seeing my expression, realization clicked in. *"You're the human they've been looking for, aren't you?"*

My body went rigid at the sudden accusation. "Who, me? No! That's crazy." One look at Tidalwave and I knew I was busted. "I'm sorry," I caved. "We're not all bad, I swear!" I stared at his cute little face. "I'd never tell anyone about Atlantis. I love it here too much to have it destroyed. You must be ashamed to have me as a rider." Silence followed. "Please say something."

"Well, I reckon this place is still standing even after you escaped the first time, so that's as good a sign as any. I suppose merpeople have their good and bad qualities, as well. Crystal, if a little guy like me can figure it out, how long do you think it's going to be before they put the pieces together? I trusted you the moment I bonded with you. I couldn't hate you even if I tried. I'll be with you 'til the end. Do you think I want to see you die? Even so, you must tread carefully from

now on. You're a terrible liar…"

"Is it really that obvious?" Here I'd thought I was doing a bang-up job.

"You don't want me to answer that. Dolphins have a higher I.Q. than most sea creatures, but, even without it, a merperson can tell there's something a little different about you. We will talk about that tomorrow. You better get inside. The storm is on its way!"

I locked the door behind me, my heart beating faster than normal. I felt vulnerable now that my secret was out in the open, a feeling I hadn't been accustomed to in years. I swam to my bed and lay there listening to the storm starting to rage outside the window. My life was now in Tidalwave's hands. I fell into a fitful sleep.

Bang, Bang, Bang.

I woke up with a start and looked out my window to see sand and water swirling back and forth in a dance that only they knew the frantic rhythm to. The banging wasn't coming from the weather, though.

"Open the door!" Someone outside bellowed.

I jumped. Tidalwave must have snitched. Sadness filled my heart. I had hoped it wouldn't have come to this. I was going to have to make a break away to the Forbidden Area. I grabbed a long stick that was leaning against the wall and took it with me. My heart was pounding. I placed my hand on the diamond knob and counted to three. I opened the door and smoked the merperson on the head. I dashed out the door to confront the rest of the King's warriors.

There was nothing there except flying sand.

I turned around to face my opponent. "What do you want?" I yelled, arms positioned to strike again.

"You're crazy, you know that, don't you?" That's when I recognized the voice and I started to feel like an idiot.

"Jeremy? Jeremy, is that you?"

"Ow...my head." He sat up slowly.

I threw the stick on the ground. "Well, what did you expect? Who comes over to a mermaid's house during a water tornado?"

"I was going home."

"Your house is in the other direction," I said, as I steered him over towards the couch.

"I came to apologize about today. We were going to pick you up but the girls wanted to get to the spa and they assured me you knew where the place was. I'm really, really sorry. Then you turned up late..."

"So, you came all this way to apologize to me?" I looked at him incredulously.

"Um, yes." He looked down at the ground.

I smacked him on the head with the back of my hand playfully. "You could have gotten yourself killed!"

He laughed. "It was worth it to see you smile."

I was speechless, but I still managed to choke out, "I'll get you something to fix that bump." My heart was doing cartwheels as I went into the kitchen.

I came back to find Jeremy passed out on my couch. His blonde hair was ruffled, his tail was bent and his arm was hanging lifelessly over the side of the couch. I sat down next to him wondering how this world could create such perfection.

"If you want to get a real good look at me then maybe you should come a little closer. I don't bite. Much." He grinned as I blushed. "So, what did you and Prince Sebastian talk about? I heard it was quite an interlude, from what he tells me."

"Things." I spoke quietly, not wanting to talk about Sebastian at the present time.

Jeremy frowned. "You should stay away from him. He's nothing but a mermaids' man."

"He showed me around the school. He helped me get through my first day. He's a friend." I defended Sebastian, trying not to show how happy Jeremy's jealousy of him made me feel.

"Is that all you think he is? A friend?" Jeremy opened his eyes inquiringly.

"Perhaps," I said. Instinctively, my fingers roamed around his head where the bump was and I touched it, tenderly wiping away the blood. They roamed from the bump to his cheek, then hovered around his necklace.

"I killed three sharks myself," he said softly, as I felt each tooth. "A few years back. Ghastly things. The one in the middle was known as Jaws. He was the biggest one I ever dealt with. Just look at his tooth compared to the others. We were out hunting and he caught us unaware. Monster of a shark, the ones outside Atlantis that want the war will be much smaller."

"Weren't you scared?"

"With as many battles as I've fought, you get used to it. It was either me or him - and I wasn't ready to leave yet."

My fingertips strayed to his chest as they traced his abs.

Jeremy's eyes fluttered open as my fingers ran over a scar. I bit my lip and stopped abruptly, feeling like I had been caught doing something bad.

He grabbed my hand and stared into my eyes. His eyes crystallized, making me smile that I could have created such an effect on him. Knowing that he was having such a happy moment confused me even more since he was supposed to be with Shell. His eyes never crystallized when he was around her as far as I could tell. What was going on here?

"It's time for you to go to bed," he said in barely a whisper as he forced himself to let me go.

I left the room regretfully and headed towards the bedroom, very aware of his sleeping form on the couch for the night.

CHAPTER 10

Attack!!

The next day, Jeremy woke me up bright and early to teach me the basics of dolphin riding. "Now, make sure your stronger caudal fin is on the back and place your caudal fins between Tidalwave's dorsal fin and tail," Jeremy instructed, as I followed his directions and grabbed onto his shoulders for support while Tidalwave echolocated to me in a whisper.

"I've thought it through and I've decided I'm going to have to teach you about merpeople culture, since you can't be a dunce about this forever. Your first lesson starts today, since you are so keen on a certain male merman here is how love works. When a mermaid and merman want to have a baby they must have their pearl broken. The merman picks out a beautiful shell for his lover, showing how strong his feelings are for her. It contains a pearl that he gives to her. That is the first step to showing commitment. It is the step called pearl breaking. Many lovesick merteens get to this stage in a relationship but it never progresses much further than that before they break up.

"When the pearl breaks, it means they love each other. If

the two merpeople want to have a child, they take the shell in both of their hands and press it against their hearts. During this time, they kiss each other on the lips. The kiss produces a small neon pink ball of energy out of each of their mouths that combines together creating one pink ball. In turn, that ball is placed in the shell where the pearl had once been and a new life is created. A new life made out of love. After the ball is placed in the shell and closed, the shell becomes bigger as the pink ball of life inside grows. Eventually, the shell will open up and "POP," out comes the baby.

"Merpeople also have stages in life. They change from baby to child to teen and then to the last stage, adult, but only when their body and mind are ready. It can take seconds, days or hundreds of years. Some merpeople never want to grow up and they never do. Merpeople are not affected by disease and, in most cases, are immortal. You only die if you're killed by a human, in war or by a sea creature. If you live down here, you can live forever. Also, if a merperson calls you a human, they may not actually be signalling you out as a human but it is meant to be taken as an insult to everything that you are."

"Crystal? Crystal? Hello? Did you hear what I've been saying?" Jeremy shook me as I stared into his green eyes, giving him my full attention.

"Yeah, sure, something about balance," I said distractedly, trying to digest the new information Tidalwave had given me. *I was immortal! I could stay like this forever. The thought scared, fascinated and intrigued me. What if I was the only one who didn't want to grow up? What if Jeremy, Coral, Star, Sebastian and Rainbow all grew up before I did?*

I would look like a child in their eyes. When was anyone ever ready to grow up?

"I said when you get really good balance you'll be able to ride on Tidalwave's front or back, in any position you like. Keep your shoulders straight with Tidalwave; otherwise, your whole body will be in front of the current, which will slow you down. When it comes to something like a barracuda turn-pike in a competition, you better be ready to drop down and forget about balance and hold onto Tidalwave's pectoral fins for dear life! No amount of balance will keep you from falling off and that'll bring down your score. Performing a new trick or style of riding will bring your points up."

"Alright, sounds easy enough." I liked a challenge.

"Go on, Tidalwave. Take 'er for a spin around the back-yard and let her see how 'easy' it really is," Jeremy smirked.

He let go of me and, as soon as that happened, I hit the sandy floor with a thump. Right on my butt. Tidalwave snick-ered. "Don't say a word." I huffed and looked at Jeremy.

"My lips are sealed. Round two?" Jeremy extended his hand. "It'll be easier when you're moving with a current in-stead of in still water. Try again." Half an hour went by with me repeating the same thing over and over again. I was un-steady, but at least I wasn't falling off anymore. "See, you're catching on! You're a pretty quick learner. Balance and read-ing Tidalwave's movements is the key to success."

An alarm went off across the city making all three of us jump in surprise. Jeremy let out a sigh. "Thought I had more time. Crystal, I have to go get ready, say goodbye to Shell, and suit Sunrise up. Get inside and stay safe."

"I'm coming with you!" I said stubbornly, refusing to let

him out of my sight. I didn't want this to be the last time I got to see him.

He smiled slightly at my stubbornness. "Not this time, Superstar." He swam away towards his home without a backwards glance, not giving me a chance to speak.

"Boy! You sure missed a perfect opportunity," Tidalwave said, amused. *"I bet you'd let him break your pearl any day."*

I blushed at such an intimate conversation. "Shut up, Tidalwave!"

"You do realize this little alarm situation IS kind of your fault?"

"Thanks. You sure do know how to cheer a girl up," I said sarcastically. "Why can't mermaids fight in battle, anyway?"

"They used to be able to, but a while back a group of giant squids invaded the city. The King and Queen, Sebastian's parents, went out to fight along with their children and a swarm of warriors. The oldest daughter didn't make it. Since then, the King has never wanted a merman to have to deal with seeing a loved one die in front of his eyes. With no females fighting, males can focus on the battle, not on protecting their families but fighting for them while they are safe and secure.

"Well, I don't have any family, not here at least. Do you think the sharks care about who they eat?" I relaxed my shoulders and unclenched my fists. "We're going out there."

"Where did this WE come from?"

"Come on, Tidalwave. Let's show them what we're made of. Let's go kick some shark butt!" I said boldly, ignoring the sinking feeling in my stomach.

We ducked behind two swaying anemone plants, crouching atop a small sand hill that gave us just enough coverage. I heard the sounds of hundreds of mermen and the clatter of armour, which sent chills through me. I poked my head around the corner of the red anemones, scaring a clown fish as he darted away. My eyes widened as I saw the mermen gearing up for battle. The King was at the front of the line with a red hippocampus in gold armour, shouting orders that I could not hear from so far away. I didn't even think we had this many mermen in Atlantis.

Hippocampi and abnormally large seahorses were the mermen's mounts as they fitted them with armour. Steel pointed plates were fastened to their tails, chest and heads for protection. Swords were being handed out and shields fitted. Very few dolphins were headed to battle as I searched for Jeremy. Misery lodged deep within my chest. *This was my fault. If I had not come to Atlantis this would not be happening.* It seemed wrong for the sun to be shining so brightly when death was on the horizon. The mermen's eyes searched the darkness that surrounded the dome, looking for any sign of the enemy.

"Take a good look at what you may never see again. You sure you want to do this?" Tidalwave nudged me seriously. *"War is not for the faint of heart. It changes merpeople."*

"I have to make things right. It's never going to end as long as I'm around." I took a deep breath, feeling my decision lock into place. *There was no turning back now. Chances of survival: 0%. Chances of doing some ass kicking before I died: 100%.* "This is going to be more than a school yard rumble. I'm a little out of my element. You have any tips for a rookie battle fighter?" I asked Tidalwave, not expecting an answer.

"Keep calm, be cool and don't die," Tidalwave instructed.

"Great," I spoke unenthusiastically at his astounding advice. "Do we have any chance of winning this war?" I looked at him grimly, holding onto a small piece of hope.

"Merpeople pack more of a punch than you give them credit for. Just wait. You'll see how fearsome they can be. Let's save the dramatics for after the war, shall we?"

The King began to swim down the line on his hippocampus as he rallied his troops, who cheered every so often. I was too far away to hear what he was saying. His armour glinted in the sun. He had blue and silver jewels splashed across his gold chest plate. I still saw no sign of Jeremy in the massive crowd.

"Felicity?"

"Yeah?" I bit the bottom of my lip nervously.

"Don't fight this fight because you want to clean up your mess. Fight for your love of the city and the merpeople. If the sharks win today, all of Atlantis will be destroyed. They will move to other colonies and soon merpeople will cease to exist and the darkness will take over."

I nodded silently. The impact of his words hit me hard. *I couldn't lose this place. It was all I had.* "If a fight is what they want, a fight is what they're going to get."

With one last cheer, the King led the army up to the dome as the troops followed him. My body tensed when I saw Jeremy for the first time. Even from so far away, I knew it was him, as he rode Sunrise at the front of the line, close to the King's side. I found it hard to swallow. I knew only too well from watching movies how being on the front line ended up for a person.

"You ready?" I asked, allowing my mind to focus on the task at hand as the last soldier disappeared into the darkness.

"Let's dance!" Tidalwave's muscles were coiled tightly as I grabbed onto his fin and he dived down to the abandoned area. We scoped and scrounged the area looking for armour that would fit us. Each second wasted could have meant Jeremy's death. In my haste, I stumbled upon a sword. I picked it up and examined it. My fingers grasped the hilt. The design on it was beautiful. On the hilt was a black dragon with bright red jewels embedded in its eyes. The dragon's tail was wrapped around a large, emerald green jewel that was placed at the bottom of the hilt. *How could such craftsmanship be left behind? It had to have had an owner.* This was the kind of sword that you would want to take with you to a fight and it was extremely light. *Mine now. I'd need all the luck I could get!* I stared at it blankly as I realized I didn't have a clue how to use it. People trained for years with these things and were still mediocre at best. I strapped it awkwardly to my side as the steel rested against my hip.

"I'm going to assume you don't know how to use a sword. What kind of a place did you come from anyway? Everyone knows how to use a sword!" Tidalwave scoffed.

"Back home, swords aren't much good against guns. But that will be a step up!" I pointed at a silver bow with vine carvings engraved on it that was propped up against a rock with three packs of arrows. The arrows had a type of green reed as the rod. In place of feathers, fish scales were used for the feather fletching and sharp shells were used for the head, which would puncture the enemy. "I did a lot of archery in high school." I slung the three arrow packs and the bow over my shoulder as I felt myself weighted down. *How could anyone fight with all this armour and these weapons?*

"Beechwood makes a very strong bow. The string is really tight, but your arms aren't as strong as most mermen. You think you can shoot it?" Tidalwave queried.

"If I want to live, I'm going to have to." My heart hammered in my chest as I heard a merman's piercing scream. The battle had begun. In that instant, my mind conjured up images of gleaming teeth coming out of the shadows, bodies being torn apart, my head getting decapitated, Tidalwave shredded to pieces and Jeremy with lifeless eyes. *This was madness!*

I suddenly felt anxious, anxious to get in and get it over with. Be done with this once and for all. I looked at Tidalwave and patted his forehead reassuringly. "To die would be an awfully big adventure…"

We entered quietly and swiftly into the dark. Dozens of glow fish flickered in multicolours of green, blue, purple and red, lighting up the dark water. The battle wasn't too much farther. A red glow fish flicked out and plunged us into darkness for a few seconds, then glowed red again giving the area a sinister and creepy look. A merman's dead body floated towards us. I choked down the urge to vomit as we pressed on, our eyes avoiding the body as I realized half of his head was missing.

I hopped up into surfer position and knocked an arrow to the bow shakily, taking a deep breath to settle my nerves. The darkness around Atlantis seemed to come alive, thriving with the sounds of death and war. This was no ordinary darkness. Somehow, I was missing the whole picture. I shook the feeling away, realizing this was not the time or place. If I survived, it would be something to examine further. I could see the blood floating in the water as thick as soup in some places. The glow fish were flickering like a lightning storm. I let out a scream when the light flicked off, then back on, and I saw a shark's dead body hurling towards us.

"Steady Crystal. Get into dolphin rider stance. You can't fire, let alone fight, if you're gripping my dorsal fin," Tidalwave said rather shakily.

Hearing the fear in his voice made me want to be stronger and braver for him. I had forgotten he was as young and inexperienced as me, yet he still came to fight with me, a human. Adoration for Tidalwave bubbled up inside me. *He'd risked so much so I wouldn't have to do this alone.*

I got unsteadily into position as I heard a growl behind me and all the hairs on my neck stood on end. As my hands tightened around my bow and arrow, Tidalwave flipped around and I almost lost my balance. Standing in front of me was a monstrous hammerhead shark. It was triple the size of

Tidalwave. I felt the blood drain from my body. *"Aim for the gills or for the centre of the skull. That is where they're most vulnerable,"* Tidalwave said, never taking his eyes off the shark, his red eyes piercing our souls. Before I could loosen an arrow, he charged us and Tidalwave swerved to the side, narrowly avoiding the beast. He came at us so fast I fell off Tidalwave. My bow slipped from my hands and spiralled down into the depths. I cursed at my lack of experience. It was going to get us both killed. This was not a good start. I disconnected the string that had me attached to Tidalwave's tail and swam after the bow with the hammerhead chasing me.

The crevice the bow had fallen into wasn't much farther. The shark opened his mouth trying to bite me when, suddenly, I put on a burst of speed. Still, I could feel my tail touch his teeth. He chomped down and I screamed. He had just torn a chunk off the bottom of my tail. It felt like the skin had been ripped off my body. I reached the crevice and plunged between the rocks. The hammerhead pursued me, managing to get stuck between the two rocks I just dove into. His face and teeth were inches from mine. I could reach out and touch his head if I wanted to. Adrenaline coursed through me. I always thrived under pressure. It was easier when you didn't have time to contemplate things, such as your impending death. I sucked in bubbles. I had no room to move without the shark biting something off of me. Suddenly, a thick silver hunk of metal was driven into his skull and a cloud of blood surrounded me. The hammerhead thrashed once and laid still. Tidalwave yanked his tail dagger out of the hammerhead's head. *"Are you okay?"*

"My tail, he bit it." I winced, trying not to look at it as I swam up to Tidalwave and showed him the damage. It was red, swollen and a blue bent vein stuck out from the side of it. I felt myself going lightheaded as shock began to set in.

"Crystal, next time you need to tell me what you're going to do before you do it. I could have distracted the shark until you got your bow back and you could have fired your arrows into him while I was providing a distraction. Instead, you drew too much attention to yourself and almost got killed," Tidalwave said angrily, while examining my tail. *"We have to be able to communicate!"*

"I'm sorry. I didn't really think…" I trailed off, at a loss for words.

Tidalwave sighed. *"Wait here. I'm going to swim back down to the bottom to get you something to wrap your wound with. From now on, we must work as a team if we are to survive this."* Tidalwave dove to the bottom of the sea near Atlantis and was back in a few seconds with seaweed dangling from his teeth. *"Wrap some seaweed around it. That will stop the bleeding and protect the membrane that is poking out.*

"Things are not looking good in Atlantis. The water is dark red as the blood and bodies are raining down from above. The King had to take the dome's protective bubble qualities down during the battle or else all the soldiers would have been netted with the King's latest efforts to catch the human. It keeps the darkness out but anything can pass through the shield without a trap going off. Good thing these creatures stick to the darkness most of the time. The curse has worked in our favour today."

My caudal fin throbbed painfully as I tried not to picture

what my beloved city looked like now. Hoping to redeem myself, I hopped onto Tidalwave's back. "Come on, Tidalwave! Let's go hunting." Whenever we saw a glimpse of gray or a shark's fin, Tidalwave would steer us towards it for a closer shot. The arrows were precious and I had to make every one count. It didn't help seeing the sharks ripping mermen apart everywhere I looked. That just fuelled my anger even more. Pieces of flesh littered the area exposing the red insides of both shark and Mer.   The Mer were savage when they fought, as I saw their wild fish side come to life. Their hissing, singing and shrieking were awful sounds and stunned their opponents. Some Mer wore no armour as they wrestled sharks with their bare hands. Most of the warriors' teeth turned razor sharp like piranhas and they ripped hunks of flesh off the sharks.

My arm hurt from constantly aiming and firing. Soon, I just turned into a robot. I had no emotion, no sympathy. I became lost in the rhythm. I wanted to stop fighting but for that to happen all the sharks had to disappear. The rhythm kept me calm and sane.

Schwing. Take the arrow out of the pouch.

Twang. Release the arrow.

Thunk. Watch the arrow hit its mark.

It helped lull me into tranquility.

Schwing.

Twang.

Thunk.

My eyes roamed the battlefield for Jeremy. Everyone looked the same; everyone was moving so fast I could only catch glimpses of faces. I felt so alone with just Tidalwave and me canvassing the area from above; if there were other archers around I could not see any. It seemed the cowardly way of doing things, but we had saved many mermen from dying by using our sniper position.

Schwing.

Twang.

Thunk.

I reached around into my last quiver and searched for another arrow but, to my dismay, there were none left. I let my bow fall and took out my sword. It felt as though the dragon was alive with a mind of its own.

"Am I really ready for up close and personal combat?" Suddenly, I was afraid again. I didn't have my rhythm to concentrate on. I didn't know what to do with this hunk of metal in my hands.

"Hold on!" Tidalwave yelled and swam fast at a Great White shark with alarming speed. I wrapped my arms on his fins and tucked myself as close to him as possible. He took his tail with the massive spike on it and plunged it into the shark's heart. Quickly, I raised my sword high above my head and brought it down on top of another shark's head that was creeping up on Tidalwave from behind. My sword severed his head like it was butter. I stared at the sword incredulously; there should have been a lot more hacking involved. I whooped in delight at just how sharp the sword was, as I felt my confidence return. This might be easier than I thought. *Two down, ten bazillion more to go.*

I stared at the floating head beside me, the shark's eyes blinking back at me before they glazed over. I shuddered.

We killed a few more using the same tactic, with speed

to our advantage. The sharks were so big, we barrel rolled around them before their teeth and brute strength could hit us. The sword felt like lead in my hand but I would not drop it. Renewed hope sprouted within me as I gazed upon the faces of Jeremy and Sunrise. They were still alive!

Jeremy was a magnificent sight to see. At times, it looked like he was struggling, but then he surprised me by killing three sharks at the same time. Sunrise was no different. She could swim in a variety of formations that kept the Great Whites guessing.

Tidalwave rushed towards him. Jeremy turned himself towards me. His body and face were caked from head-to-toe with blood. "Lucky you got here," he panted. "I don't think I could have defended the King with all these hammerheads approaching."

My eyes darted toward the King who was fighting ten sharks at once. Between his bodyguard and him, it looked like an endless swarm of attacking sharks.

I didn't answer Jeremy for fear he would find out who I was, despite all my armour. With somewhat of a manly grunt and a nod I acknowledged him. I'm glad he wasn't paying attention to Tidalwave. Then he would have definitely found out who I was. Together we fought side-by-side, working together as a team. We could anticipate the enemy's every move. We were in complete sync with each other. We managed to dwindle the numbers down, allowing us a fighting chance at winning.

Just then came a small ripple in the water.

Swish.

Swish. The ripple was a little bigger this time.

Swish. It kept increasing. It started to get so big that it was throwing people from side to side and off their animals.

Swish.

"Keep your swords drawn! This war isn't over yet!" cried the King.

Out of the darkness loomed the biggest squid I had ever seen. It was like The Incredible Hulk. Its tentacles were as long as twenty of me put together. Its suction cups were the size of my head or bigger. It was accompanied by a group of swordfish, which only emboldened the sharks, who began fighting with renewed vigour.

"What in the world?" I stammered.

One of the mermen beside me yelled. "It's the…the…the Kraken!" His face went as pale as a ghost.

CHAPTER 11

The Kraken Awaits!

I started to glance where the merman had been pointing as chaos erupted amongst the soldiers.

"Don't look it straight in the eyes. He'll put you in a trance and stop you dead in your tracks," Jeremy advised. "Hold the line!" he yelled to his fellow warriors. I had heard of the Kraken, but never believed the stories. I never thought it could possibly swallow ships and crews whole, but the more I watched it the more I started to believe. *Where were Moby Dick and Rhinestone when you needed them?*

"Sneaky little blighters, swordfish. They're so light and agile. When we fight the sharks, they stick you in the back," Jeremy warned me. "Everyone get a partner and fight back-to-back. Watch the swordfish," he yelled to the frightened mermen.

I could feel Tidalwave shaking beneath me. A lot of the mermen were cowering as the massive squid approached. We were all doomed. We didn't stand a chance. I watched the King as he slayed the last of the hammerheads that had been surrounding him, ready to take on another round. *He was per-*

sistent and determined. I'd give him that. I admired the King's strength and courage. Even in the face of the Kraken, he showed no fear.

A fierce roar from behind us shook the waters as goose bumps rose on my arms. A silver dragon swam over us. Lighting its way were three purple, blue and pink glow fish. The crowd cheered as the dragon let out a burst of icicles and ice shards at the approaching enemy, the icicles embedding into the first line of swordfish like tiny crystal daggers. Seeing the dragon gave me hope as the icicles lit up the sky with the glow fish sending colours shooting in every direction, dazzling the eyes. Sitting atop the silver dragon was Sebastian. The two of them made a powerful team, pushing back the first line of swordfish with a wall of ice.

The mermen gained confidence at the appearance of the Prince and the dragon. *First Jeremy, now Sebastian, they couldn't both live in this war.* The silver dragon's ice was starting to dwindle as the swordfish began to attack, forcing themselves through the ice, many dying in the process but the mermen swam to protect the Prince and the King. The Kraken still needed to be dealt with. I eyed up the opponent. My chances looked pretty slim but that had never stopped me from fighting anyone before.

"Ah, cripes!" came Tidalwave's echolocation. *"I hope you're not thinking what I think you're thinking."*

"It's about to wipe out our entire army for fin's sake. Sebastian's arrival isn't going to be enough with that beast still in the picture. It'll kill the dragon in a matter of seconds. We need to draw it away from the army. The dragon can take care of the rest. Better to die a hero than a coward."

"Oh boy. You wouldn't happen to have a plan, would you?"

"Never do," I squeaked, hoping he couldn't hear the tremor in my voice. "We gotta distract it."

"Leave the speed to me. Hang on." Fast as a bullet, Tidalwave swam towards the Kraken. *"Don't let the ink touch you. It will blind you. He can only ink every ten minutes or so. The suction cups will drain your blood - and his teeth will slice and dice you like a piece of coral."* I braced myself as Tidalwave prodded the Kraken with his pointy tail, jabbing him in the head but barely causing a scratch, and I poked him with my sword. The Kraken inked all over the place and the chase began as we guided the Kraken away from the army. We were swallowed up by the darkness, totally alone as a few red glow fish trailed behind us. *"Take out the eyes,"* said Tidalwave as he swooped down low towards a floating shark. I pulled two spears out of its body with the Kraken hot on our heels. *"When you aim the spears, they have to be right in the centre of both pupils to get rid of his full sight."*

I swallowed. The main battlefield was long gone. It was just the Kraken and us. My grip tightened as Tidalwave whipped around and headed back towards the beast.

I stood up and clutched one of the spears and zoned in on the eyeball. "It's the bottom of the ninth, Felicity," I whispered to myself. "You need this to win the game."

My hand tightened. I threw the spear as we passed the huge black orb.

A deafening roar escaped the Kraken as he spun around and his eyes locked on us. The spear was right in the bull's-eye and it wasn't about to come out anytime soon no matter how much the Kraken struggled.

The Kraken stared at us in disbelief with his good eye. Someone had already hurt him, giving us the advantage. I whispered excitedly to Tidalwave: "I looked him in the eye and he didn't do anything to me. I must be immune to his influences because I didn't become entranced. I'm not a natural mermaid, but a human." My excitement was cut short, though. "Tidalwave, swim!" I kicked Tidalwave frantically as the Kraken chased us down in a passion of fury.

"Round two, here we go." Tidalwave panted.

He back flipped around and the Kraken's reddish pink, bulbous head barrelled straight at us. Tidalwave moved just in time for me to see the creature's other black eye fly past me. The Kraken's stench alone made my eyes sting. *"You missed!"*

"I know! I'm sorry, it was too fast."

"I can't do that again. I know I won't be quick enough next time. I'm running out of steam."

The Kraken turned around. We were on his bad side, the one without sight. "Quick! Put me on your tail and fire me in his direction. Aim for the other eye. He hasn't seen me yet." I gulped. I wasn't sure if I wanted to do this. One quick movement from the squid and he could have me wrapped around his tentacles.

Tidalwave went flying in his direction. Time was the enemy as we swirled around in between the tentacles and popped up on the other side. "Steady, steady, steady. NOW!" Tidalwave front flipped and I went shooting towards the Kraken. I grasped the spear with both hands. The Kraken's eye widened but it was too late. I had hit my target. I hung off the spear as it went into the centre of the disgusting black pupil. Black goo oozed out of it. I could hear the squishing as I thrust the spear deeper and deeper as a nasty smell perfumed the air.

"Hop on!"

I didn't need to be told twice. "I thought I was fish food." Tidalwave swam a fair distance away from the Kraken so we could catch our breath and we watched him ink out in anger from the loss of his sight.

"You did great! His sight is gone so he will have to use the waves and vibrations in the water to find us. The eyes were the easy part, but at least it will dull his senses. Now we have to go after his heart. From what I've heard about the Kraken in stories, it's located in one of his orangish pink tentacles."

"That's your grand idea? We're going to risk our lives on a hypothesis?" I asked touchily, not in the best of mood after having his eye goo all over my hands.

"Not we, Crystal, you have to be the one to do it. I'm not immune to the Kraken like you are. Heck, the ink might not affect you, but it will kill me. Don't worry. We won't have to find out if we do this quickly. He just inked a few minutes ago so we should be okay for about 10 minutes, give or take, before he can recharge himself for another go. I don't know how much protection you have but I don't want to test that theory if we don't have to. We need to do it now. Just remember, you can't touch the suction cups. By the look of all the spears and arrows embedded in him, you can use those for handholds. I'll keep him distracted on the outside. You just have to hold on tight because he's going to be chasing me the whole time."

I shook my head at the sheer irrationality of it all. My body was already bruised and battered, and my muscles were stretched to their limits. This had been a true testament to my strength and sheer willpower. I stayed silent as I realized that when the sharks' numbers had decreased I thought I'd have a chance to live. Now, I wasn't so sure. Going after the Kraken might be the mission I wouldn't be coming back from. Terror seized me from head-to-tail.

"You'll be in and out in no time. I'll try and keep him from moving too much. If I could go with you, I would. I haven't abandoned you and it's killing me to have to now. You will not die, you understand me!"

"Alright," I spoke quietly as I embraced Tidalwave tightly, blood rushing to my ears.

"We have to go now while he's nursing his wounds."

I said a short prayer hoping my God and Poseidon were listening. "Bloody hell! Let's go." I wrapped my left arm around Tidalwave's dorsal fin and held the sword in my right hand. We made sure we approached the Kraken with the water currents so he wouldn't be able to notice the difference in fluidity and discover our position. Both of us stayed silent. The Kraken's tentacles were trembling in rage, moving this way and that, feeling around in the water, searching. We spiralled around him slowly, looking for a good opening or any sign of his heart.

I pointed excitedly near the first row of tentacles, about four layers in and almost up to his teeth. There was a huge square. You could actually see the thumping of his heart. Relief surged through me. *Tidalwave had been right. The heart did exist! It wasn't too far in...*I saw an arrow protruding from his skin. As soon as I left this water current he would be onto us. Taking a deep breath, I leaped off Tidalwave and latched onto the arrow, grabbing a second one that was inside the first layer of tentacles and solidifying my grip.

Sure enough, the Kraken noticed. Tidalwave moved out of the current and into the Kraken's line of fire as the creature bunched his muscles and swam after Tidalwave, yanking me along for the ride. The strength of his take-off made me lose my grip. As I fell, I managed to reach out and grab another arrow a few feet down, while the water pressure was trying to force me to loosen my grip again. I ducked inside another layer, taking away most of the current's pressure on me, then I grabbed onto other arrows, getting me closer to the Kraken's heart.

The fall had knocked me down, making me lose sight of his heart as I swam through the forest of tentacles. I gagged at the stench. The Kraken's jerky movements stopped as Tidalwave jabbed his tail into different parts of the Kraken's head, keeping it busy. I saw a tentacle bat at Tidalwave, send-ing him in the opposite direction. As soon as he recovered, he was on the attack again. I sighed in relief and carefully hauled myself upwards towards the Kraken's mouth.

Bodies of mermen, seahorses, hippocampi and sharks were stuck to the suction cups, which were feeding off the blood from their bodies. A merman with half a body hung lifelessly with his intestines spilling out and a tentacle was wrapped around a shark's body, popping out its eyeballs. I felt a lurch and grabbed onto a spear as the Kraken swerved hard to the right. His roaring made my ears bleed from the pressure and caused my body to shake. I felt sharp stings as the suction cups pressed against my left arm. I lashed out with my sword, causing them to squeal and release me.

As the creature rolled in another direction, I cried out, knowing Tidalwave didn't have much time. His energy was just as spent as mine. I cut off a few more suction cups that had latched onto my back and shoulder from that last swerve. Following Tidalwave's advice, I began to climb, using spears and arrows as handholds. The Kraken was really riled up and his speed suddenly clicked into a higher gear. I gritted my teeth and paid attention to his body movements, allowing me to avoid getting stung by most of the suction cups. I passed more bodies that were still wriggling around attached to the suction cups. They looked like puppets. I wanted to cut them loose but had no time. As I passed each of the dead mermen attached to the Kraken, I searched for Jeremy's face hoping that he and Sebastian were still alive.

With my body stinging and weary from the climb, four spears away I spotted the pulsing of his heart. My body gave out its last burst of energy. Blue and red veins ran along the creature's heart, pumping a constant supply of blood into his body. This was definitely not on my list of top ten favourite things to be doing. I grabbed my sword and began slicing a square of skin open so I could expose the heart. Blood started pouring out and covering me. The Kraken stopped abruptly, realizing I wasn't just his food squirming around. I was the real deal. I screamed out as two suction cups tore into my tail.

The heart was a beautiful purple like nothing I had ever seen. It was as hard as a diamond with golden strands inter-twined in the centre making it mesmerizing. I wasn't going to be able to plunge my sword into it after all. The heart was massive. It was going to take two hands just to carry it. I squeamishly grabbed a green fish net off a dead merman. I dumped out his herbs, ointments and bandages and slung it across my chest. This would be perfect to carry the Kraken's heart in.

The veins and aorta held the heart firmly in place as I tried to rip it out of his skin. *This was going to be messy.* I hacked at the aorta first, which was thick and solid. It took me three tries before I cut through, spraying blood in every direction as I quickly cut the other veins attached to the heart. Instantly, the area began filling up with blood. I jabbed my sword into one of his tentacles, submerged both my hands inside his flesh, and yanked the heart out.

The Kraken gave a blood-curdling squeal as his cavernous mouth opened, causing me to scream as he showed me his layered razor sharp teeth. He started to move around, stinging me like crazy. I threw his heart into the fish net and yanked the sword out of his flesh, stabbing at the suction cups that had latched onto me. I heard a huge rumble as black ink started to eject from his body. This was his last attempt to kill me before he died.

I dove straight down, hoping that Tidalwave was there to catch me so this beast wouldn't crush me when he fell. When I tightened my arms closer around my body, I felt a suction cup graze me and cursed under my breath. My heart was pounding as I raced against time and my vision became blurry with the more stings I received. I felt my sword leave my hand and let out a cry of anguish as a suction cup stole it from me. I closed my eyes, hoping I would make it. I felt a thud as I landed on Tidalwave's back and grasped him blindly, letting him take me away, the Kraken's body sinking into the darkness.

"Crystal! Crystal, wake up! We still have unfinished business."

I sighed wearily. "Boy, you sure are pushy. No, hi. How are you? Nice work," I said, trying wearily to lighten the mood. I trailed off when I noticed his condition was no better than mine. The bottom of his right tail fin looked like it was broken and he had a big bruise that covered most of his body, which I assumed had happened when the tentacle hit him. "Oh!"

"Crystal, you were incredible and I'm proud of you. Come on. Let's finish this together. If we can take on the Kraken and live, then this should be as easy as krill pie."

My body hurt everywhere, but if he could do it so could I. "Well I'm not about to let you show me up."

By the time we found our way back, most of the sharks were either dead or fleeing. I saw the King bending over someone, so we swam over to see if we could be of any help. I looked at the merman. He was very young, about my age, coughing up blood. Sand and blood were covering his face and his hands were clenched into fists; a huge chunk of the side of his stomach was ripped out. My stomach heaved at the sight. "What happened?" I asked, as manly as I could, and hopped off Tidalwave. "Is there anything I can do?"

"He sacrificed his life for me, otherwise I would have been in the position he's in. A shark bit him hard in the ribs. There's no way to save him." The King drew his sword, ready to end the soldier's misery.

"Wait!" I cried, as I looked into the soldier's eyes and recognized a muddy shark tooth necklace. "What's his name?" When no reply came, I asked again, this time more firmly. "What's his name?" This time I demanded to know, as dread filled up inside of me. "Tell me his name!"

"His name is…is…Jeremy. He saved my life, one of my finest soldiers."

I stared in open-mouthed horror. *No, no, no! We won! This wasn't part of the plan. I diverted the Kraken away so the mermen wouldn't have to fight as many enemies.* I began scraping off all the blood and dirt to see him better. It felt like a lifetime ago since I had seen his face. "He can't die!" I said, tears streaming down my eyes.

"Do you not see how much pain he's in? I must do this, just as I would hope any of you would do the same for me," the King said, ready to bring down the sword and end Jeremy's life.

I yelled frantically, "I can fix it! I can fix it! Just don't kill him yet!" Sunrise was anxiously watching her companion a few yards away.

"You can fix it? How?" the King asked in desperation.

"I don't know! Just let me think of something." I had to get the King away from Jeremy's side. Maybe I could give him a task that would make him feel helpful, something that would keep him away for a while. "What he needs is some new skin…yeah, that's it, new skin."

"And where can I get that?"

"Tidalwave and I killed the Kraken. If you can bring back one of his tentacles, I might be able to save him," I said in what I hoped was a confident voice. I couldn't believe I was lying to the King, of all people!

"You slew the Kraken? How?" The King asked, surprised.

"I'll explain later. Just get me the tentacle."

As soon as the King left, I threw off my helmet, my blonde hair spilling over my shoulder. I cupped my hands around his head. I heard the soldiers murmuring around me in shock but I no longer cared. "Jeremy, Jeremy, Jeremy! Wake up. Oh, what do I do? What do I do?" I whispered, wiping my hands on my tail hoping to get rid of the blood. I had abandoned my manly voice.

"Crystal?" His voice rasped.

"You're not going to die. Not today!" I took both of my hands, cupped them together and brought them towards my mouth. His voice gave me hope. I didn't know what I was doing. It was all instinct. Something was telling my body to do this. I gave no thought to the process, but I knew I had to keep him breathing. I wanted to see him smile again, to watch him open his eyes and look at me. "Heal." I whispered into the palms of my hands with all my heart and soul and breathed into them. "Heal!" I said, with as much kindness and love as I could muster.

I felt my body heave as I moved my hands away from my mouth. I felt myself weaken as a neon pink ball the size of a pearl slipped from my mouth. My breathing came in short gasps. I brought my hands towards Jeremy and placed them on top of his rib cage, covering the wound with the pink neon ball until it was completely enveloped.

"Heal!" I muttered with the same intensity. I saw Jeremy's eyes flutter open, as soon as the word finished leaving my lips.

I smiled at him weakly, and then darkness overwhelmed me.

CHAPTER 12

The Plain Truth

When I opened my eyes, my vision was blurred. As I began to focus, I was shocked by all the white that surrounded me. I realized I was looking at the ceiling of a white tent. The material was woven together with bits of green moss mixed in, making me wonder what the tent was made of. I was lying on my back on something soft and spongy. Mermen were lying in neat, tidy rows around me. Some were missing limbs. Mermaids went up and down the rows checking on everyone or attending to the mermen's wounds.

Obviously, this was some strange kind of hospital. My wrists, tail and side of my stomach were tightly bandaged with seaweed. I had a lime green salve spread over all the suction cup marks, making me look like I had a major case of the chicken pox. I wrinkled my nose. The stuff didn't smell too good, either. I noticed some of the wounds were infected and oozing over my body.

I tried to sit up but sharp bolts of pain shot through the bandaged areas. I gritted my teeth and was clenching my hands into fists when I realized someone was holding my right hand. I recognized the blonde shaggy hair immediately and my heart gave a lurch. *Jeremy!*

"Crystal!" he said with relief, as he gripped my hand tighter. "You're awake. How are you feeling?"

I spoke slowly, finding it hard to answer such a question. "Confused. Aren't you supposed to be dead?" I looked at his stomach and noticed pinkish skin had been replaced where the shark had ripped out a chunk but the teeth marks still remained. I shuddered at the memory.

He spoke quietly. "I was, but you brought me back to life."

"How's Tidalwave?" I asked, both alarmed and drained of energy at the same time.

"He's alive and well, anxious to see you. The Kraken took quite a toll on you, but we'll talk about that another time, when you have more energy."

I felt a weight lifted off my shoulders with the news of Tidalwave's good health. I gave Jeremy a puzzled look. "I'm afraid I don't understand. How could I have saved your life? I didn't even know what I was doing. All I know is I didn't want you to die."

"Crystal." He searched my eyes. "Don't you realize what you have done, what you have sacrificed to keep me alive?"

"No, but you're alive and that's all that matters," I said. His face was full of sorrow. I laughed uneasily. "What? Did I lose a limb or something?" I asked self-consciously, checking everything to see if it was still intact.

"Crystal," Jeremy moved closer to me as he took my hand comfortingly. "In the week that you were unconscious..."

"I've been out for a whole week?" I raised my voice incredulously.

"A lot of merpeople didn't think you were going to make it. It has given us time to research how you saved my life." When I didn't speak, he continued. "Every merperson has a ball of life within him or her. It's blue, representing the water and all that we are. Then there is another ball, a pink one, which is the ball of love and represents fire, heat and passion. Not many mermaids are willing to give it up unless they've found their mate and, even then, it's difficult for them. Many times, mermaids will give out little pieces of their ball of love, or their 'pearl' as it is commonly known, to potential suitors. You had never broken your pearl and, in that moment, you gave all of it to me. Love is a very strong magic but I never thought it was possible to heal or bring someone back from the dead. It helped me live but at a great cost. Many merpeople would never be as brave as you. Do you see what I'm saying?"

"Um, not really." I laid back down on my bed. I was still trying to wrap my head around being asleep for a whole week.

"There is no easy way to say this, so I'll just cut to the chase. You'll never find true love."

I laughed then. "Don't be ridiculous, Jeremy. Of course I'll find love. A silly little pearl can't take away what's in my heart."

"You may love but it will never be the right kind of love. You will go through life in loveless relationships. Please try to understand you gave *all* of your pearl to me, willingly. I had no choice but to accept it, since I didn't know what was going on. Shell is awfully upset about it. I will always be drawn to you, but I love Shell. This bond we have will affect you, too, so I'm just warning you now, please don't think I'm yours."

I had a lump the size of a walnut in my throat. "Of course not." I closed my eyes as my throat swelled, trying to absorb all the information. "You never were."

"I—I made something for you. A gift so that you will always remember what you did for Atlantis and our colony." I opened my eyes as he attached a thick leather band to my wrist. A purple jewel glittered in the middle as strands of gold lingered and moved in the centre. "I made it myself," he said proudly.

My eyes widened in recognition. "That's a piece of the Kraken's heart!"

He smiled timidly. "We found it on you when you passed out, didn't have a clue what it was at first. I just figured since you gave me your heart, this was the closest I could get to giving you mine."

Emotions welled up inside of me. *Why would he say such a thing? I didn't want to hear it!* I pretended to yawn, not having a clue how to respond. "I'm tired, Jeremy. I'll see you tomorrow?"

He straightened up. "Of course, I'll stop by everyday if you like, whatever it takes." I nodded distantly, closing my eyes until I heard him swim away, wanting to be alone. I realized this was a feeling I was going to have to get used to.

The next day Tidalwave hovered around my bed and set something heavy on my lap that was wrapped in seal hide. *"How's the tail doing?"* He hadn't left my side since Jeremy had informed him I was awake, his body looking just as banged up as mine and a big suction cup scar on his one side from where the Kraken had swatted him with his tentacle.

I glanced at my tail, trying to hide how distraught I was. They had removed the bandages from my caudal fin last night. "They say it'll never fully grow back. It'll heal over as more of a stump," I said sadly. "What's this?" I pointed at the seal skin.

"A gift to help cheer you up. It's something that belongs to you and no one else. I also have some good news. They say they have most of the poisons out of your system. They're working on trying to get your heart back to normal after that little stunt you pulled with Jeremy."

"I appreciate their efforts but it'll never beat as fast as it used to and there will always be a dull thud until my mate picks out a shell for me with a love pearl in return. Unfortunately, that has to be Jeremy and he made it abundantly clear that was never going to happen..."

As my voice trailed, I looked at the seal hide and noticed a metal handle peeking out from underneath it. Pushing the seal skin to the side, I grasped the handle and pulled out my sword with the dragon's familiar red eyes. "You found it! I thought it was a goner." Happiness tore through my body as all sad thoughts disappeared. I grasped onto the emotion firmly. I hadn't felt this good since regaining consciousness.

Tidalwave smirked. *"I didn't find it. The King did. He was pretty reluctant to give it up. Turns out this sword has been around since before the gods even swam in these waters. Your sword is called Mystical Illusion and it's found very rarely. Only in a time of need does it appear - and it picks its owner.*

It's alive, Crystal, with a mind of its own."

"So you're saying that this little bug," I said, pointing to the metal dragon, "is alive?" I had my doubts but, nowadays, nothing would surprise me.

"The sword has fought in many wars and whoever wields it succeeds in battle. Mystical stays with the person it chooses until the end of his or her days, then just disappears again into thin air until the next merperson is worthy of it. Many have wandered the sea world searching for it. It's called Mystical Illusion because many merpeople have illusions and dreams about the sword. Many mermen claim that sometimes they believe their sword is Mystical Illusion during a war. They can see the dragon with fire in its eyes wrapped around their sword, and it fills them with hope and courage before the battle."

"So, why are you telling me about this amazing sword now?"

Tidalwave began to fidget at my side. *"I just want you to be aware of how powerful it is and how it can draw the wrong kind of attention, especially the attention of the King. I don't want him to use you as a pawn. He has a lot of enemies in the world. If he could, that sword would already be in his eager hands, but that is not how Mystical Illusion works. The side that has this sword in battle never loses. The King might want you to fight for him to ensure victory. He's always wished that his son had it, and he's probably not too thrilled that you've got it, instead. You disobeyed a rule that he made known to all: that no mermaids can fight. You think he wants you flaunting it around, questioning his authority?"*

"That's not what I intend to do!"

"Well, when you meet the King, tread carefully. The penalty is death, or total ostracism, for disobeying such a law."

The words echoed in my head. "Wow, he doesn't give a merperson much wiggle room, does he?"

"That sword might be the only thing that's keeping him from enforcing his edict."

I felt anger rise inside me. "After everything I've done for him - for his city - he would still have me killed or alienated?"

"He must show no weakness or fear, because his enemies are always watching. How else do you think he's been King for so long?"

I leaned back, silently wondering how things had gone from good to terribly bad.

Later that night I looked into the depths of the dragon's eyes and muttered, "Why did you pick me? What good can I do?"

Silence.

"Wake up!" I shook the sword.

Nothing.

I sighed in frustration. "Listen, you little pest, if you don't wake up, I'm going to melt you down so you're nothing but liquid."

I saw bright orange flames leap across the steel. I threw it across the room in fright. Suddenly, my right shoulder began to burn. I watched in fascination as a small gold circle formed on my shoulder with a dragon and sword connected together in the centre. Another tattoo.

"Pretty darn good for a little pest, if I do say so myself."

I turned around and saw a black steel dragon with fiery eyes sitting on my bed examining his claws arrogantly.

"A simple hello would have sufficed," I said casually, resisting the urge to throw the rodent against the wall. He didn't look all that powerful, not compared to the brute strength of the Kraken or the sharp teeth of the sharks.

"That symbol on your shoulder is for me to know when you are in need of assistance or in danger and for merpeople to know that I belong to you from now until the day you die. All you have to do is rub it with your hand." He hopped onto my arm as I felt his cool steel claws dig into my arm. "I'm yours for eternity!" he grinned.

"Great," I said unenthusiastically.

I saw his ruby red eyes flicker in agitation. "Oh, I can already see the doubt on your face. You don't honestly believe it was you who did the sword fighting in the war do you? You wouldn't have lasted two seconds without my help. Watch this!" He opened the maw of his mouth as orange fire blazed all around me. I rolled off the bed and began to toss around in the sand, trying to put out the fire. My body did not turn into a crisp as I had expected but I felt my old skin burn off and a new layer of clean skin take over. When the dragon was finished I stared at it in bewilderment. All the bruises and cuts I had on me were completely gone. My tail was transformed back to its former glory. He puffed out a spew of smoke from his nostril and snorted. "Now, do you still have doubts?"

I touched my tail over and over again, hardly believing it was back. "Sorry," I mumbled. "I just thought you'd be bigger."

"You aren't exactly tall either. If you want to talk short,

who do you think saved the sea world from Albony's Bane? That would be a shrimp! Who do you think saved the baby whale, Nightwatch, from having a run in with the humans? A sea monkey did!"

"Okay! Okay! I get it." I laughed. "What I want to know is why you picked me?"

"Are you testing my judgement? It doesn't matter what you were or will be but who you are inside."

I rolled my eyes as I grabbed his neck tightly to keep him from escaping. "Enough with this nonsense. The truth, please," my eyes begged.

"Fine," he sighed. "It was an obvious choice. You clearly needed help. I couldn't have you die, not just yet anyway. It isn't your time, but it would have been if you went into battle without me. I always pick the weaker ones that no one believes in. They always have the best stories, even if one is a foolish human."

I looked around, shocked that he had said it so loud and out in the open. "Quiet!"

"Don't worry, everyone's asleep. No one can hear me. But, I sure am tired. Been awhile since I've been awakened. It takes a lot out of me." And, with that, he curled up into his original position on the sword and turned back into steel, as though nothing had changed. I glared at it. I had so many questions and clearly I wasn't going to get the answers tonight.

Tidalwave was waiting for me outside the tent. *"Well, you're looking much better. Not so green around the gills."*

I tapped the sword at my side appreciatively. "Pays to have friends in high places."

I took a big whiff of the saltwater. It smelled so good, way better than the stale water in the hospital. Never again would I have to take the nasty medicine they shoved down my throat and never again would I have to eat the mush they served for meals.

"So, you awakened it! What was he like?" Tidalwave asked.

I snorted. "Not as noble and majestic as you'd like to believe."

Atlantis looked like it was back to normal, gleaming and clean, dome back in place, almost as if a battle hadn't just taken place. Rainbows were out high in the water, glittering brightly. The merchildren were actually bottling some of the rainbow in small shells and tossing them about all over the city, reminding me slightly of a water fight.

Tidalwave noticed my glance. *"It's pretty rare for us to have a rainbow. Come on, I want to show you something."*

We approached the gold and diamond castle of the King's. The castle winked brightly in the daylight. "I wonder what it would be like to live in there?"

"I think you'd have one massive headache."

Tidalwave gestured towards the front of the castle, where I was shocked to see the corpse of the Kraken. *"The King has injected the Kraken with a never-aging liquid so he will stay here forever and never change. It will be a spectacle for the whole world to see. Sure hope we don't get another one of those anytime soon."*

"What do you mean?"

"This isn't the only one in the sea, silly. They breed, too, you know."

I tried to ignore that comment, not wanting to think about how many more of these mammoth things were out there. The Kraken sent chills up my body just looking at him. The eyes had been removed and replaced with two huge diamonds. Some of the tentacles' skin had been ripped off. Two mermaids took a picture of themselves in front of it. I thought at any second it was going to wake up and impale us.

There was a shimmery silver sign posted that read:

Here lies the monstrous beast, the Kraken, who will no longer roam the sea. We leave his bones here to rot for all eternity so we can remember our fallen comrades who fought to rid Atlantis of this foul creature. For that, we thank you. Without you, we would not be here today.

Sincere thanks to Crystal Clearwater and Tidalwave the Magnificent.

At the bottom, beside our names was the Kraken's heart encased in a crystallized glass for protection, with a lock on it to prevent anyone from stealing it. "Tidalwave the Magnificent?" I laughed. "How amusing. You know, I can't believe we actually brought that thing down."

"A little more to the left and it would have landed on my castle." We both jumped at the sound of a deep voice. It was the King. "A pretty decoration, don't you think?" He stroked his long black beard as his black hair floated around his ears and his keen grey eyes watched us. I found it very easy to see Sebastian's resemblance in him.

I recalled the King's desperate attempt to save Jeremy from his pain in the battlefield. His voice had been filled with panic and I found the stern man beside me was not the same one as in battle. Apparently, everyone has their moments of weakness, even Kings. He was shrewder and more calculating, flowing with the power of the sea. Both of us nodded our heads, but I couldn't find anything to say to someone so important.

He stared at Mystical Illusion on my hip. "May I see it?" Reluctantly, I handed it over to him. "It's exquisite. I've seen a picture of it in a book once, but it doesn't compare to the real thing. I wondered about all the stories it could tell. Have you awoken it yet?"

"Yes, just once," I said defensively.

"That's good, that's very good," he mused. His look turned desirous and then he sighed and passed it back. "I may have need of you yet, Crystal Clearwater. You and Tidalwave are very skilled warriors."

"Thank you." I stammered from the compliment. "I will do anything to aid the kingdom in any way." After having heard so many times that female warriors would be killed or ostracized, I was practically in shock at the royal treatment afforded me by the King. But, I sure wasn't complaining.

The king nodded at us and turned toward the castle. "Follow me. I want to show you something."

Tidalwave and I found ourselves in a spectacular gazebo in the backyard of the King's castle. It was pure crystal, just like his house. It was twinkling brightly in the daylight, sending rainbows shooting in every direction, reminding me of my crystal sun catchers at home. The gazebo was surrounded by plants of many colours. "I only let a select few see what I am about to show you two. You have proven yourselves worthy of my trust by saving the Kingdom, killing the Kraken, saving my daughter's boyfriend and the lives of my loyal subjects. Just as the Kraken has a heart, this city has one, too."

As we walked inside, something black and poisoned stood on a pedestal. It didn't have the beauty that the heart of the Kraken possessed. It looked decrepit and foul, as though it were rotting away slowly. It was not of the human heart variety like the Kraken's with veins and blood, but more of a Valentine's Day heart, the type that little girls doodled all over their binders.   "It used to be a beautiful sea blue," the King announced. "Then the darkness came and surrounded the city and the city's heart. I haven't been able to get rid of the darkness since. I don't know if it's doing any damage to the heart. I used to stare at it for hours. Now I keep it hidden away.

I think this heart holds the key to getting rid of the darkness, but I don't know how. I believe the heart of Atlantis will never die as long as merpeople live. It may weaken, but nothing can pierce Atlantis' heart. It is unbreakable. The heart used to be accessible to the public, but I do not need them to know that darkness now surrounds it.

So, now you know what worries me - and why it needs to stay just between us. I don't need to stress how important it is to keep this quiet." He stared at us, making sure we understood and, with the look he gave us, I can tell you, my lips were zipped, buttoned and locked on this subject.

"Yes, sir," I answered, as we swam out of the gazebo. He went in the direction of his castle and we headed back to the Kraken's body.

"*Uh oh, we got company!*" A pack of hording merteen fans spotted us by the Kraken with kelp paper and cameras in their hands, wanting to get our autographs and pictures.

"Run!"

"What?"

"You're a celebrity now. If they get a hold of you, they are going to tear you limb from limb just to get your attention. It'll die down eventually but, trust me, I know from experience that you don't want to deal with it now! Just turbo swim!"

"I doubt they'd like me very much if they found out I was a land walker, any more than the King would. He showed me the heart of Atlantis and he, of everyone, must never know I'm a human. If he finds out, I will have disobeyed his rules and his trust."

"Yes, well that's never going to happen. We must split up. Don't go into popular areas or else they'll morph into bigger groups and you don't want that." He sped off and left me to deal with the crazed merpeople.

Great.

I took off to the main part of the city. I could lose them in the crowd milling about the city at this time of day. I flew past the school and into a jewellery shop. The shopkeepers looked at me and I put my finger to my lips for silence. They went about their own business as the mob passed by. Someone grabbed my shoulder. I yelped, turning to face a startled Sebastian.

"Oh. Hey, you wouldn't happen to have a place to hide, would you?" The mob was splitting up into groups now, searching every store.

He noticed my gaze, grabbed my hand and said, "Come on," whisking me away out the back door.

We swam to some kind of park. It was small and secluded. Little pink and blue plants dotted the ground. There were more green weeds than sand and there was a crystal sea-horse merry-go-round in the centre with merchildren hopping on it, squealing with glee. I stared at the merry-go-round in awe. Each seahorse had different crystal colours. How do they create such beautiful things?

"You missed the medal ceremony for all the mermen who did heroic deeds."

"Aw, shucks," I said. "I've been in that war once. I don't need to relive it again. I still get nightmares."

"You and Tidalwave each got one."

"Really? But I disobeyed orders."

"Even rule breakers deserve recognition. Don't worry. I'll try and talk to my Dad but, for now, just enjoy being a hero." He tucked a strand of hair behind my ear.

"We wouldn't have won if it wasn't for you," I said, looking him in the eyes. "You gave all the men confidence."

"Don't change the subject." He tutted as he held out a package that I had failed to notice. "You were amazing out there." He unwrapped a gold medallion and placed it around my neck. I stared at it. It never stopped shimmering and, inside it, something was moving. It had an animated picture of me riding Tidalwave. My sword was raised high. It was incredible. "War is a dangerous thing, but there are some who stand out." He grabbed my hand and squeezed it lightly.

I felt my breath catch at such an intimate look, but no fuzzy feeling entered my body. "Feels almost as if I was there again." I stared back at him. "Thank you. Who else got awards?"

"I have never seen so many mermen's eyes turn crystal in one day. It was the greatest honour they could have been given. It's no wonder they were at their happiest. They all dined with the King that night. Jeremy received the highest honour for saving the King's life. A few mermen received medals for saving the King's higher up soldiers and so did the families of mermen who lost their lives performing heroic acts."

He opened his bag and pulled out a long, slender pointed object. It was my bow. Then he pulled out a thin stick. My arrow. "These arrows were found in many of our enemies. We were thoroughly puzzled. A lot of the sharks were killed with one of these in them. Someone who killed so many sharks deserves recognition, as well. Each arrow is colour coated for each merperson and the merperson who owned it said he never brought it to battle."

I stayed silent sorting through my thoughts. I can't claim these as mine because they would think I was lying. The King would never believe that a *mermaid* could kill the Kraken and shoot that many arrows, too. I felt a small feeling of triumph that it was I who had did that with my own skill and not with the aid of Mystical.

"You don't have to say anything. Deny it all you want, but I know it was you. You are the bravest and craziest mermaid I know, no matter what rumours are spread or what happens in the future. I was supposed to fight the Kraken with my dragon but a dozen swordfish attacked us all at once, puncturing Silvertongue's wings badly. By the time she recovered, I saw you disappear into the darkness. I thought I'd never see you again. I was so angry. I should have fought the Kraken by your side. You saved Atlantis."

"We all did," I said quietly, thinking of everyone who had

died and the human who had lived.

CHAPTER 13

Stuck in a Loveless life

Being back home, lying in my shell bed as daylight crept into my window, I began to grow a conscience. Now that Tidalwave and Mystical Illusion knew my identity, I wanted to tell everyone. I wanted to stop all the lies so the merpeople of Atlantis could start liking me for me. Everyone admired me for my bravery and courage, something I was not accustomed to back in Lakewood. Once they found out my secret, they would never look up to me again.

Maybe I should go back to Lakewood, where I wouldn't have to hide. Let the merpeople of Atlantis believe I'm a hero, not a human and leave it at that. If only I could turn back the clock to the days before the war, before I sacrificed my love pearl to Jeremy. A sour taste filled my mouth. *Who was I kidding? I would have done it all over again.* I feel like I've lost more than I've gained. I cannot love. I'm destined to be a spinster.

"You won't be." Mystical Illusion unfolded himself from the sword and sat on my lap. "Because you're a fighter - and fighters never quit."

"I'm lucky I'm even here at all," I said miserably.

"You're here because fate has brought you here. It's fate that brought us together, it's fate that you met Tidalwave and it's fate that you saved everyone from certain death."

"Then how come it doesn't feel like it? I can't help but think that if I had sacrificed my life a lot of merpeople would still be alive."

"The war would have happened regardless. The sharks have been after this colony for a long time. Perhaps the war wouldn't have started as early as it did, but it would have happened eventually. Being a human had nothing to do with it."

"Even so, I still feel responsible. Jeremy doesn't want me. Instead of messing everything up, I could easily have stayed in the human world. But, I chose this life and I am endangering everyone with my presence. I'm like poison. Sooner or later, the truth will come out. It always does. It's hard to keep spinning this web of lies. Eventually, I'll have no one on my side."

"You'll have Tidalwave and me," he stated firmly, his whisper rippling through the water, full of compassion. "By the way, someone's waiting outside for you," Mystical said.

I let out a deep breath, hoping it was Jeremy. I opened my door and leapt back in alarm. One big golden eye was staring through the door, almost taking up the entire frame. A dragon! Her claws were as big as my head and were kneading the sand. Her silver scales, thick as armour, were shimmering in the water and her teeth showed their razor sharp points. "Wanna go for a ride on Silvertongue? One of the rarest creatures in the whole ocean." I looked up to see the Prince sitting high on the dragon's neck with a wide smile.

"Are you kidding me?" I swam up onto Silvertongue's neck and felt the coarseness of her scales, trying to ignore the fresh battle scars on Silvertongue's body. *All my fault.* I looked behind me to see the glares of about twenty beautiful supermodel mermaids who were sprawled all over Silvertongue's outstretched wings and tail. "Um—unless you have more pressing matters that need to be attended to," I said, tilting my head.

"Well, stop gawking at us. Bow to your Prince and show him the respect he deserves," spoke a mermaid from the tail end of the dragon, the comment directed to me.

"Oh!" I blushed. Maybe I *should* bow, maybe I have been insulting Sebastian this whole time. I was unaccustomed to the rules of royalty.

Sebastian put me protectively behind him and stared the mermaids down. "Crystal bows to no one, least of all to me. She is a guest and I expect you to treat her as one." The mermaids grumbled amongst themselves quietly. "Pay them no mind."

Silvertongue let out a snort of bubbles and lazily drifted through the water. Below, I could hear the mermaids trying to get the Prince's attention. "What's with the parade of mermaids?" I asked curiously.

Rolling his eyes at the females below, he grabbed my hand and put it in his. He was handsome and courteous but I had no feelings for him, except friendship. I felt empty inside. "Father's orders. I am to choose a bride soon." The girls sighed dreamily and fanned themselves.

"Aren't you a little young?"

"I'm the King's son. I've come to terms with the fact that

I will never get to be normal. I can't live my own life. I have obligations that must be followed. I want to make a difference in this world as my father has. I'm no coward when it comes to marriage. My father can be very strict."

Suddenly, my little family squabbles didn't seem like a big deal. "Dude, I'm just going to say it. No offense, but that blows."

"I just hope I can find someone who truly cares for me. Look at Jeremy and Shell. Everyone knows they were meant for one another. That is what I wish to have." I stayed silent. The truth stabbed me straight in the chest. I no longer wanted to be sitting on Silvertongue talking about things from which I was going to be barred forever. Noticing the pained look on my face, he apologized. "Sorry Crystal. I forgot. Must be pretty hard…"

"So, where are you taking me?" I said, changing the subject and trying to hide my discomfort.

"It's a surprise." He perked up, grateful for the change of topic.

"If you're not going to kiss him, then let us have a go at him!" yelled a spirited blonde with big boobs. Her caudal fin was fanned out long and wide. It was a beautiful light green. Her tail stood out the most amongst the rest.

"Vertoni, one more comment out of you…" Sebastian warned.

Suddenly, the girls turned on me. "Look at her face! It's bright as a tomato. Sebastian, I don't think she's ever been kissed," said the one named Vertoni.

Another girl laughed. "You sure know how to pick them."

I wasn't embarrassed by the conversation, I had never had

much luck with boys let alone the time to put into a relationship. I was angry at the comments. I was just about to swim back there and shut them up when Silvertongue lurched to a stop.

"Alright ladies! I've had enough for one day. Off you get, you can swim back to the castle," said Sebastian angrily. The mermaids pouted and began jumping off Silvertongue's outstretched wings. Sebastian patted Silvertongue's neck and she continued on with a snort of relief as all the weight disappeared off her back and wings. She had gills on her neck and I watched them open and close. "So, is it true?"

"Is what true?"

"That you've never been kissed?"

"I'll never tell you," I joked. "Wait!" I pointed to the darkness as Silvertongue showed no signs of turning. My body went rigid. "I...I don't want to go in there." Instantly, my hands reached for Mystical Illusion. There could be more sharks in the water, ready to gobble up whatever they saw. I didn't like the feeling of being unprepared in the dark waters with no one but ourselves to defend us. During the war, they had surrounded us like a pack of bees protecting their hive. I shuddered at the living memory inside my head. The Kraken, along with hundreds of sharks and swordfish, had outnumbered us, knowing we wouldn't be able to survive. Still, we kept on trying, even if the situation had seemed hopeless.

Suddenly, Sebastian interrupted my thoughts. "Crystal, why do you think I'm *on* Silvertongue. If there is anything out there, she'll be the first to know, she has great night vision. The war is over. You have nothing to fear. You can close your eyes until we're out of the darkness if you want. You can trust me. I have a special access pass for us to leave Atlantis so all the traps are deactivated. I would never risk your life if I didn't know it was safe. Granted, I *was* supposed to take the other mermaids to The Surface, but I'd rather be with you."

"The Surface!" I said excitedly, forgetting my fears. Just hearing him mention the word reminded me how eager I was to see land and breathe air again. As much as I loved Atlantis, I was starting to miss my friends and even my annoying family.

"I've never been there myself. Dad assured me Silvertongue knew the way. I wanted to share my first experience with you. After what you've been through, you deserve to see something beautiful. If you're too scared, we don't have to go into the darkness."

"I'm not scared, just cautious." I pulled out Mystical and sat him on my lap, which gave me some comfort. Meanwhile, Silvertongue continued to flap her wings, pushing us through the dome and enveloping us in darkness. I did not close my eyes. I hated the feeling of not knowing. It felt exactly like my first day in Atlantis, pure darkness. I could feel the coldness and weight of water all around me. The heat of Sebastian's hand was the only thing that told me I wasn't alone. It kept me anchored and prevented me from freaking out. It was a vast area of nothingness. I knew that much, because with every flap of Silvertongue's wings the ripples seemed to never stop, just fade into the distance.

Sebastian grabbed a bag that was hanging from one of Silvertongue's horns, removed an orange glow fish and stuck it into a lobster trap, giving us a small area of vision. *How had they found all these human made objects?* "With Silver-tongue, it shouldn't take us too long to get there. If it wasn't for the darkness and its dangers I could show you Silver-tongue's underwater ice city, it's a three day trip. Not many dragons roam the water anymore for they are becoming rare. We used to go once a year to see her family but we dare not go anymore, in case the city should need protection. The darkness can be very disorienting. Should we try and find it, we may get lost."

My eyes roamed around and I strained my ears listening for anything unusual. It was strange being in the darkness without Tidalwave. I concentrated on the dragon's wing strokes, which took my mind off the creatures that scurried out of our way. I began to tremble and Sebastian wrapped his arm around me for comfort and security. "I bet it's beautiful."

"Let's just say it comes close to Atlantis's beauty."

"So, what's the story on this darkness? It hasn't always been this way," I asked curiously. I have to admit, my body was wishing I could feel more than friendship for Sebastian, but I was still trying to forget the bitter sting of the conversation Jeremy and I had when I was in the hospital.

"It's not something I like to talk about. One day it wasn't here, the next day it was. There is something about it that makes it feel like it's more than just stagnant water, like it's waiting for an opportune moment to pounce. It has been like that for a while but the war just solidified my assumptions.

At one time, we had some of the best farms and farmland available. Atlantis was once a thriving city selling our goods to neighbouring cities. We used to have tons of tourists who came to eat our food and see the Forbidden Area.

When the darkness came, it wiped out everything - the merpeople who were living on the farms and all their crops. The land is now dead. Nothing grows. It happened not too long after the first code red. Merpeople are more paranoid than ever that, with the second code red, history will repeat itself, that the dome will not hold and that, once again, our city will be covered in shadow. If it wasn't for my father putting up the dome when the darkness arrived, Atlantis wouldn't even be here," he sighed. "So much death comes with code reds."

"This will be my first time leaving the darkness. It doesn't surround the other mer cities, just Atlantis. Some mer say it's our punishment for not destroying Atlantis when the Forbidden Area was created. Destroy Atlantis and the human's entrance into our world would also be destroyed.

"This city has too much history. I was born here and I want to die here. It is still one of the nicest cities in the world, but you should have seen it before all the code red business. See how the darkness over there is lightening up?" He pointed to a lighter batch of black. "We're almost out of it. You see that glowing green light up ahead? That's crystal. There's tons of it here. All of these crevasses, boulders, bedrock and mountains are filled with these green and blue crystals lighting the way to The Surface."

We passed by an underwater cavern, which took my breath away. It looked like we were in a huge geode. "Silvertongue just has to follow the path of light. That little hole up ahead will take us into the Seaweed Desert. It's going to be a tight squeeze. You might want to hold on," Sebastian said.

I felt Silvertongue let out a roar of frustration as everything began to get smaller the closer we got to the hole. Coming to a stop on the opposite side of the hole, I felt her legs scrape against an underwater mountain that was beside the cavern. Her muscles bunched up as she prepared to spring. Silvertongue folded her wings against her side and kicked out with her feet as we burst through a patch of seaweed and into open water. There was no rock, just green seaweed on the floor. Miles upon miles of seaweed stretching as far as my eyes could see.

"Wow, they didn't exaggerate when they called it a desert," he said, looking at the endless amounts of seaweed. "We have now entered the human realm. Notice how the colours here are so bland compared to home," Sebastian said, recovering from the initial shock. The colour wasn't as vibrant in Atlantis but it felt like I was back in the human world, with fewer magical properties. I looked closer. We were in a gigantic cavern, the seaweed colour illuminating it and turning everything green.

"I thought only whales like Moby Dick and Rhinestone could bring merpeople here," I commented.

"Usually, it's a safety precaution. In the human world they have whales, too, so ours blend in, especially if a ship spots a whale with merpeople on them. They think we're just myths and fairy tales. We like to keep it that way. Sometimes, merpeople like the sun so much they follow it across the ocean trying to catch it. None of them ever return. We think they become so disoriented they can never find the door back to our world or they die chasing their dream.   That is why the whales watch over us. They keep us a secret and make sure everyone does as they are told. Our guardians. I wanted to see if The Surface was everything merpeople were saying. The human world may be a cruel one but merpeople say the sun is the prettiest thing you'll ever lay eyes on." I looked down and saw dashes of silver and blue fish dart in and out of the seaweed, their scales gleaming. "I wanted you to see the sun. I'm sure once I'm married I'll be making regular visits with my wife but it will never be the same as the first time."

Wife. Husband. One thing I would never be called and another I would never have. I realized we were swimming on an upward angle. I began to get anxious. It felt like so long since I had seen the sun. "Thank you for this." I spoke truthfully.

"I feel kind of foolish around you sometimes, Crystal. This is probably the most bravest thing I've ever done. I've never been this close to the human realm."

I laughed. "Sebastian, you fought in a war. I don't know about you but, to me, that sounds pretty brave."

"I'm not as brave as you. You fought the Kraken and lived to tell about it - and you have Mystical Illusion. I've been so sheltered since my sister died in the war against the squids. This is all I can offer and I feel like it's not enough."

"I was only brave because I was forced to be," I said. I looked around at our new surroundings. "It's perfect. After so much ugliness, it's nice to see something beautiful."

Sebastian grinned. "Look! There it is." He pointed upward as we came through a wide opening, the only one in the cavern. The clouds, heat and sun were beckoning to us from under the water. "It looks almost like the Forbidden Area, just bigger." White light infiltrated the area as we neared The Surface, lines of sunlight rippled all around us and everything was a beautiful blue. I had seen the ocean before, but never like this. If there was such a thing as magic, this was it.

I saw Sebastian wrinkle his nose as he pointed to a big catfish. "Not a very nice looking fish compared to what we have. They probably taste terrible, too. And look at their skin. They're really plain looking, but they sure do move fast." I chuckled briefly. These plain fish were the kind I had grown up eating my whole life.

"Hold on!" Sebastian cautioned, as Silvertongue picked up speed. Faster and faster she pumped her wings until we broke through the water's surface, spraying water droplets in every direction and arcing high into the air. The sun wasn't as bright as I had imagined it from underwater. It was close to setting but still dazzling. When I saw Sebastian's reaction, nothing could have made me happier than to be with him at that exact moment. His eyes were wide as they crystallized, his lips parted and his hair moved in the breeze, as he felt its gentle motion for the first time. It must have been his first time feeling a lot of things. Silvertongue dove back under the water, the world disappearing before us. "Wow, that was incredible! It felt weird out of the water. Almost heavier," said Sebastian.

We stared at each other in happiness as Silvertongue headed back down into the depths. "What are we doing?"

"Going home," Sebastian said glumly.

"Why?"

"Because we can only see it for a second. We don't want to risk getting caught. Silvertongue isn't a whale."

"But there was no one around. Come on, the sun is setting. We've come all this way. You - I mean we - have to see what a sunset looks like. Don't you want to spice up your life a bit, do something daring for once? This is a once-in-a-lifetime opportunity. If someone comes, we'll quickly dip back under the water. We are just fairy tales, after all," I smiled.

Sebastian was a little hesitant but, after one longing glance, up we went. Silvertongue was enjoying herself immensely as we floated along the water watching the sunset turning the sky a kaleidoscope of colours. Silvertongue's body hummed as her tail splashed lazily in the water.

It was dark by the time we returned to Atlantis. We had stayed on The Surface until the rays of coloured sunshine had disappeared over the horizon. "I wonder where the sun goes, only to return the next day?" Sebastian asked. "Sure wish we had a sun as warm as that down here. No wonder so many merpeople have chased after it. I could sit under it all day. I don't like all that open water, though. The human world must be very large. Nowhere to hide. It doesn't feel very safe. Anyway, it feels great to be home!" Silvertongue gave a snort of tiredness as we rode through the centre of Atlantis towards the castle. The street glowed with multi-coloured glow fish lighting our way. Many merpeople were out tonight enjoying the quiet waters.

As we passed the statue of the King, many merteens who were hanging about the area went silent, some staring, but many gawking at seeing Silvertongue swim past. I spotted Shell and Jeremy along with Coral, Rainbow and Star. "You *do* realize my brother is getting married," a curt voice spoke from the crowd. Shell sashayed her way through the group as Rainbow came up. She couldn't disguise her jealousy at seeing me with Sebastian. "Sebastian, she's a commoner!" Shell pointed out in front of everyone. "Why do you think father picked out the mergirls that he did?"

Sebastian halted Silvertongue and said, "Even if I did want to marry her, what's it to you? Crystal is just as much a warrior as Jeremy and I don't hear dear ol' Dad complaining about you two."

Shell crossed her arms, unperturbed. "Because, we do not marry liars," she stated firmly.

"What's that supposed to mean?" I said indignantly, sliding off the dragon and getting ready for a fight. Besides my little human lie, I hadn't a clue what she was talking about.

"You *can't* honestly expect us to *believe* you brought down the Kraken singlehandedly? Or that you just happened to get the sword that is so rare that not even my Dad, the King of Atlantis, could get it?"

Everyone was silent. Jeremy would not meet my gaze. I could tell from the looks of Rainbow, Star and Coral they believed everything the Princess had said, despite all the accolades I'd received from the King. I could care less about what everyone else thought but, even before the war, I had hoped Jeremy would have been the one to stick up for me. Before I could comment, however, Sebastian spoke angrily. "Crystal did what she had to do to save this city. If it wasn't for her, your *boyfriend* probably wouldn't even be around. If anything, you should be *thanking* her, not yelling at her. Stop being so paranoid that she's going to steal Jeremy from you. She isn't like that."

I looked at Sebastian appreciatively. *Mandy or Faith*

would have gone right up to Shell and given her a piece of their minds for causing such a scene. So, that was what the merteens thought of me. I patted Silvertongue on the snout. "You go and take Silvertongue home. I'll be fine. Don't worry about me. I can handle myself."

He gave me a worried look then left as I swam away from the crowd. I sat down on a rock thinking how perfect the day had been and how horribly it had finished. I heard a slight shuffle behind me and looked up to see Coral staring down at me. I turned my back on her, trying to ignore her presence, and watched some merkids building a sand castle. *They were so innocent, so carefree, so trusting. How I wished I could go back to those days where love didn't matter. All that mattered then was having fun.*

"I'm sorry for what happened back there, Coral's melodic voice said. "For the record, I don't think you're a liar. I guess I just kind of got a little jealous when I heard Sebastian had taken you on a dragon ride."

I snorted. "Jealous of me? Yeah, trust me; you don't have to worry."

"I guess I'm used to Rainbow doing those kinds of things. It's just, I really like you, Crystal, and when I saw you doing something that I would have expected from Rainbow, I was upset and hurt. It's hard for Sebastian to see me the way he sees you or Rainbow."

I let out an annoyed sigh. I could really care less about her romance problems. This is why I didn't hang out with this sort of crowd, so I could avoid such conversations. I turned to yell at her to leave me alone, but those bright violet eyes reminded me she was probably one of the few friends I had left, since everyone else thought I was a liar.

"I cannot love. Sebastian and I are just good friends. He's just being a flirt. It's his nature, so don't take it to heart when he goes after another mermaid. I am linked to Jeremy, heart and soul, whether I want to be or not. There is nothing for me here." Talking about someone I could never have made me feel very depressed. I would never again get the anxiousness, the nerves, the butterflies or the sweaty palms when it came to a crush.

"To win Sebastian, you need to get yourself noticed and show him the real you, not the side you show Rainbow and Star, but the side you show me. You both like history and learning. I'm sure he would love to hear your thoughts on how to improve the Kingdom. Be yourself. Enjoy every second of it. Don't lose your chance. He will be married soon, so let your intentions towards him be known." I swam away, wanting nothing but to be left alone with my thoughts.

I found myself looking towards the Forbidden Area, the metal fence sparkling in the moonlight as I gripped Mystical Illusion tightly in my hand. My mind wandered to The Surface and I yearned to be there. *Maybe this wasn't the world for me. But how could I go back to that life after I'd had this one?* I looked up to where the puddle was located, contemplating my options. Atlantis was making me go soft. I was losing my hard, stern attitude that I had developed in Lakewood. I realized I was a happier person without it.

I felt something crawl up my arm and saw that Mystical had woken up. "You can't take me."

"And why not?"

"Because, I belong to the sea."

"And I belong to the land, yet here I am underwater."

Mystical flicked his tongue. "Poseidon has blessed you well by keeping your secret hidden. That's the only reason you haven't been discovered yet."

"Or it's pure dumb luck," I laughed nervously. "I just can't help thinking about how accessible Atlantis is for humans. It's not like it's hidden all that well and if the wrong kind of human ever found it, this place would be ruined. It would be used as some kind of tourist attraction. People here are already scared of just one human. Imagine hundreds. Or thousands. It *must* be moved to a safer place."

"Figured that out all on your own, did you?" Mystical smirked jokingly. "I guess you don't need any of my well-guided wisdom today. Just try not to spill the *entire* ocean while you're up there trying to move the entrance. And don't get caught. Simple enough."

I smiled at the confidence he had in me. "I don't know where I could possibly hide it to keep it safe." I thought of Lakewood, which was swarming with humans.

"The fate of this world will be in your hands, once again, Crystal." Mystical folded back into steel leaving me to my thoughts.

I groaned in frustration and began pacing about the area. *Just one thing after another. What if this time they caught me before I got a chance to leave Atlantis? Delaying this any longer could have jeopardized everything.* I took Mystical Illusion and buried him deep inside a patch of moss. "Stay safe until I come back." I glanced around and saw a merperson swimming fast in my direction. It was Jeremy.

He came up to me, his eyes searching the area. He

grabbed me and hid me behind the rock where I had just been sitting. "Jeremy? Wh-what are you doing?" My heart hammered in my chest at the sight of him as I tried to calm my hormones down.

Before I could say any more, he clamped his hand over my mouth and whispered in my ear, "Be quiet or they'll hear us." I felt tingly all over, as his breath was warm against my skin. At the same time, I cursed myself for even having such feelings. His body was pushed up against mine. Excitement fluttered inside my body, filling the empty space. These feelings were ten times stronger since I'd given him my love pearl. He was making my body sizzle and pop. I closed my eyes, savouring the feelings, breathing in his scent. These kinds of emotions could not be ignored. How could he not feel it, too? Maybe we were meant to be. Maybe he *was* mine, maybe Shell had been lying to me, and maybe he loved me just as much as I loved him. I shook my head, ridding myself of such notions. How did I know what was real?

"Where did he go?" I heard a girl ask. I peered over the rock and saw at least 12 mergirls searching frantically.

He whispered in my ear again, "See what I mean?" I nodded in reply.

"When I see him…I'm gonna kiss him so much that his eyes are gonna pop out of his head and then he'll be begging for more."

Jeremy glanced at me with a horrified look. I choked down a laugh, resisting the urge to say, "He's right here, ladies. Step right up'. Then I remembered that he thought I was a liar and all feelings disappeared as his betrayal stabbed me. "I think they're gone," Jeremy announced, after taking a second look to make sure the coast was clear.

"They're quite taken with you," I said harshly, pushing him off me and brushing the sand off my body. "Tell me, do merteens only think that you and Sebastian exist in this world?" I leaned my back against a rock as he sat across from me. "Stop looking at me like that," I warned, as his green/blue eyes stared back at me.

"Listen, I came to apologize. I'm *really* sorry. This hasn't been easy on me either. Everyone's hounding me about you and Shell doesn't trust me anymore. You saw all those girls, how crazy it's getting. It's out of control. I'm sorry I didn't stick up for you the way Sebastian did," he said sadly. "I've been trying to stay away from you, Crystal. I really have. The problem is, every time I see you I fall less and less in love with Shell."

My hopes went sky high at his comment. I stared at the ground, stunned by what he had said. "Was that before or after the war? Or after I broke my pearl?" I stared hard at the ground not wanting to look at him. Everything I had wanted to hear spilt from his lips. The way he answered this question would determine it all.

"Before, I think…" he sighed. "Crystal, I can't give you an honest answer. My feelings are all over the place. While you saved my life during the transfer of your pearl I must have given you a piece of my love pearl in order to care about you this much. When I saw you with Sebastian, I was envious. I…I don't want to lose you."

"You never will, Jeremy. I want you to like me in the right kind of way and not because of the pearl breaking. I want to make sure it's genuine. How can I be happy with you if I am not of your own choosing?"

Jeremy stared at his hands. "I do like hanging out with you. It's going to take some time."

"That's understandable," I reasoned.

"Crystal?" Jeremy asked. "Why did you go and fight in the battle?"

"Because, I don't take orders from merguys," I joked, not wanting to tell him the real reason.

He laughed and nudged me in the arm playfully. "There has to be more to it than that? The truth...."

Ding! Ding! Ding!

We both jumped and I looked at Jeremy in confusion as I left his question unanswered. "City Hall meeting. We should get going. It's mandatory for everyone to attend." He started to get up and held out his hand for me to take.

"Um..." I looked towards the entrance of the puddle. I needed to get up there before nightfall.

"You coming?" I grabbed his hand in reply as we both swam towards City Hall. *This shouldn't take too long, should it?*

CHAPTER 14

Decisions, Decisions

As we entered the cave through a tunnel, I could hear different voices bouncing off the walls. When we approached the centre of the cave and the main source of the commotion, I was reminded of a baseball stadium. In the middle stood an impressive large starfish statue lying on the floor and there were three tiers of seats surrounding the starfish in the centre. Most of the stone seats were already filled.

"Look over there." Jeremy pointed to a mermaid who was abnormally tall. "She's from the South." When she turned around, my eyes widened in wonder. She didn't look like any of the mermaids I had ever seen. Her slanted eyes were a piercing yellow and her body had a blue tinge to it. Her hands were webbed like the feet of a duck and her lips and eyelids were sparkled with the same colour as her black hair. She was exquisite. "They say that breed of mermaid shoots venom from their mouth but it's a rougher country out there. I wouldn't stare too much if I were you."

He glanced around the room at the large crowd. "Looks like the King has representatives from all over. This must be really important."

A group of mermen swam past with big black spikes coming out of their skin. I waited until they were out of earshot. "Who are they?" I asked, puzzled as they reminded me of a hedgehog.

"Warriors from the North, very scary that lot. When they're agitated or going into battle those black spikes shoot out of their skin. They can control it but they have been known to impale a few merpeople by accident when they get too close. They remind me of blowfish. You never know when those spikes are going to come out. This breed of mer-people is hard to spot because they look just like us until pro-voked. I'm sure with the talk of a human, though, you will be able to pick them out of the crowd."

My stomach suddenly felt queasy. "Then I guess we shouldn't sit by them, eh?"

Jeremy laughed, "They have a special area designated for them to sit in."

I felt a dolphin tail lightly hit the top of my head. As I looked up, I noticed the ceiling was covered with dolphins. I saw one in particular staring down at me. I smiled slightly trying to show Tidalwave how indifferent I was to this meet-ing and failed miserably, noticing his concern deepen.

"Look!" Jeremy waved to Coral, Shell, Rainbow, Sebas-tian and Star up on the second tier where there was a better view of the starfish. "Come on, they saved us seats."

I noticed Shell and Rainbow didn't look as thrilled to see me as the other two. I sat by Coral and Star, while Jeremy sat in-between Shell and Rainbow, which seemed to please Shell tremendously. Sebastian and Jeremy struck up a conversation with each other immediately, making me wonder if Sebastian had anything to do with his apology or if he had smoothed things over with this group.

Coral spoke up quietly beside me, her breath ruffling my hair since we were sitting so close together. "Don't you think the starfish is so fitting for a place like this? That was my idea," she boasted proudly. "There was a competition 20 years ago and whoever had the best statue idea for City Hall won."

I looked at the centrepiece. "Why a starfish?"

"This is where all the council meetings are. A starfish is patient, which is key to meetings like these. Being hasty never works. It's a good reminder."

I thought back to the school's mascot. "Why not a snail? It does the same thing."

Coral laughed a little. "They aren't exactly known for their intelligence. Starfish are known for rebuilding things when they have nothing." At my look of confusion, she continued. "If one of their arms get ripped or cut off, they will regenerate a new one and deal with everything as it comes in an appropriate manner. Starfish are not known for war but for the choices they make. It should be the same at these meetings…Oh, look! There's the King. He's magnificent, isn't he? Good as new after the war. Not a scratch on him. I heard he talked with you. What was he like?" she asked.

"He's strong and made me nervous. You know Sebastian, how have you not met his father?"

Her excitement disappeared. "Apparently, he doesn't approve of Sebastian hanging out with us. But that's what's so amazing about Sebastian. He always makes the right choices.

He'll make a great King someday."

I felt a pang of jealousy because of the feelings Coral had for Sebastian. I sucked back a rude comment, realizing that not being able to love may turn me bitter. I thought about the way I acted towards people in Lakewood and realized I didn't want to be like that. I didn't want to start acting like Felicity from Lakewood here in Atlantis. I was Crystal and I wanted to keep it that way. "And, hopefully, you'll be by his side," I whispered, as she blushed profusely, looking around to see if any merperson had overheard, then smiling brightly.

The chatter in the room died down as the King stepped onto the starfish. The starfish glowed orange and lifted him high up into the air as bubbles under the starfish kept him afloat. He sat with his golden tail hanging down. "The time has come for us to be rid of the human!" His voice boomed inside the cave as merpeople cheered. "It is time for action." The merpopulation nodded in approval.

I heard Jeremy let out a whoop. "'Bout time!" he hollered as I sank lower in my chair, not liking this conversation one bit.

The King continued on. "I do not think the elimination of the human should rest solely on my city when it concerns not just Atlantis but the whole sea. I will not have history repeat itself. That was a disaster but we learned from our mistakes and are stronger for it!"

"What does he mean history repeating itself?" I whispered to Coral as she put her fingers to her lips telling me to keep quiet.

"After the human is dealt with, I believe it would be wise for us to destroy the Forbidden Area. It seems that it is not a gift, as I had once perceived it to be, but a curse. If we destroy it, we will never have to fear humans again." An uneasy murmur rippled through the crowd as Coral shook her head negatively with that decision. "We must do this as quickly and swiftly as possible. Who knows how many other humans it has told about Atlantis? How many humans could be in this cave right now? My representatives and their most intellectual merpeople are here to help flush this human out. If you have any information, you can go to them and they will investigate the matter. They will stay here until this matter is resolved. You will see them everywhere in Atlantis."

I couldn't help but purse my lips in irritation. Just when I was about to help them by moving the puddle, they have to pull a stunt like this. "We will be investigating all newcomers from the day the code red began. In order to stop any more humans from entering or leaving Atlantis, we are going to build a tube that attaches to the Forbidden Area and then connect it to a cage. An alarm will sound when something is caught, just like the code red. Our hurricane tunnel is failing us, along with the dome's protective qualities. Once this is complete, maybe, just maybe, we can find a way to drive the darkness away. I believe it will go away with the disappearance of the Forbidden Area, but we must all work together. Keep your senses alert and let this be the end of it!" The crowd roared as the starfish descended to the ground and the King swam out of view with his guards and trusted friends at his side.

I stood up, preparing to leave, and searched the ceiling for Tidalwave. Everywhere I looked there was a mess of arms and fins trying to get out the one exit, chatting nervously about the events to come. There would be no privacy for anyone from now on. Time was of the essence. If I hurried, I could get to Lakewood, move the puddle and then be back down here lickety-split and no one would be the wiser. This tube project was going to take some time to build. The only thing that made me nervous were the investigations they would do of the new merpeople, but I would have to deal with that later. I had to leave now before everyone was out of the cave and vigilant. No one would even know I had left.

"Felicity! You're home. We've been so worried." Mom ran into the front yard and pulled me into a hug as I inhaled her sweet scent of perfume. All around me the street was ablaze with lights as stars peppered the sky. I wondered how late in the evening it was. "Where have you been?" I felt my stomach twist at all the stress I had caused them. "And no note!" Mom kissed me on the head as she yelled at me sternly. "You've run away so many times, but never this long! No matter, you're home now." As much trouble as I had caused, it was still nice to see how much they had missed me and how much they cared. It felt good to be wanted instead of judged. It was nice being back in familiar territory where I no longer had to lie. I had my swimsuit on underneath the baggy clothes I had stolen from someone's clothesline earlier.

Dad walked up and ruffled my hair affectionately. "Good to have you home, sport." He turned to Faith who was standing by the doorway. "Call the police and tell them Felicity is home."

"You…you, you called the police?" I said stunned.

"Duh!" Anna Bell's replied. "What did you expect when

you were gone for over *three* days without contacting us, right after you had a big fight with Mom and Dad? None of your friends knew where you were. We weren't going to sit around twiddling our thumbs. "

Dad jumped in before I could issue an apology. "All that matters is that she's home safe and sound. Your mother and I want to apologize. We didn't mean to be so…" he searched for the word "…brash. We thought you would have been strong enough to handle our criticism."

I felt a sliver of irritation at the comment and my right eye twitched. I am anything *but* weak at this moment in my life. I weaseled my way out of Mom's arms. "It's okay."

"Come on, everyone inside." Mom ushered us into the house. "The neighbours don't need to be privy to what goes on in our household."

"It does get to be a little too much sometimes," I admitted, walking into the house. "Critiquing me on everything I do and then getting mad at me. A person can only take so much before they snap. It's exhausting."

Mom's eyes welled up with tears. "Oh, how I've missed your melodramatics!"

"I'm being serious!" I looked at her incredulously. *How could she say something like that? Did she really believe everyone in this family was flawless? How could she be so ignorant?*

Faith bustled in. "A police officer will be stopping by to make a report on Felicity's return before they can officially remove her from their computer system." Her eyes locked on me. I kept my eyes from rolling as I realized I was about to get an earful. "Do you *know* how many sleepless nights this family has had? How many times we went out searching for you? Mom cried almost every night! How could you be so thoughtless? You always have to be the rebel. If you wanted attention, you got it. I hope you're happy." Faith stormed upstairs as the rest of the room was quiet.

Dad whispered in my ear, "Don't take it too personally. She was really concerned about you. This is just her way of letting off steam, knowing that you're alright. Come into the kitchen and I'll heat up some dinner for you."

I walked into the kitchen as Dad rummaged in the fridge, with Anna Bell bringing up the rear. Mom had gone upstairs to console Faith. I fidgeted on the island stool, unsure of what to say, as Dad popped leftover lasagne in the microwave. "I'm sorry," I managed to croak out, rusty from the lack of using apologies in my life. I couldn't remember the last time I had said that and actually meant it. Even though I found my family's presence suffocating, they were still family and nothing would ever change that. Anna Bell sat down beside me as I inhaled the smell of lasagne cooking. I began to fidget, waiting to eat as my stomach growled loudly. Human food. I almost passed out in delight.

The microwave beeped and Dad placed a steaming plate in front of me. "All that matters is that you came back. Are we really that bad that you had to run away for so long? When you usually run away it's just for a day or two. What was it about this time?"

I swallowed as I thought up a lie that wouldn't harm Atlantis. "I needed to get away and be on my own. I wanted to make my own decisions. I'm not the same person I once was."

"Are you going to stay?" Bell asked quietly.

I took a bite and mulled over the question. I realized I didn't have an answer for her. "I don't know."

I heard her and my Dad suck in deep breaths. "If there is anything we can do to get you to stay, just say the word. I don't want to lose a daughter."

"I'm sorry, but if I choose to go I'll go. You won't be able to stop me. I'm not leaving right this second anyway." I ate the last of the lasagne and headed upstairs to my bedroom. I hated seeing the looks on their faces, hated the decision I was going to have to make and hated the fact that I came back to see them like this. Guilt tugged at me. While I was out having adventures, they were busy worrying about me the whole time. How could I be so insensitive? I'd hardly even thought about them while I was in Atlantis.

Tucker was sitting on a pillow on the floor chewing on my black sock when he heard me come in. He lifted his head and gave a small puppy bark. His furry little tail wagged uncontrollably as he ran towards me all excited. "I see some things haven't changed." He jumped on me and started to lick my face. "Hey!" I said, laughing. "Cut it out!" I placed him on the bed and flipped him over onto his back and scratched his tummy.

Then I set him back down on the floor and sat at my desk pulling out a piece of paper and a pen. I could already feel the tug of the sea calling me. The next time I went to Atlantis there was every possibility I wouldn't be coming back. I started to write:

Dear Mom, Dad, Anna Bell & Faith.

If you find this letter then I'm sorry to tell you that I've left home and will never be coming back. I thank you for all that you have done but this is not where I belong.

Maybe someday, I will come back and visit but, for now, I have to find my own path. I love you all. Please do not worry about me. I will be fine. Trust me, it's a lot better this way.

Please take good care of Tucker. I know it's better if I don't take him with me. He deserves a good home.

Whatever you do, don't send a search party for me, or the police for that matter, because you will never find me.

I hope that you respect my wishes for I am really truly happy about where I am going. I have discovered a new life and can't return to the one here. I hope you can move on with your own lives and just be content that I have found a place were I finally belong.

Love always,
Felicity

I set my pen down and reread the note again. *Short and to the point, just the way I liked it.* I knew it wasn't much of a letter for a final goodbye but I had never been much of a writer. I stared down at the little puffball that was contently gnawing on my sneaker. "You are *so* lucky. You're so *little*. You don't have to worry about anything. You just get to have fun all the time." He cocked his head to the side with those big brown eyes peering up at me.

I heard a knock on my balcony door and looked up. I saw Jesse's face close to the glass and quickly shoved the letter into a drawer. I noticed a leaf on his shoulder from climbing up the tree to reach the second floor. He was dressed in nothing but jeans, a backwards baseball cap and a partially zipped up sweater that exposed his chest. I couldn't blame my sister for liking him when he wore an outfit like that. Even I had a hard time not staring. I opened the door and let him in. "Well, what brings you to my humble abode?" I smiled, happy to see a different face besides my family, someone who understood me better than most.

"Oh, I was just in the neighbourhood and wanted to make sure you were alright. Saw the lights on in your bedroom. When you said you were going to run away, I didn't think you meant literally."

"I thought I'd give you a break from the drama in my life."

He shrugged. "That's what friends are for, Felicity. We have no secrets." He picked Tucker up off the floor and petted him, as Tucker licked him on the cheek. "I don't want you to run away again. You can't leave me with Anna Bell. I'll go insane!"

"There's so much on my mind right now, running just seems easier," I sighed.

"Do you want to talk about it?"

"Felicity?" came Bell's voice. "Is someone else in there with you?" I heard my doorknob rattle as I ran to keep my door from opening.

"No. Don't come in, I'm just getting out of the shower," I lied from behind the door. I gave Jesse a pained expression and apologized as he slipped out the balcony door.

"Oh, for a minute there I thought I heard Jesse's voice."

I opened the door. "Why would Jesse be in my room? It's just Tucker and me."

Bell walked around the room and noticed the bathroom door was slightly ajar. "Why isn't your hair wet? There's no steam coming out of your bathroom," she asked suspiciously.

"Because I took a bath."

"You said a shower."

"Well, I mixed up the two. Are you the bathroom police or something?"

She stared at me. I could see no speck of trust in them. "The police officer is here to take your statement." She walked out the door, not waiting for me.

I let out a breath of air as I flopped onto the bed, hugging Tucker to my chest and hoping everything would just go away. Then, I headed down the stairs.

The next day, I was up and ready for school, eager to enlist Mandy's help in moving the puddle so I could get back to Atlantis. I looked at Tucker. "I'm going to miss you most of all." I kissed him on his fluffy head and ruffled his ears, then headed down the stairs for breakfast as he followed behind me loyally.

"Hey, Mom." I walked into the kitchen and grabbed four slices of toast.

She was surprised I was awake, out of bed and on time for once. "Morn—morning, Felicity."

"Where's Faith and Anna Bell?" I said, looking around the room.

Mom looked away from me. "They already left for school."

"Without me?" I asked. It had been a tradition since we were twelve that we walked to school together and, even though I'd been gone for four days, I thought they'd still want to walk with me. "That's weird." I stopped mid-chew. "It was Faith, wasn't it?"

"Since you left, they've walked to school together on their own. Faith is still hurt. It's going to take her some time. You know how she is. She just wants to be left alone. You could've at least *told* us where you were, a phone call would have been nice." Mom began scrubbing the pots and pans to keep herself busy.

"I already told you I'm sorry I didn't leave you a note. I was gone longer than I planned to be and, no, I won't tell you where I went."

Mom set the dishcloth down. "Your father and I aren't trying to push. When you're ready and you want to talk, we will be here for you. If you need help, I can arrange to have you talk to someone. Sometimes it helps."

All the fire in Mom's eyes was gone. Her tone was layered with sadness. "Mom! I don't need a shrink. I'm *fine!*" I walked out the door towards school, wondering if I was actually as fine as I thought.

Mr. Darnel's head poked up behind a hedge, spying as usual. He was not someone I wanted to deal with this morning. "I heard you were dead," he said in a somewhat disappointed voice.

"Afraid not, old man." I mused at his crackpot hallucinations. "Where did you hear that from?"

"Oh, you know. The old grapevine." He stared down the street where my neighbour, Mr. Rosinski, was putting out his garbage.

A second later, Mrs. Darnel came to the door. "Who's that

you're talking to, darling?"

"Oh, it's nobody, dear," he said gruffly.

I pursed my lips. *This old geezer needed a firm knock to the face.* "Who are you calling a nobody?" I looked at him nose-to-nose, daring him to say something. He wouldn't call me a nobody in Atlantis.

Alex came up and stood beside her father. I thought she would have left for her "private" school an hour ago driving her pink mustang convertible, but there it sat gleaming in the driveway. *How I hated that car.* I should have known better. *Great, just great. Now, I'd have to deal with the whole family.* "Daddy, come on. Leave her alone. She's had a rough time. Mental facilities must take an awful lot out of someone with all that shock therapy."

She was sneering at me and I was about to wipe that look off her ugly, plastic face. I said, "Not as much as *this* is gonna take out of you." Her face turned into a look of confusion until the light bulb went off in her head, but it was too late. My swing was already in action and I popped her one right in the jaw. "Man! That felt as good as I imagined it would after all these years. It really was everything I had hoped for," I said in a choked-up fake voice while I wiped away a fake tear.

"Daddy!" Her eyes watered as she stared at me venomously. "You're not going to let her do that to me, are you?"

I saw Mr. Darnel getting ready to pounce. Thank God he tripped over a rose bush or else he would have grabbed me. Instead, he snatched up a hoe that was sitting off to the side. I ran my little heart out realizing Mr. Darnel was taking this a little further than I expected. He started chasing me down the street in his pyjamas. Talk about a redneck moment. I wondered if this would make the front page of the local newspaper. As I flew down the street, I could see the neighbours' surprised and amused faces. I looked behind me and could tell he was running out of steam. I knew he wasn't going to be able to catch me. It felt good to have my feet back again.

He gave me the evil eye and yelled, "You had better watch your back and sleep with two eyes open!" Then he did some weird voodoo stuff with his hands and stomped back to his house. *Was revenge sweet or what?* That old rivalry connection gave me a small sense of contentment.

Since I was feeling extremely mature, I stuck my tongue out at him. "Can't wait! Bring it on, Grandpa!"

CHAPTER 15

Ridiculous Fiddle Fuddle

I entered the school and could already smell cologne and perfume clogging the hallways. I rounded the corner to my locker and stared in shock. Mandy was wearing a pink top and a black skirt, no less! Her arm was wrapped around a guy with short brown hair and she wasn't wearing her usual layers of makeup. I think the guy's name was Jeff and he just happened to be Karl's best friend. Karl had his usual cocky smirk. I felt my fists bunch up. If Jeff breaks her heart, he is going to get a beat-down. I could use another fight today - Alex was just a warm up.

I ducked behind a corner before I did anything rash and noticed Mandy was smiling and laughing. All my anger disappeared. *Who was I to run someone's life? I couldn't even run my own.* I shuddered as I realized I was on the verge of becoming my mother. Mandy isn't stupid. She wouldn't fall into something without knowing what she was getting herself into. She was glowing, the centre of his attention and I almost ruined it for her. At that moment, I knew I couldn't ask her to help me with Atlantis. I couldn't tear her away from this.

She might be killed for helping me if they ever found out someone else knew Atlantis existed. I wouldn't be able to live with myself if that happened. This is where *she* belongs.

Frustration welled up inside me. What was the purpose of defeating the Kraken if I couldn't think of a solution to move the puddle? Mandy was always the one with the best ideas and now I had nothing and nobody. She was the only person I trusted on land with Atlantis' safety. Tidalwave couldn't help me. He'd die if he came on land. If a merperson found out the truth, he would kill me on the spot. I wished Tidalwave was here to help me or Mystical, at least. *Why couldn't I have had more brains than brawn?*

"Felicity?" Mandy ran up to me with stars in her eyes and gave me a hug. My back went rigid. *When had she become a hugger?* "Where have you been? I have so much to tell you!"

I cursed inside my head. I couldn't make my getaway fast enough. "I can tell," I said, as I glanced back at Jeff who was talking to Karl. "How long has *this* been going on?"

"Almost a week," she gushed. "Isn't he something?" *Since when did Mandy gush?*

"Oh, he's something all right," I said bitterly. "If he hangs out with Karl, I'm sure he's a real charmer."

"Come on. Give Jeff a chance. Besides, that little thing with you and Karl was years ago. People change."

"Not him," I stated firmly. "Listen, Mandy. I'm truly happy that you found someone but I don't want to talk about Karl."

"We could go on a double date!" she said giddily. Clearly she had been thinking about this a lot.

I cringed as her voice went an octave higher, which is

what my sisters' voices usually did when they were excited. *Had the whole world gone topsy-turvy?* "Mandy, I'm really going to have to catch up with you later."

"But you just got here," she pouted.

"Yeah, I know. I'm sorry." I left without feeling the least bit sorry. I wanted to knock on her head and say, 'Hello, Mandy? Come out, come out, wherever you are?' because this is not the Mandy I knew. My earlier victory against the Darnels felt hollow and empty, useless if I didn't have the old Mandy to boast to. It was such a creepy transition. I hoped I didn't have a case of the Stepford wives on my hands.

I went to the puddle and sat down by the tree, willing myself to think of a plan as I stared into the water. I ended up with more questions and no answers. *Where should I put it? How should I move it?* A headache was starting to form from stress. I was under a time limit and it was drawing short. I didn't want to be stuck on The Surface when I could be in Atlantis. I massaged my temples to stop the throbbing. I wish I didn't have this responsibility. I went to Atlantis to get away from responsibility. My mind kept drawing blanks.

Someone would find this place someday. A few years back, they had talked about moving the baseball field somewhere else to make room for a mall or hotel here, to bring in more tourists. I know one thing that would bring in more tourists and they would find it while marking and surveying the area for construction. With that in mind, I was going to have to bite the bullet. I trusted no one on land with Atlantis. Maybe I could find a merperson who cared as much about Atlantis as I did, rather than worrying about my human presence. If Jeremy was a true friend, he would forgive me like

Tidalwave did. Sebastian was out of the question. I didn't want him to get into any trouble with his father. He couldn't have any knowledge of this. Maybe Coral wouldn't be a bad choice, but I needed to consult Tidalwave first. My only hope was that I wouldn't be too late.

CHAPTER 16

Mission Impossible

When I jumped into the puddle, I felt the familiar pull of the vortex. As I tried to escape the current, I felt glass all around me. *Oh no!* I felt myself sucked down the glass tube to the bottom of the ocean as sirens screamed and red lights flashed everywhere. I was momentarily blinded. My hands touched the cold, hard metal bars that surrounded me like a box. I swallowed. I stared up at the Forbidden Area to see a gigantic clear tube stretching up to the puddle and down to the cage. I began to dig, my fingers clawing at the sand frantically. If I could just make a tunnel then I could slip under the bars. My fingers hit something hard. I felt around as my body began to quiver. More bars. I was trapped. I curled up into a tight ball, hoping no one would be able to guess my identity and wishing my tail wasn't so distinctive. I threw as much sand over my tail as I could to try and camouflage it. I closed my eyes cursing myself for being so stupid.

"Human! Show yourself," came the loud voice of the King as the lights and alarms ceased their constant blaring. I buried my head deeper, heart pounding. "Get the eels," commanded the King.

I felt my skin peel away from my body as the eels' tails licked my back. I cringed but didn't cry out in pain as I stuck my fist in my mouth and bit down. This was nothing compared to the stings of the Kraken. I could hear murmuring all around me as I realized the whole city of Atlantis must be out to get a look at the human.

"I knew you would slip up sometime as soon as the dome was punctured we began building the tube all through the night knowing you would return at any moment. Why are you here? What do you want from us? Do you want to kill us and stick us on your wall as a trophy? We all know your kind can talk," the King persisted. I stayed silent. "Fine," he said, clearly not amused. "Guards!" the King barked. "Keep all corners posted with men, and have your spears at the ready at all times. If she moves or speaks, I want to know about it. 24/7 surveillance. She can't stay in that position forever. Give her a day or two with barely any food and she'll crack sooner or later. Don't spare the eel whips either. Clear the crowd. Give her total isolation until tomorrow. Then, we shall let the public have a better look at her."

As the crowd left, I was beginning to feel like I was part of some kind of circus and I was the main attraction. Doubtless to say, I'd see everyone again tomorrow. Five guards were posted at my cage with their spears at the ready and eel whips in the other hand. I could feel their eyes boring holes into me. My back began to throb in pain and my arm went numb from being in the same position for so long. I choked back a quiet sob. Getting caught had always been on my mind when I was in Atlantis but I had never actually believed it was going to happen. Night was beginning to settle in, cloaking me in shadow. I looked between the strands of my hair and saw the guards' arms were starting to droop as boredom began to set in. I heaved out a deep breath causing the guards to jump in alarm as I felt an eel sting me again. I started to rub my shoulder where Mystical Illusion's tattoo was. I felt it heat up and a golden glow lit up the cage. The guards backed away and one swam to alert the King.

"We're coming!" Tidalwave's voice echoed across the water.

I paled. I had wanted Mystical to come alone. "Don't, please," I echolocated into the water, hoping it would reach Tidalwave's ears. "I don't want them to kill you, especially if you're linked to me. Just go away and pretend you never knew about me being human. Act betrayed and angry."

"No way. I've never had a family before, Crystal, and you're the closest thing to it."

A lump the size of a walnut formed in my throat as I thought about his tragic upbringing. "Tidalwave, you must stay away from here!"

"A little late for that, don't you think? This is not up for negotiation. This is a rescue mission."

I saw a slender object hurtling towards me, leaving a trail of fire in its wake. Mystical Illusion hit a merguard right in the gut and bunted him on the head with the hilt, causing him to crumble. The guard closest to me pointed his spear at my body as the other two guards began to fight Mystical, who was using his tail to wave the sword around.

Tidalwave leapt up from a rock and smashed one of the guards hard on the head with his tail, leaving the other one for Mystical. The guard who had the spear pointed at me was distracted by Tidalwave. I leapt up and grabbed him through the bars, putting him in a chokehold until he passed out, as Mystical finished his duel.

Tidalwave pressed his nose into the bars as far as it would go. *"Piece of kelpfish."*

I smiled as Mystical Illusion floated in through the bars. As I grabbed the sword with my hands, he unwound himself and crawled to my shoulder. "As much as I'd love to chitchat, the King will soon be here and this place will be crawling with guards."

"Good point. I assume you have a plan?" I looked pointedly at Mystical who nodded enthusiastically. "Okay great. Tidalwave, you need to leave right now!"

"You can't make me, Crystal. I'm with you till the end."

"They can't damage a hunk of metal like they can a living creature for helping me escape. I don't want a guard waking up and recognizing you. With Mystical by my side, I'm as good as free, but I won't break out until I know you are far away. Time is ticking. Tick tock, Tidalwave. You stay, I stay. It's as simple as that." I crossed my arms stubbornly.

Tidalwave lashed out with his tail and hit the cage causing it to shake and clang from the impact. *"You're not giving me much of a choice!"* he spoke angrily and swam off.

"Tut, tut. Well, that was a bit harsh," Mystical observed. "It was him after all who fabricated this whole plan."

I gritted my teeth. *"Enough* from the peanut gallery! How do I get out of here?" I took the sword, placed it in the rusty lock and began twisting it, hoping it would break from all the pressure.

"Well, in the most polite manner possible for a mermaid such as yourself, I would be happy to explain the process. It would go a lot faster if we combined our strength and you weren't being so serious all the time."

"You wouldn't exactly be in a cheery mood if your whole life was on the line. I never thought I'd survive the war but, now that I have, I want to live!"

"Alright, alright, fair enough. There's a reason why I am such a powerful sword. I'm not all about looks, you know, dashing as I am. I know it's hard to believe. That reminds me of the time when..."

"Mystical!"

"Oh yes, right, we're escaping. Feels good to be doing something useful. I'm almost like, what does your world call them...ah, a genie! That's it. Stuck waiting around for some-one then, when we are called upon, we do what we're sup-posed to do. After that, we're stuck waiting around for the next person. A fair comparison, don't you think?"

I grunted. "Do you want me to die or not? Pretty soon you won't have a master to boast to!"

"You're hacking at the lock. You have to slice it perfectly and evenly. I can make the sword slice through anything, but we must combine our strength. Take the sword out of the lock. You were never going to open it that way. The King has enchantments on it." I felt my eye twitch as I refrained from screaming at him. "Grab hold of the loop on the lock with one hand. Hold it tight and in one swift motion you have to slice through it."

I did what I was told and felt the sword slice through the metal, nearly slicing my fingers off in the process. I unlatched it and cautiously stepped out. *I was free!* Horns blared around the corner as the guard by the door began to wake up. I swam fast with Mystical in front, only to feel strong arms grab the bottom of my tail, dragging me back to my cell. "No!" I yelled as I was thrown back in. The guard took out a newer lock and replaced the old one, as Mystical ducked quickly behind a rock.

The King loomed over my cage. "Trying to be tricky, are you?" I focused on the sand to keep my mouth from opening and pushed my hair across my face, thankful for the night to help hide my identity. Once he heard my voice I'd be done for. "You've been nothing but trouble from the start!" Each angry jab sent sadness into my heart. "You will die for all the sorrow and panic you have caused my city." I heard hushed tones in the background, realizing that another crowd had gathered in the dead of the night. With me locked up securely, they no longer had to fear my existence. Blue glow fish circled the cage, casting shadows on the merpeople.

"Throw her to the sharks!" I heard a voice off to my right yell, accompanied by a few cheers as I felt pebbles hit my back. Then a few turned into many as the crowd began pelting me. The guards tried to get everyone under control. I cried out slightly as a stone nailed me on the head painfully. Betrayal settled in the pit of my stomach. I had fought for them, laughed with them and some merpeople had even admired me at one time. I wanted to tell them to stop, that I was not someone to fear. They were so accustomed to hating humans nothing would change their minds. All their lives, they'd lived in fear of us. They would never forgive me.

I looked upon the crowd again and saw Jeremy right at

the front of the cage. My old friends were with him, too. "Oh my God!" squealed Rainbow as she pulled on Jeremy's arm. "It's looking right at us. How ugly."

I saw Coral with a confused look on her face as she stared down at me inside the cage. My eyes locked with hers and she was startled as recognition kicked in. She became the master of the poker face, but I could tell her mind was reeling. I realized it was probably my crystal eyes that had given me away. Even in the worst circumstances I could never manage to get it to change back to normal. I covered my head with more hair, praying that Coral would stay silent.

"What's that on her back?" I heard a merchild speak, his head craned as close to the bars as he could get, trying to get a better glimpse.

I froze in panic as I started to hastily cover the tattoo on my back with my hair, hoping the kid didn't know what it was. "It looks like the Mystical Illusion mark," came a male's voice.

"Impossible!" murmured another.

"It has to be a fake," yelled someone else.

"It's real," came Jeremy's voice, as hurt overwhelmed me. "No one can fake that tattoo. Didn't you see the eyes on it?"

There was no sense in hiding it now. "It's true…it's me." I stood up slowly, stretching my back and arms as I moved my hair to the side of my face, exposing my identity.

"You lied to us," the King said blankly.

"I didn't lie! It's not what you think." I stared at all the faces and found myself lying to save my skin one last time. "I…I just wanted to see what it was like up there. That's all.

You don't actually think I'm the human, do you? After all I've done."

"Then why did you hide this information from us for so long? Why didn't you speak up, instead of causing so much trouble?" came Jeremy's voice with a hard edge.

"She's lying! The traitor. She is the human. If you all recall the code red was from someone coming *into* Atlantis not leaving it," Rainbow piped up. "Don't let her mermaid façade sway you. She is a human and very dangerous."

"And will be dealt with accordingly," the King said, as his voice trailed off and he suddenly noticed Mystical Illusion trying to sneak into my cage. He chased after the dragon. Mystical swam quickly into the cage, mere inches separating him from the King's grasp. It gave me one last look and hopped onto the sword, turning it into steel. The King picked him up and grasped the handle tightly. "I want everyone to go to City Hall now. Until her fate is decided, she will stay here for the night. Certain things must be taken into consideration before a decision can be made. Tomorrow, she will go underground to the dungeon. We may even experiment on her. See what makes her tick, what her weaknesses are and how we can control her."

"Don't I get some kind of trial?" I exclaimed, not liking that last statement at all.

Not one merperson answered as they left me alone with the guards. It was then that I finally let the tears come.

Chapter 17

My Final Days

I lay on the sand resting while City Hall decided my fate. I heard a muffled cry as a guard went down, then another and another until no one was left guarding my cell. This wasn't a Tidalwave and Mystical escape plan. This was different. *Did the merpeople want to kill me personally?* I heard the sound of keys and the door clang open. Baring my fists, I was ready for a fight, except no one came to the cell. I heard a deep yet strangely familiar voice. "Well, are you coming or not?"

"Sebastian is...is that you?" I peered into the darkness wearily.

"Of course, it's me! You didn't think I would believe that you're a, a..." he couldn't help but stutter, "...a human, did you? Once I found out it was you it made me sick at everyone who had thrown things at you, had hurt you! I should never have taken you to The Surface. This is all my fault. You just wanted to see the sun."

I swam up and gave him a big hug. "But...but, what about your father?"

"My father is wrong! Somehow I'm going to prove to the

sea that you're not the human we've been searching for. Someone is just playing a sick joke."

"What makes you so sure that I'm *not* the human?"

"It's a cover-up. You must be protecting *it* and you would probably tell me why but now is not the time. You saved Atlantis. How can we condemn you to death?"

I snorted. "Ironic isn't it?" I said. As much as I wanted to tell him the truth, my freedom and my life were more important.

"Shhh, quiet!" He put his fingers to his lips. "Do you hear that?" He tilted his head. "They're coming for you, the decision has been made. This is your last chance before you're imprisoned. They're on seahorses. You must be quick! I can't stay. My father will have my head if he finds out I let you escape. Swim fast and be safe. Go now, while you still can!"

"You're a good friend, Sebastian."

His voice was quiet. "Crystal, you were never a friend. You are much, much more than that. Now go!"

We both swam in opposite directions. I saw the first guard round the corner, not giving me a chance to think about what Sebastian had said. I saw Sebastian tuck himself neatly into a small crevasse as mounted soldiers discovered I had escaped.

I cut through alleys, backyards and tiny spaces forcing the riders to circle around. The street was empty as the horsemen searched the side streets that branched off from the main road. I looked both ways and saw nothing. I looked at the darkness that battered against the dome of Atlantis and swallowed my fear. If I could slip through the dome, the darkness would hide me. Maybe then I could find another colony and start fresh. After that, I could figure out a way to move the puddle and maybe enter through The Surface where Sebastian and I went to see the sun for the first time. There was only one problem. I had no clue what area of the world The Surface opened up to it could be in Japan, the Caribbean or Hawaii for all I knew. My mind flashed back to the present, I could hammer all the details out once I was free. No one was around, allowing me to have a straight dash into the darkness. I gulped in some air bubbles, stretched my arms and quickly took off at full speed. No matter how tired I got, I must not stop. Only after I was safe could I stop.

I flew past the main area and headed towards the end of the road. Right around the corner came the horsemen. The sea horses bounded after me, leaving a trail of bubbles in their wake. I refused to look behind me but I could tell they were hot on my tail as I put on another burst of speed. I was so close, just a few more strokes.

Suddenly, as I got closer to the darkness I noticed that the seahorses were reined in. The guards realized what I was about to do. I smiled slightly. *Finally some luck!* They must still be shaken from the war. Bracing my arms to protect my head on contact, I shot towards the dome, letting out a cheer of victory, only to hit a solid wall. *Bang!* I smashed into the dome, jarring my teeth and vibrating my whole body. I felt myself crumble in pain and saw spots dance around my eyes. Purple glow fish lit up the area as the guards rode up and held me at sword point.

"A new addition the King added after your first attempt at escape tonight. Pretty clever. Looks like you're not going anywhere," came a guard's voice. The guards' bodies were

blurry before me and ringing echoed in my head. I felt someone bind my hands behind my back with a thick rope and
hoist me onto a seahorse as they carted me away to a desolate
dungeon.

Time didn't seem to play a factor in the underground
prison. What felt like days could have been hours as the
chilled water seeped into the marrow of my bones. Little light
was provided down here. I breathed on my hands to try and
warm them. I found a dark side of Atlantis I wished I'd never
known about. The bars of my cell were covered in grime from
age. The sand was muddy and black and the stench caused
me to gag. Bones littered the floor, causing me to shudder
and hoping that I wouldn't be joining them anytime soon.

I had no fight left inside me. I was drained, body and
mind. Goosebumps lined my arms as I heard a wail in a cell
close to me. The unbearable sound bounced off the walls. A
lot of the occupants muttered to themselves. Obviously, the
merpeople and other creatures had gone mad from the isolation and neglected living conditions. I wondered what they
did that was so terrible. I slept very little down here and ate
even less.

Suddenly, I heard the door open up above as the light
pierced the darkness and prisoners hissed at the brightness. I
squinted at the figure. No one could have mistaken the golden
tail, the broad shoulders and the long black beard of the King.
The very one who put each and every one of us in here. His
blue eyes pierced mine as he floated down to my cell with
three guards behind him.

My eyes narrowed at the sword attached to his hip. Mystical Illusion was firmly strapped down with belts wrapped

around the King's waist, a chain keeping him secure. Anger boiled within me. Mystical should never have been subjected to such a prison. He was meant to be free. "Mystical doesn't belong to you!" I shouted, as I noticed Mystical was in his steel form, frozen on the hilt of the sword. He had some sort of muzzle on his snout. I noticed the King had a puncture hole on his arm. Mystical didn't go down without a fight.

"He may not belong to me, but he is on the rightful hip. Now, shall we get down to business? I'm a very busy man." I moved to the back of my cell and crossed my arms defiantly. Seeing my look the King shouted, "Guards!" I saw the eel whip lash out at me. This time it made contact with my arm, packed with a much higher voltage than I remembered. I felt blood trickle down as I yelled out a curse and reluctantly rubbed my arm as I went to the front of the cell to face him.

"That's more like it. I have a proposal for you. If you accept, your life will be spared." Hope flickered inside my belly as I nodded for him to continue. "Should you accept my offer, this will be your permanent home. You will get to see daylight once every few weeks."

"What's the offer?" I said, thinking it wasn't much of a bargain living in these barbaric conditions.

"You will command Mystical to do my bidding, since he is in your control."

"Never!" I yelled outraged. "I will not condemn him to be a slave and I will not live in this filth."

"Very well, a day or two more in here and you might change your mind. Now, you will tell me how you found this place."

"Oh, you know. The Munchkins told me to follow the yellow brick road and I did."

"Who are these Munchkins?" He stared down at me seriously.

I smirked. I saw him flick a glance at the guard on his right and I fell to the floor, gasping in pain, as the whip went straight to the bone.

"Not so funny, now, are you? I have no time for lies! How did you escape?"

When I didn't answer, he signalled for another eel strike. "Wait! Stop, I'll tell you." I sighed. "It was a large group of sea monkeys. They gathered and shaped their bodies into a key and unlocked the lock for me." I shrugged my shoulders, knowing I was stealing one of Mandy's crazy comments. "I told them to stop, but they loved me." I smiled innocently. *Of course, your son had absolutely nothing to do with it.*

"Sea monkeys! Confounded!" the King hollered in anger.

"Yup, that's right, sea monkeys and a whole pile of bananas." I sighed, trying to act indifferent in front of him, but it was difficult. "I want you to know that whether you believe me or not, I *never* told anyone about this place." I pleaded as I searched his face for any kind of acceptance to the statement.

He scrutinized my face but that comment seemed to please him. I had hoped he would actually believe me. "Your execution, I thought you should know, will make Atlantis one of the biggest tourist attractions in the sea world. Many merpeople are coming to watch you die. You're really going to raise the bar. By the way, someone wants to talk to you."

I looked behind the King, hoping to spot Sebastian but, instead, Jeremy swam down the stairs. I wasn't ready for this conversation. Not now, not ever. His hostile voice sent shivers down my spine. "How could I have been so blind? Everything I know about you is a lie. It all adds up," he spat.

"Not all of it was a lie. You don't understand. The reason I was caught was because I was on my way back here to tell you everything."

"Don't you even try to bewitch me with your trickery." He shook in rage and disgust. "I can't believe you're bonded to me like a leech."

"No, it's true. You've got to believe me!" I reached out to him, searching for the old Jeremy, my friend.

"Why believe a human?" he said coldly. "You not only betrayed me, but you betrayed the whole colony. We looked up to you."

"And you *still* can, Jeremy," I said frantically. "Nothing has changed. I'm still that merperson! For the first time in my life, I actually believed that I belonged somewhere."

"You don't belong anywhere. None of your kind does."

Anger boiled to the surface. How can he be so cruel? "You know what? This hasn't been easy on me either! Why can't anyone understand? I am not here to hurt Atlantis. Is that so hard to believe? Everyone is so paranoid. I'm tired of hiding who I am. Why else do you think I stayed quiet for so long. I was scared of this exact thing happening. You're one of the reasons why my eyes turn a jewel colour. Every day since I have been down here they have stayed this colour, even now when I'm about to die I know they are still the same because this is where I belong whether you like it or not. Why would I want to destroy a place that makes me so happy? You said it yourself that when merpeople's eyes turn this jewel colour it means they are at their happiest. Talk to Tidalwave, he'll tell you everything. My name is Felicity O'-Conner, but in my heart it will always be Crystal Clearwater." My voice cracked as I became upset at showing such weakness.

He leaned up close to the bars, hatred showing in his eyes as I backed away. "The next time I see you, *Felicity,* it will be when your head is no longer attached to your body." He turned away and began to swim up the stairs behind the King.

His face was ugly and serious, he truly meant what he said as an ache spread through my body. "I saved your life! That has to mean something!" I yelled at him, desperately gripping the bars. I had lost him forever.

The light from the door closed as I collapsed in the corner sobbing. Nausea kicked in as I tried to keep my emotions in check. No one had ever spoken to me like that. I ran my fingers along my tail's smooth and slippery scales, tracing the diamonds that were embedded in them. *This is what I had wanted. This is what I got.* I closed my eyes and let down my walls as waves of pain engulfed me. Maybe dying would be better.

CHAPTER 18

A Beautiful Day to Die

Why should I not be extra cranky, extra sarcastic and, above all, extra grumpy? The King had graciously decided to stop feeding me in the hope of wringing some more answers out of me. Unfortunately for him, I'm made of tougher stuff than he thinks, even though I've been without food for two days. Why not go for three? After all, today was my execution day.

The guard who was passing by my cell had a glow fish trailing behind him in the dungeon and slid a cup through the bars. I cupped it between both of my hands, staring at it suspiciously. "Did you poison it?" I looked at him as I peered at the thick sludge inside.

"No," he spoke gruffly. "I wouldn't want to deprive the King of slicing off your head."

I slurped it as the liquid burned down my throat like whiskey. My hunger pains disappeared and I found I had renewed strength. "What is it?"

He shuffled. "Helps keep the stomach settled. We do this for everyone on the day of their execution. It has fireweed in it."

The door upstairs opened and shut hastily as a figure cautiously swam down the stairs. The guard froze upon seeing Prince Sebastian. "I won't tell if you don't," he said to the guard, who bowed and started to swim away. "If you happen to have second thoughts about telling the King, I know all your dirty little secrets. How else do you think I got in? Secrets you or anyone else doesn't want my father to know about," Sebastian threatened.

I clung to the bars. I stared at his beautiful face. It would probably be the only friendly one that I would see before I died.

He grasped my hands in his and smiled weakly. "Crystal, I have a plan. Do not give up hope. Do not give up on me."

"I never did," I lied. I had given up on everyone and everything but I didn't want him to know that. I couldn't tell him that whatever he was planning wasn't going to work. It was the King's word against his. The King always won. Still, it was nice to see someone smiling at me for a change.

"This little issue could all be resolved if you would just tell my father where the human is hiding instead of pretending to be the human." He looked at me with a hard-headed stare.

I swallowed. I was as good as dead anyways. What's one more person hating me going to change. "I'm not hiding the human, Sebastian. I *am* the human." My voice cracked and swelled with sorrow. "Can't it be like before? If you didn't know I was the human, we would still be friends, right?"

He blinked in anger, surprise clearly on his face, and he stayed silent for a few minutes. Then he spoke quietly. "This has been a crazy few days, Crystal. For the past few days, I have done a lot of thinking. I'm still going through with my plan to save you. Human or not it is morally wrong to kill someone for this. I try and try to put myself in a humans shoes - your shoes- and I suppose I would never want to leave Atlantis either if I was in your position it is too beautiful. Then again maybe if I entered your world I would like it better and never want to leave. But that is not the way the world is suppose to work. Merpeople are not meant for land and humans are not meant for the sea. It's just the way it has to be."

Something clanged on the bars causing us to jump. "Fifteen minutes till death row," a guard muttered farther down the cells. My body shuddered violently. *It was so soon.*

"Keep it together, Crystal." He grabbed my hand and squeezed. "You're not dead yet." Sebastian continued talking to me as the clanging of the bars got closer and closer. "Have faith!" He turned and swam up the stairs just as the guard reached my cell.

"Time's up. Let's go!" As he opened the door, I noticed he wasn't one of the friendlier guards who worked down here. "Hands out where I can see 'em'."

I held them out as I felt manacles clamped onto my wrists. The brief span of happiness I had from seeing Sebastian was snuffed out. The guard bent down and attached a ball and chain to my tail, making it difficult to swim. I forced down a scream as I worked up the courage to speak. "Honestly, this is a bit much, don't you think?" I asked, surprised at the lengths to which they were going. "Look at the size of you and the size of me," I said, waving at his big frame and massive muscles.

He gave me a dangerous look and said, "Let's move." He steered me up the stairs as the ball and chain slowed me down. All I could hear was the crunching of the ball over bones and shells, and the pounding of my heart.

I swam into City Hall. The arena's seats were filled to the rafters with spectators. Angry shouts and threats were issued to me from everywhere. However, some mer I noticed didn't look as enthused for my death as others in the crowd. Gratification flowed through me as I realized not everyone wanted me dead. Some still cared. The starfish in the centre of the arena still sparkled, reminding me of the brilliance this world held. A world I was never going to see again.

I heard the sound of steel against stone and my mouth went dry. My throat tightened as I looked up to the right of the starfish at the stage. On the chopping block, one of the King's guards was sharpening an axe, inspecting it every few minutes as he glared at me. They were going to lop off my head, King Henry style! Panic spread from the top of my head to the tip of my tail as it finally began to sink in. Chains rustled to the far right of me. Tearing my gaze away from my soon-to-be death, I looked towards the source of the noise and was startled to see Tidalwave. He was pinned to the ground with lots of rusty, metal chains wrapped around him so he wouldn't break free. Guards were surrounding him and holding eel whips in their hands. My eyes widened. They were going to make him watch as a punishment for keeping my secret.

I stopped swimming, shocked, as a guard pushed me roughly forward. I didn't think I could handle much more of this. I screamed my hatred for what they had done to Tidalwave. "You're all monsters!" I called, as my voice echoed across the walls. "Every single one of you! Don't you see how wrong this is? He didn't know he was choosing a human as a bond! You can't do this to him. This isn't fair and it isn't right!" It was one thing to threaten me. That was easy enough to tune out. After all, I had been doing it my whole life. But, to threaten Tidalwave for something that wasn't his fault was something completely different. I began to see red as adrenaline coursed through my body.

There were only two guards escorting me to the chopping block. My body tensed as the guards sensed my rebellion. I punched one in the face and stomach and wrapped my chained hands around the other's neck. The crowd began to scream, shout out and point. Some even got out of their chairs and headed in my direction to help out the guards. I had to act fast. The guard I was choking passed out. I grabbed the chain that was strapped to my tail and yanked as hard as I could, pushing myself towards Tidalwave before the other guard recovered. My strength surprised me as I made it there faster than I had expected, giving us extra seconds. The guards that surrounded Tidalwave began to whip me, keeping me just out of reach of my companion. Taking a deep breath, I felt my body weaken on the third stroke. When a whip shot out at me, I grabbed hold of it as it snapped at my flesh, electrocuting myself, but still managing to yank it out of the guard's grip. I dove for the handle and began waving it around, making the guards back up and giving me the space I needed to close the gap between Tidalwave and me.

"Tidalwave!" I embraced him, trying not to cry as I saw all his deep gashes and bruises. The crowd was almost upon me, but were still a little hesitant since I had the whip. A cork with a pint-size hole in the centre blocked Tidalwave's blow-hole, making it extremely hard for him to breathe even with his gills. I yanked it out and he began to take big breaths to fill his lungs.

He smiled and wheezed out weakly. *"Heya, Crystal."*

"I need you to do one last favour for me," I spoke quickly.

"Anything for family."

I felt tears brimming as I forced them to go away. I glanced at the guards who were a few tail strokes away. "When I'm gone, I need you to tell Jeremy everything." I winced as another guard from a farther distance hit me with the whip as I lashed my whip in his direction keeping my eye on the crowd. "The puddle was never moved! I need him to do it. He will, if it means saving Atlantis. I know he will. If he doesn't listen then go to Sebastian."

"I promise," he spoke quietly.

I took a big breath, feeling lighter as if a burden had just been lifted from my shoulders. "Thanks, Tidalwave. This is a fitting end for me. This is where I want to be, even if I must die. I could have stayed on land but I chose the sea." All I could think about was Jeremy and whether he would believe what Tidalwave would tell him.

"Do you think I like seeing you suffer? How am I going to live if I have to look at your murderers every day? No one will ever trust me again. I promise I will make sure he knows, even if I have to shove him up into that tube myself to make him see the truth."

"I'm sorry, Tidalwave. I never meant for it to come to this." I felt the guards grab my arms and yank on me painfully. The crowd roared their approval as I felt two punches to the face that sent my head spinning. I began shouting at the crowd and the guards, waving my whip around, hurting anyone and everyone until a guard wrestled it from my hands. *"Mystical,"* Tidalwave echo-located to me, frantically. *"He knows how to get the darkness away from Atlantis! Use that for your freedom Crystal."*

I stared at him not really registering what Tidalwave meant until the guards placed my head forcefully on the chopping stone and held it there tightly. My vision was starting to get fuzzy as the coolness from the rock seeped into my face. *Talk about leaving it to the last minute.* They chained my hands around the chopping stone as I struggled and attached new chains secured in the sand so I couldn't escape, let alone move. I wondered if this would be quick or if it was going to take a few swings for my head to come completely off. I felt bile rise in my throat I hope it was clean, swift and fast.

The King approached the stage and his voice boomed across the cave, drowning out my attempts to talk to him about Mystical. "Today… will be a day for the history books. Today… a human will die and not a creature of water! The time has come to rid the world of this evil." The crowd started to cheer.

My heart hammered painfully in my chest as I found it hard to breathe. I somehow managed to let the words squeak out. "Please…don't. I'm so sorry, sir. You must listen to me. Mystical and I know how to…"

"It's a little late for that. I gave you weeks in prison to explain yourself. You should have used your time more wisely," replied the King, cutting me off as he motioned to the guard to raise the axe. I was starting to get lightheaded. All thoughts of Mystical were driven from my head. I focused on some happy moments in my life. The first thing that popped into my mind was when I punched Alex and saw the look on her face. I had to crack a small smile picturing it.

I felt the cold sharp edge prick my skin as he lined up the axe and lifted it up for the final strike. I closed my eyes allowing a single tear to fall and my heart hammered in my chest. "Sir," I whispered, "Mystical and I know how to destroy the darkness that surrounds the city." I opened my eyes and looked every guard in the eye so they would know the truth, that the King might be destroying the one person who could save them.

One of the guards standing beside me was Jeremy. The same guard I had punched in the nose, his sense of duty masking any kind of emotion he felt for me. I pursed my lips and sucked back some tears, he wants to make sure I'm 100% dead that he had to personally escort me to my death! A human had to die, simple as that. Our eyes locked and I saw the worry lines that crinkled around his eyes. Relief spread through me that he didn't really hate me - or at least not as much as he made it seem. That maybe he regretted the words he had said to me a few days ago. I also knew I had made him feel like a big fool in front of the entire Kingdom. Was he really angry with me - or was it all an act since death was imminent? Despite my confusion, hope surged within me.

The King turned. The word *stop* hovered on his lips...

"Stop!" The crowd showed surprise as a body suddenly covered mine, protecting me. "I said stop! Or else you're going to have to kill me, too."

The King hissed as anger surged in his eyes. "Get out of the way, Sebastian!"

"No, I have an announcement," he said stubbornly, stretching to his full height.

"Can it not wait?" the King thundered.

"No, because it concerns Crystal. Father, I wish to take her as my bride." Sebastian grinned. "She is the one I want. Only she will make my life complete."

"You...you can't be serious," the King sputtered, stunned.

The crowd was silent, shocked. "Yes, I want her to be my bride."

"Your wife?" Jeremy choked out. "That's absurd. Never before in the history of any Mer has that ever happened. It has to be illegal."

Sebastian ignored Jeremy's comment and faced his father. "She is more than qualified. Who better to tell us about humans than a human herself? She has Mystical Illusion, Father. She helped us in the war and she defeated the Kraken. Is this how we repay our heroes? Mystical saw something in her that no one else seemed to see. If we can't trust his judgement, then who *can* we trust? By getting rid of her, you are doing more harm than good. She can help us! Let me marry her and she will do great things for this Kingdom."

Clearly overwhelmed by what had just taken place, the King could not find his tongue to say anything. The whole room was quiet, waiting for him to speak and seal my fate. I would either be dead or married to someone I could never love.

The King looked at me and, in that instant, I knew I wasn't going to live because of Sebastian's love or his marriage proposal. The King would never allow me to swim around in his castle, let alone his city. The King spoke, tapping Mystical Illusion's sword absentmindedly. "Sebastian, your choice in a wife is denied but I will not kill her for your sake." He spoke sharply and briskly to everyone in the crowd and I heard disapproval clearly in their voices.

"What?" Sebastian roared. "I should get whomever I want. I am a Prince!"

"You are not yet King," Sebastian's father rumbled. "You are lucky that I am sparing her life! She does not belong here. For your happiness, she will not die but will be returned to her world. She will take an oath of silence. It will *not* be easy on her. She must promise us that she will never return. If caught again, she will be executed - and that is a promise.

"Let's send her on her way immediately and get this nightmare over with. We will figure out how to seal the Forbidden Area once we have dispatched this filth."

I felt guards unchain my tail and hands as they prodded me with a spear in the direction of City Hall's exit. "Put a blindfold on her!" the King ordered. "I don't want her to glimpse anymore of the city than she already has."

I was worn out with no intention of trying any funny business. "Can I at least say goodbye to Tidalwave?" I asked the King.

"No, you might as well get used to it," he grunted. I stared at Jeremy, hoping he would help me. He stayed silent as he looked at me with pitying eyes before seaweed covered them and I was pushed out the exit. Tidalwave was too far for echolocation.

"May I have a last word with her?" came Sebastian's deep voice as we reached the Forbidden Area. "Since you are taking the love of my life away from me."

The King made a mild motion allowing it.

"I've got something for you." He took my blindfold off as the King leaned in, wondering what it was. "Do you mind, Father? It's kind of private. It has nothing to do with the destruction of your Kingdom." Sebastian rolled his eyes as his Dad swam away. He pulled out a bag and placed it in my hands. "So you won't go insane while you're up on The Surface, a few reminders that Atlantis exists and that you were here. Just keep them hidden away from prying eyes, will you?"

I peered into the burlap sack and looked at the glittering goodies - seashells, jewellery, a golden dagger, my medallion, jewels and an abnormally large lily. "Thank you!" I leapt onto him and gave him a huge hug.

"Sebastian, go and do crowd control," the King ordered. "Keep everyone away from the area." Sebastian gave me one last look and swam away.

"Now that Sebastian is gone, guards take her to the back of my castle."

I was shoved into the gazebo, hands free and blindfold removed, as the King ordered the guards to stay posted outside so that it was just the two of us. The black heart glistened as the poisonous darkness surrounded it. Bits of brilliant blue would flash out every few seconds until the darkness swallowed it. "You better know how to destroy this darkness, Crystal, or else your sacrifice will have been in vain." He tapped his sword thoughtfully. "If you don't destroy this darkness, it will mean you lied to me again. I will kill you. No one will know and everyone will be happier for it. Sebastian thinks you are back in your human world, so he will never know if you made it there safe and sound."

I swallowed. "I need Mystical in order to do so." I eyed my sword, fastened to the King's side, and thought about the five guards outside, one of them Jeremy.

The King took a key that was wrapped around his neck and undid the chains strapped to his waist and passed Mystical Illusion into my hands. I felt the dragon's power as it surged through me. Mystical came alive with his red eyes blazing. Suddenly, I realized we could kill the King, we could kill all the guards and I could escape.

Mystical snarled, "No one keeps me chained like some kind of pet and lives to talk about it."

The King swam back a few steps as his face paled. "Get that dragon under control or I will have my archer shoot you right between the eyes!" He pointed towards a merman posted at the top of the gazebo.

Mystical let out a burst of flame in irritation and then a snort. "You are lucky." Mystical calmed down and crawled onto my shoulders.

"Come now, Mystical. I will be dead in a few minutes if we cannot destroy the darkness."

"And when your master dies, you disappear," the King said, trying to reassure himself.

"I guess we will just have to wait and find out." Mystical smiled showing his white teeth.

"Mystical!"

"Oh, alright. Your Highness, I'm all for the good of your Kingdom, but you guys have some *serious* trust issues. Thick-headed, pea-brained, ungrateful…"

"Mystical! Stop! Can we just get this over with so I can go home? I'm tired of everyone hating me."

"Fine! You will see someday, King, that what you have done to her, to me and to Tidalwave was wrong. I will blow on the heart and burn as much of the darkness off as I can. Then Crystal must wipe away the rest, for only my master cannot be burned by the touch of my fire. You must wipe away everything or else the darkness will return. Ready?"

"Ready." I breathed in a few air bubbles to keep myself calm.

The King did not like this plan. He pursed his lips and his body tensed. "If any harm comes to the heart…"

"Yeah, yeah, we know, you'll kill Crystal. You're not giving her many options besides death anyway. If she gets a scratch on your heart - death; if she so much as looks at a guard -death; if she makes any forward move towards you - death. We know the drill."

Mystical opened his maw as orange flames licked at the heart and the darkness began to smolder. Smoke began to fill the gazebo, as black as the ink from the Kraken. I grabbed the heart in my hand. As Mystical kept blowing on it, I rubbed the thick black sludge from the heart. It was caked with many layers. We used all our strength as the darkness battled against us. Mystical would burn it off and then rest, as I wiped more layers off. Then, he'd light the heart with flames again as the darkness dissolved in the water.

The whole process took up all our resources of energy. I

started to see a deep blue shine as I got closer to the last layer. It was mesmerizing. It was squishy. It wasn't like the heart of the Kraken or the heart of a human, but more like a large stone. It was bright and bursting with life, the size of my palm. As I held it in my hand to wipe away the last bit of darkness, I was reminded of the necklace that Rose threw into the water from the movie Titanic.

"The darkness is fading, my King!" one of the guards exclaimed, delight showing on his face. In awe and wonder, he stared at Mystical and me. Mystical did one last burning to cleanse the heart of any darkness.

"Guards! Blindfold her! Her duty is done. Send her back to where she came from. She will *never* see Atlantis in all its glory." Three of them pinned me down, one of them being Jeremy, as seaweed was wrapped around my eyes. The excess force was unnecessary. I was weak and Mystical fell to the ground, drained of all his energy. The darkness had almost killed us in the process.

A guard prodded me with his spear. "Get moving." After he led me towards the Forbidden Area and into the cell, another lone guard accompanied me into the tube to assure I did no funny business.

Jeremy! I could tell by his touch as he grabbed my arm. "Do not take that blindfold off until I say so. I will take you back up to your world." He stated as he escorted me up the tube as I wondered what my life would be like now. "Everyone will think the King destroyed the darkness but few will know it was you."

I felt a lump form in my throat not sure how to take the remark. "Please let me see Atlantis one last time," I begged as my lip trembled, wanting to see the glistening city that I was to be forever barred from. "Please."

Jeremy swam me upwards and stayed silent for a minute, thinking. "It would be better if you didn't. It will only make leaving harder. Now go!" He pushed me one last time up to The Surface of Lakewood as I emerged coughing, sputtering and crying

CHAPTER 19

Oh Happy Day

I opened the door to my home and found it empty. My Mom and Dad were at work and the twins were at school, which suited me just fine. It felt strange to be back here. The fact that I could never go back to Atlantis frightened me. I was going to have to start being a part of this family again, which was going to be no easy feat, after all the bridges I had burned. It didn't help that they probably thought I had run away again.

I clutched the burlap bag tightly to my chest, bounded up the stairs to my bedroom and dumped the contents onto my bed. The house was eerily quiet. I didn't want to be alone after the time I had spent in prison so I went in search of Tucker. I found him sniffing the bottom of the bedroom door to my sisters' room. He let out a small bark. I grabbed him into my arms and nuzzled his head. Puppies make everything better. "You're going to help me get through this. Now, let's go get those cats, shall we?" Tucker's tail began to wag wildly. If the freaks ever found out I went into their room, they would kill me. I walked right in because they always know when I sneak into their room anyway. This time, though, I don't think it would have mattered. The cats had torn and scratched the room to within an inch of its life. It was a disaster area.

I gathered all three animals into my arms, closed the freaks' door with my foot and walked back into my bedroom. It felt weird to have feet again. I set the animals down on the floor and watched them play. All of them were oblivious to the world as Tucker became engulfed in white puffy fur.

I watched them for a little longer, then I turned to the glittering objects on my bed. The seashells gleamed as I traced the ridges and I could hear the sound of the ocean in the biggest one. I hoped that the sound was from Atlantis. A few jewelled necklaces and bracelets were scattered on my bed sheets, making me wonder if Sebastian had punked some of his Mom's or sister's jewellery. I put my treasures in a small box, including the gold dagger, which happened to be a replica of Mystical Illusion. The medallion went in last. Then, I shoved the small box into my closet. It would be better if I never looked at the treasures again. I should burn them - but I couldn't bring myself to do it.

The only thing that remained was the closed lily. I stared at it curiously, wondering why Sebastian would have given me something so fragile. It needed water. I went into Dad's study and sitting on his desk was the most humongous brandy glass I'd ever seen. I took it into the kitchen, polished off the leftover brandy, rinsed the glass out and ran back into my room. I filled it with clean water from my bathroom sink and set it on my nightstand. I placed the closed lily gently in the water. It didn't look withered or dying, so that was a plus.

As I watched it, I saw something moving in the flower. I stuck my index finger on the top of the closed petals and slowly it began to open up. As each layer peeled back, a kaleidoscope of colours burst forth, lighting up my room. Dolphin music filled the air. I shut my eyes and listened to its soothing sound. Once the flower was fully opened, a golden globe rose up and floated to the top of the opening in the lily. Inside the globe was a moving image of me riding Tidalwave and battling a huge wave. I started to miss him. I never even got to ride a wave or a whirlpool with him. *Now I would never get the chance.* Maybe I would have liked it. I needed to find a place to hide the flower, other than my bedroom nightstand. I stuck it on the highest shelf in my closet. No doubt my Dad would be searching for his glass by tomorrow. I eyed the little box and grabbed the medallion out of it and shoved it under my pillowcase. I wanted to keep it close to my heart. Defeating the Kraken was my biggest and scariest accomplishment.

I heard the front door open and voices fill the downstairs. "Maybe my parents will still think I'm gone," I said, more to myself than to the pets who didn't offer up any advice.

I sat in my hammock, as quiet as a church mouse, listening to all the noises down below. I heard pots and pans being taken out of the cupboards as Mom began making dinner. Not long afterwards, the smell of food wafted into my room, causing my stomach to growl. I sat there grumpily, wishing I had thought to smuggle some food up here before they came home. I didn't want my presence known yet. After an hour of waiting, I had had enough. If I was quiet, I could slip into the kitchen while they were in the dining room and they'd be none the wiser.

I tiptoed down the stairs with my troops play-biting at my heels making my sneakiness a lot harder than I had planned. Tucker and the two cats stumbled down the stairs, blindly chasing each other, causing all kinds of racket. I heard laughter come from the dining room as two male voices joined in. There wasn't much protection from the dining room and kitchen as I edged along the wall.

I noticed my sisters had invited two guys for dinner. Our new guests had their mouths stuffed with mashed potatoes that should have been mine. Their cheeks were puffed out like hamsters gathering food. Both of them, as I recalled, were on the football team. Linebackers, I think. Go figure. I bristled. One was sitting in my seat, the more muscular of the two. As I sized him up, I wondered how fast he would pummel me to the ground if a fight ensued.

I sighed. *What did it matter to me anymore? They have moved on without me, just like I was going to do with them.* My stomach twisted painfully as I remembered my mission, pushing those thoughts aside for when I was alone in my room. Another hearty laugh came from my father in the dining room, as my sisters' voices chatted away about who knows what. I felt somewhat reassured to hear their happy voices. A nice change compared to what I had to endure my last few days in Atlantis. I heard the scraping of a chair across the hardwood floor as footsteps headed towards the kitchen. *Busted!* With empty plates in hand, Mom flicked on the light and jumped in surprise. "Felicity! You scared the death out of me," she said, as she set the plates in the sink.

I ignored the comment. "Glad all of you are having a good time in there," I said, angry at how easily they had forgotten about me. My thoughts drifted back to Atlantis. *Did anyone there even stop to wonder if I was happy or if they actually missed me?*

Mom glanced back at the dining room. "It's not like that. It's been hard but we've been trying to give you your space." She came towards me and started to do the motherly thing, checking me over and poking my stomach. "I even tried not to worry when you disappeared the second time. You look pretty thin. Haven't you been eating?"

"He's in my seat. How could you let him sit in my seat?" I asked, trying to avoid her questions.

Mom grabbed a plate from the cupboard and loaded it with leftover scraps from dinner. "You're not dead, Felicity. It's not a shrine. We have company. You know their comfort comes first."

"As it's always been," I said quietly, grabbing the plate and going back up the stairs to eat my food in silence, trying not to remember the pained look on my mother's face. *Why did I have to be such a trial to her all the time?* I moved my food around and stared at myself in the mirror, not liking the person I had become. *Something needed to change in my life and the only person who could do that was me.*

After I ate, I changed into my swimsuit and dove into the pool, feeling the satin of water embrace me. My body ached to be underwater with a tail and to be surrounded by the beauty of Atlantis and all of its colourful fish. *Something was missing.* I swam towards the edge of the pool and walked to the small green shed, which my parents had filled with all sorts of pool toys and equipment. I dug until I found a pair of flippers and strapped them to my feet. I kicked out in the water and found them to be too big and clumsy so I threw them off in frustration. Nothing beats a tail.

It began to rain and I didn't want to come out of the pool, so I swam to the bottom wondering how long I could hold my breath. *I never wanted to surface. This was the closest thing to Atlantis that I could have - and that wasn't saying much.* I tried to imagine what Atlantis would look like without all the darkness surrounding the city. *I bet it would look beautiful with golden sand as far as the eye could see.* Staring upwards as the raindrops hit the water's surface and caused it to ripple like millions of crystals, my mind became a blank canvas. The droplets painted a nice picture up above for me to focus on. If I could hold my breath this long, surely I could reach Atlantis and maybe I could find The Surface's entrance. That thought evaporated from my mind quickly. Without any protection, I would be dead before I reached the Seaweed Desert. *Maybe Sebastian would come and find me,* I thought, twirling a few water bubbles around my finger. *It would be like finding a needle in a haystack.*

A blurred shadow stared down at me from the edge of the pool as the rain increased in intensity. I swam up to the top. "Jesse? What are you doing here - and in the rain?" I asked, surprised, as his white t-shirt clung to him transparently.

"Your parents told me you were out back. Besides, I could say the same for you."

"I'm already wet. Can't do much more harm than what has already been done." I lifted myself up onto the edge of the pool, keeping my feet in the water as I sat on the concrete and loving the feel of the rain kissing my skin. "Looks like you're off the hook with Anna Bell now," I joked. "She has a new man in her life."

"It's about time! You should have seen her face light up when I was at the door - and the scowl she gave me when I asked for you. How about you? Any new guys in your life?" he nudged me playfully.

The question caught me off guard. This was not the sort of stuff Jesse and I talked about. "Nope, I'm still solo, as usual."

"Good." He grinned, as confusion lined my face. He placed one hand on my cheek and leaned in. My eyes widened as his lips met mine. I felt something, a tiny little fluttering in my stomach. *I could feel. I had lost my lip virginity!* I began kissing him back to see if I could make this rush expand and grow. It quickly sputtered out and I stopped kissing him. Maybe in time I would love again but it would be a really, really long time. As the kiss ended, he smiled and stroked my cheek tenderly. "I've wanted to do that for a really long time. I'll see you tomorrow." He got up and left, leaving me dumbstruck. *I should have been happy that I could have someone like Jesse. He's a great guy. Why couldn't I be more excited?* I smiled, feeling lucky to have him as a friend, even if I only considered him a platonic friend. He deserves so much more. He deserves someone who cares for him just as much as he cares for me. The truth is that I need him a lot more than I let on.

I walked into the kitchen, towelling off and ignoring all the water droplets that went flying in every direction, which was sure to mortify Mom. Dad stood quietly with a coffee in his hand watching the rain. He turned when he heard me come in. His eyes stared directly at all the dripping water, as he forced himself not to reprimand me. "Hey, sport! I thought you were never going to get out of the pool," he smiled. "Then again, you always loved the water. You've become quite the fish."

I smiled back at him, unsure what to say and wondering if he had seen Jesse and me kissing. I blushed at the memory. My love life was not the kind of conversation I wanted to have when my emotions were so mixed up. I knew my parents deserved some answers about everything that had been going on over the past few weeks. Plus, they were now the only people in my life I could emotionally and physically feel love for, since I'd been forced to give up my entire love pearl back in Atlantis. I shrugged, "Like father, like daughter. At least you always *used* to be a swimmer back when we lived on the lake."

He stared out the window once again as I joined him. "A pool isn't the same as the openness and freedom of the lake. You know, it's really good to have you back, Felicity. But, I think it's time we had a chat. You have to understand that I can't have you popping in and out of our lives like this."

"Don't worry, it won't happen again. I'm…I'm here to stay." I hugged him tightly, happy for his warmth. "Hey, Dad?"

"Yeah, kiddo."

"Do I have to go to school tomorrow?"

He kissed me on the forehead. "I'll let you have the day off, just this once. If your Mom *ever* found out she'd gut me."

"Thanks, Dad!" I hugged him tighter, surprised by how easy he made it for me.

"On one condition," he said in a serious tone.

"Name it."

"You have to start giving your mother some slack. She is trying her hardest to raise three girls. You will find out someday that it isn't as easy as you think. She worries an awful lot about you."

"I'll try, for you," I promised and headed up the stairs as I realized children were never going to be a part of my life or marriage or even a husband, unless I was with Jeremy.

I was awakened when I heard my door open and saw my mother's plump figure walk in with a basket of laundry, humming to herself and placing the basket on the corner of my bed. Sunshine streamed through the window as I glanced at my clock. It was early in the afternoon. The humming stopped as she noticed me bundled up in bed. She placed her hands on her hips with her eyebrow raised and her lips pursed. "Why aren't you at school? You should have been gone hours ago!" She threw off my covers, her voice becoming hysterical. "Get up!"

I stared at her groggily, upset that Dad didn't have the common sense to tell her that I was skipping school. "It's okay. Dad said I didn't have to go," I reasoned, as politely as I could at being disturbed from my peaceful slumber.

Mom snorted. "Like I haven't heard that excuse a million times before. Get up. I will not have a daughter of mine expelled from school." She ran to my drawer and began throwing clothes at me. "Hurry up. Put this on. You've missed half the day already."

"Mom, please, don't make me go today. If I've missed half the day, what's the point in even going?" I stared at my clothes, trying not to show how frustrated I was at her going through all my stuff. "Please try to understand."

"The only thing I understand is that you've missed enough school already and I will not lie to your principal anymore when you are more than capable of sitting in a classroom. I will not have you flunk this year." A scowl appeared on her face when she could see I hadn't moved. "Come on, hop to it!" Reluctantly, I got out of bed, realizing this conversation could very well turn into a full blown argument and remembering that I'd promised my Dad I'd try to behave, at least for a little while. "What's that?" She pointed at my back.

I paused. At first I thought she noticed the medallion that was still clutched in my hand. It was circular in shape and had left a mark on my hand. "Nothing." I quickly threw the medallion under my bed sheets and covered it with blankets.

"A *tattoo* is not nothing, Felicity."

"What are you talking about?" I snapped. I looked at where the tattoos should have been on my body when I was down in Atlantis but nothing was there.

"You *know* I don't approve of mutilating the body!" I looked in the mirror and realized Mystical Illusion's tattoo was still there. I smiled, happy that I had something to remember him by. How was it possible that his tattoo remained? "We will be getting that removed as soon as the weekend hits."

"No! It's my body and I can do what I want with it." I would not let anyone touch it. "I might even get a dolphin tattoo right beside it, so you're just going to have to deal with it! Just let me get ready, okay? I should have told you about the tattoo, I guess," I mumbled, hoping that would put out some of the fire.

She nodded her head. "You guess! You guess you should have told me? Don't think we're finished with this conversation. Get to school. We will talk more when you get home and your father is here."

"Can't wait," I said sarcastically.

I was so mad, I decided it was time to prove a point. *No one was going to tell me how to run my life.* I went downtown to a tattoo shop I'd heard about, where no one would know my whereabouts. Unfortunately, that meant I had to take the Lakewood bus for the first time in my life, which was a pretty tedious experience. It was sticky and hot due to the humidity outside - and some of the strangest people were riding it. A man dressed in feathers sat in the seat beside me. He reeked of rum. I wondered if I could get my hands on some rum to get me through this ride? Needless to say, I can see why mother never wanted us to ride the bus and go to this part of town.

Realizing I was close to the tattoo place, I pulled the cord to signal my stop was coming up. I was more than happy to get off the bus. I trudged down a few blocks and there it was, Black Ink. It wasn't classy or extravagant but it would get the job done. I opened the door and the bell rang to signal my entry. A woman riddled with tattoos, piercings and black clothing looked me up and down and smiled. "First time?"

"It is that obvious?" I asked, looking around at the walls and the artful displays of tattoo choices. It was a small building. Only three other rooms branched off the display room. I could hear the buzzing of a needle in another room. I wrinkled my nose wondering if I actually wanted to go through with this.

"Do you have a tattoo in mind or are you just browsing?"

I stood there awkwardly, not knowing what to do. I had felt so strongly about getting one but, now that I was actually in the room, my plan was dwindling. "Well, I wanted a dolphin tattoo."

"Sure thing, I'll let you look at some designs. I have no appointments until later so if you want we can fix you up right now. My name's Rae, by the way." Rae pulled out a book and began flipping through it. "These three pages have different dolphin designs, but if you don't see anything you like you can describe what you want and I can draw it for you."

"It's now or never," my voice wavered slightly. "I'd want a small one to go on my back. I pointed to one of the designs in the book that drew my attention. "That one will do fine. But with two different colours for shading."

"Alright then, come on back. I have just the colours; a nice blue and a light grey for the underbelly and tail. How does that sound?"

"Sounds great." I was led into the room and sat down in the chair. "What's it going to feel like?"

"Besides the noise of the machine, it's like being punctured with needles. It usually depends on the spot and the type of person you are. The shoulder won't be too bad. It goes numb after awhile."

I pulled off my sweater and one side of my shirt, showing her where I wanted the dolphin, right beside Mystical.

"Whoa," Rae said, seeing Mystical's mark. "This is some tattoo. I thought you said it was your first time? Who drew it? The detailing is exquisite and the colour is like none I have ever seen. It's the gold that shimmers and shines. The eyes pierce right to the soul."

I thought fast on my feet. "It's a stick-on. I liked it so much that I want to get a real one."

She laughed. "Who do you think I am? I wasn't born yesterday. This tattoo is real and let me give you a piece of advice. The tattoo I put beside it will never look as good as what you have now. It will be dull compared to *that* and it will look out of place. This tattoo doesn't need anything beside it. Too much clutter isn't good."

Looking at her arms, I held back a snarky remark. It was nothing *but* clutter. "That's the only place I want it."

"Okay." She kept staring at the tattoo, touching it and examining her hands for sparkles. "I have *never* seen anything so beautiful and well drawn. I would advise you to go to the same person and get them to draw your dolphin. I don't want to make it look tacky. My name and the business would be given poor advertising and put to shame beside something of that quality. I'm sorry but, as an artist, I will not do it. I will draw it anywhere else on your body, though."

Disappointment flowed through me, only to be washed away as I found myself smiling. Mystical will always have an effect on people even when he is not in his true form. I readjusted my shirt and grabbed my sweater, heading for the door. "It's okay. I understand." I pushed the door open and inhaled the fresh air, clearing my head from all notions of getting a tattoo.

I came home to see my Mom sitting on a chair with the cordless phone in her hand. Her fingers were drumming on the side of the chair. "Guess who I just got off the phone with?"

"I dunno." I really didn't feel like arguing right now, but she wasn't going to give up until I gave her an answer. "The gingerbread man?"

"The principal of your school, the school where you need an education in order to get a good job in life."

Freaking jobs! I was so sick of people stressing over my career choices. I was tired of people telling me what to do and how to run my life. Money wasn't everything! I didn't want responsibilities. I wanted to be back in Atlantis where none of this mattered. "Dad said I didn't have to go to school today, so I didn't."

"This is not O'Connell behaviour."

"Just lay off, okay? I've heard this speech a million times before, Mom. Maybe I don't want to be an O'Connell. I am not my sisters. I'm sorry if I don't live up to your expectations or I don't jump at your every beck and call. That will never be who I am. I'm trying, I'm really trying but this change isn't going to happen overnight. I need you to accept the fact that I am not the same person I once was."

I walked upstairs, not wanting to waste another breath. My emotions were running hot. Tears came streaming down my face. I wanted to go back to Atlantis. I clutched the medallion hard in my hand and brought out the lily, trying to lose myself in the scene and wanting nothing more than to feel the thrill as Tidalwave and I crested over our first big wave. When I was all cried out, I climbed out the window in search of a friend and headed over to Jesse's.

We chugged back cartons of chocolate milk and watched movies long into the night as I tried to forget the life I once had. I knew there was only one solution to all of this. I needed to move on.

CHAPTER 20

Memories

The first step in moving on was going back to Lakewood High School. I walked down the halls zombielike, as everyone else talked about their classes and what they did last night. It was the same old boring thing. Mandy wasn't at school today, which made my return even more horrific. I realized not having many friends at school wasn't a good thing. What I needed right now was distractions - and lots of them. At this rate I was going to go insane if I didn't find a way to get my mind off Atlantis. The bell rang across the schoolyard, signalling the start of class and reminding me of my first day at school with Sebastian.

I headed to my next class, where the teacher handed me heaps of homework. All that did was make me realize how much school I had missed. It's not like I had a lot of wiggle room to begin with for my grades to slip. I stared at the pile in front of me and cringed. I had lost all ambition, motivation and desire. The teacher jawed on about today's agenda but I could no longer focus. I wanted out of this world. I didn't have the energy or commitment to do all these projects and assignments. I would never get caught up and Mom would be on my case more than ever. *Hopeless.* I laid my head down and slept.

The bell rang, startling me awake as students exited the room. I collected all my work and the teacher gave me a disapproving glare, but I didn't care. The hallways were full of people, as everyone trudged to their lockers like a herd of cattle. I went to the library and grabbed a book in the fantasy section, hoping it would somehow get my mind off Atlantis. Books have never failed me before when I needed to be sucked out of this world and pulled into another and I hoped they wouldn't fail me now.

I went to English and picked the very back seat in the classroom - close to a window - and began to read about a different world. A world that would never exist. I had read this book before and it was one of my favourites. *The Daughters of Ishtar* was packed with adventure and heroism. If anything was going to help me get my mind off Atlantis, I figured this was it. But, as soon as I started to read, I knew it was going to be useless. I had been in a fairy tale story of my own. I didn't need to imagine it when I'd already lived it. I shouldn't *have* to turn to books to comfort me when I could return to something real just a few blocks away. *Was this what the rest of my life was going to be like? Always moping and pining, wondering what everyone in Atlantis was doing. Did they even think about me or was I old news by now?* Immediately, I realized that I wasn't enjoying life back here in Lakewood and probably never would, that I was just living a lie.

After I suffered through English class, I headed back to my locker, wondering what I was going to do for lunch. This

was not a good time for me to be alone. I wanted to play football. I needed to focus my energy on something with a lot of
running and hitting until I was so tired I wouldn't have the
energy to think. I needed to get out of this slump. Two girls
ran past my locker chattering excitedly. I caught the words
'sexy' and 'new guy' in the conversation before they buzzed
around the corner. I slammed my locker door, knowing I was
probably going to spend my lunch at the baseball diamond
by a certain puddle.

Four more girls ran past me in the same direction the
other two had gone, squealing with excitement. *Oh, come on!
It wasn't like we'd never had new kids in this school before!
Get some fresh meat and the whole girl population went
topsy-turvy. They'd die if they met the mermen in Atlantis.* I
smirked slightly as my sarcasm returned, realizing there was
life still left in me, filling the ache that had infected my heart.

"Well, what's he *look* like?" a girl wheezed, slightly out
of breath, as she and some friends rounded the corner. I noticed they were part of the Clone Zone.

"He's indescribable, Lanie. You have *got* to see the abs
on this guy!"

Lanie was dressed in hot pink and her eyes glowed. "How
do you know what his abs look like, Tosha?"

"Because he's not wearing a shirt!" she squealed.

"Why didn't you say so before? Let's hurry before he puts
it back on."

I headed in the same direction. *What kind of lunatic was
coming to school this time? He'd fit right in.* Curiosity burning, I followed the noise, wanting to get a look at this idiot
and hoping my entertainment needs would be satisfied for

the remainder of the day. I climbed up the long ramp and noticed the main hall had hordes of girls of every status pushing against each other like caged animals. *What on earth? This was beyond madness.*

The single guys were all watching the action intently from the cafeteria and would shout out bets while others with girlfriends had sour expressions on their faces. Karl was one of them, which perked me up. Three girls ran into me. I cursed and was on the verge of starting to do some shoving of my own. I felt a headache coming on. I could see the hall monitors running to the principal's office as I laughed at their frightened faces. *You'd almost think this guy was some kind of rock star or something. It was a freakin' riot out there.*

The principal and a troop of teachers rushed into the crowd trying to break it up as one teacher talked frantically on his cell phone. Probably calling the cops. I was trying to stay *out* of trouble so I began to walk into the cafeteria, prepared to ignore all of this and stay on my mother's good side. I was willing to bet Faith and Anna Bell were in that throng and were going to hear an earful tonight from Mom.

I walked up to Ted, a grade eleven student, who leaned against the wall watching with all the other guys. "So, who do you think will be the lucky girl?" I joked as I popped a piece of gum into my mouth casually. "They're taking this a little bit too far, don't you think?"

"Hardly! We haven't even seen a single catfight. I'm in the pool for 10 catfights while Marsh has 20. Now, I think *that's* a bit steep but, with the crowd growing bigger, so are the bets. Everyone's in on it but not a single fight yet!" he said depressed. "Once a chick named Crystal gets here, though, the action's really going to start. That's the only thing the guy's said so far, at least from what I've heard."

I choked on my gum. *Could this be what I'd been hoping for?* "Crystal? There is no girl named Crystal at this school."

"Exactly. I'm hoping it's a girlfriend. That's sure to bring on a fight and then it'll just capsize from there."

The faculty managed to make a break in the group, allowing me to catch a glimpse of blonde hair before the 'new guy' was swallowed up again. I sucked in a deep breath of air. Jeremy could be in the middle of all *that!* I rolled up my sleeves and realized I was going to have to take the plunge. "Well, Ted. Let's hope I make it back alive!"

Ted looked at me and then shouted, "I've got 100 bucks says Felicity starts the first fight!" and more wild bidding began as I was completely forgotten. *This place was a war zone! It looked like I was going to have to make my own route.* I ran up and began grabbing girls by the backs of their shirts, picking them off one by one, trying to get deeper into the mob. I was almost there. I squirmed my way through the wall of girls as dirty looks and kicks were issued, which spurred my anger. I burst through the gap and stopped, stunned to see a very nervous and very scared Jeremy. I didn't move, too afraid to believe what I was actually seeing.

He squinted his eyes at me and croaked, "Crystal?" right as the cops burst through the school doors, making the students run in every direction. Shaking my head from the initial shock, I grabbed his hand and tugged him away from the riot.

CHAPTER 21

The Truth Comes Out

We burst out the exit door by the science hall. My mind was reeling with the fact that Jeremy was in Lakewood. I was so happy I could cry. My hands were shaking as I realized just how unsettled I was about having to live back in Lakewood for the rest of my life. I looked at him closely, afraid that I would wake up and all this would just have been a wonderful dream.

He was panting beside me as his legs wobbled, trying to get used to them. He was wearing a pair of shorts but he had put them on backwards, which made me smile. He probably didn't even know the name of them, much less how to wear them. "I've never seen so many humans in my life," Jeremy shuddered. "How many more are there?"

"A lot more than you think, this is just a small portion. There are countries teaming with cities and small towns. This is only an average sized city."

"We would have never stood a chance," he said, frustrated. "We have trained hard for the day a big human invasion would come to Atlantis. Studied your kind and skimmed

The Surface for more information, even kidnapped one or two for experiments and information..." He drifted off lost in thought.

"Experiments?" I said shocked.

"That was a long time ago." He waved it off in dismissal, as I tried not to show my disgust. I led us to a small private park where we could talk. His eyes grew accusatory. "You *knew* what kind of danger Atlantis would be in, located in an area surrounded by our enemy. Tidalwave informed me that you were going to move the Forbidden Area, but here I find it undisturbed and out in the open. If I hadn't come along, you had no intentions of moving Atlantis, did you?"

"Hey, now. Wait a minute. I don't like what you're implying. I was going to move it - eventually. I would never jeopardize Atlantis."

"That's exactly what you're doing. Every second Atlantis is near this city, someone could be discovering my colony."

Frustration and hurt welled up inside of me as all my happiness disappeared the moment he started talking. This was not the reunion I had wanted. My voice rose an octave. "Do you know what I've been going through since I've been stuck up here? How brutal it has been for me? That puddle is the last link I have to everyone and Atlantis. I fought for the lives of everyone down there. I gave up love so that you could live. I have given everything to that city, Jeremy. Everything!" My voice cracked. "I care more than anybody will ever give me credit for. If you came up here to criticize me then get it over with and leave me be." I stared at the ground, forcing the tears to go away as one slipped down my cheek. I didn't think I'd ever cried so much in my entire life as I had in the last few days.

He lifted my chin so that I had to look him in the eye and he wiped away my tear. "I'll admit I haven't exactly been there for you."

I snorted sarcastically. "You think?"

"Today, when I reached your school, I almost turned tail and went home. But then I realized how scared you must have been when you were on the chopping stone. I realized that I owed it to you to tell you the truth about who you are."

"I know who I am." I spoke firmly and confidently. If there was one thing in the world I knew, it was myself.

"Crystal," he sighed, not sure how to continue. "Sebastian did some research on the code red we had a long time ago, before our king was even king, before Sebastian or I were even born. We had mistaken one of our merpeople for a human. We had a mermaid executed. That mermaid was your mother." He looked at me, trying to measure my reaction.

I looked at him without humour. "That's not very funny. My Mom is alive and well. She's at home. Sebastian would find any excuse, any story, to get me back to Atlantis but I will not go back under false pretences. Stop trying to hurt me with your lies, Jeremy! I can't take it anymore."

"That's not your real Mom," Jeremy continued.

"Enough! I know my Mom. We may not get along most of the time but I grew up with her. Dad would never lie to me about something like that."

"Well, I'm not going to sugar coat it for you. It's not something Atlantis likes to remember, but at least listen to the story and then pass judgement."

"Why should I? I never got the same courtesy down in

Atlantis. You treated me with less respect than an animal." I turned and began to walk away.

Jeremy shouted. "She looked just like you, you know. Your real Mom, I mean, from her picture in our history books. She was an adventurous one. She was always intrigued with the Forbidden Area. When she first arrived in Atlantis, she was only in her third stage of life, a teenager. She wasn't afraid of anything. You have a lot of her in you." I stopped in my tracks wondering if that statement had any merit to it. I always thought my Mom and sisters had no resemblance to me but plenty of families have an oddball. I often dreamt that my mother was exactly like me but dreams are and will forever be just dreams.

Jeremy continued. "Monique, your Mom, wanted to see the world. We should have kept a better eye on her when she got to the fourth stage and became an adult. No one in their right mind would have dared venture up to The Surface of their own free will. We didn't have the technology that we have today for detecting the comings and goings to and from the Forbidden Area. The gate and vortex trap weren't even in place. The sun that streams from your world into ours entices a lot of mer but all are loyal to the King and his laws. Humans left us in peace and we did so in return. Heck, the darkness didn't even surround the city then.

Your Mom's presence in Atlantis became scarce, popping in and out of the city at random and gone for days at a time. She was very secretive about her whereabouts. We had reason to believe that she had met a male human up here. Turns out our suspicions were true. Her stomach began to get bigger and bigger until it was too big for an ordinary mermaid's stomach. She disappeared for a time after the King began to take an interest in her. When she returned, she had a baby in her arms and her stomach was back to normal mermaid size. That raised some eyebrows. Monique had no mate in Atlantis.

So the King went to the library to do some research to try and find an answer to this mystery. He stumbled upon it by accident when a librarian grabbed a book on human babies and the King saw it and realized Monique's process mirrored the same way as a human's of having children. He sent out search parties for her with no success. She was a dolphin rider just like you and her dolphin had warned her ahead of time about the guards, so she fled with you in her arms. Her dolphin was tortured and told us she had gone to the Forbidden Area. Your Mom had barely escaped death in order to save you. For days they monitored the area and waited for her to return - and she did, but without the baby, which was you.

They questioned her but she didn't say anything. She was very strong-minded. The King drew the conclusion that she was a human and had stumbled upon Atlantis much like you had. We have never had a birth like that and only humans can birth babies that way so we assumed she had to be a human in order to have a baby come out through her belly.

She was killed so that our secret would die along with her. Her dolphin no longer had his rider and could no longer communicate with anyone, so he soon turned wild once again. They worried about finding the baby for some time but eventually gave up, for no mer could enter the human realm. They didn't think a baby would be able to remember anything anyway. Human babies aren't smart like merbabies. After Monique's death, the King doubled the guards and created better protection for our city. Years later, the guards' presence lessened as the past was forgotten."

I had listened but still didn't believe it. "That could be anyone. This world is full of people. What made you think that baby was me?"

"Your mother found the Forbidden Area. We've had nothing happen for years and then you came along. Two code reds. Two of the biggest things in history that concern humans. That was not just a coincidence. In the end, it turns out that both of you who were thought to be human weren't human at all. Dolphin riding is a rare thing. She possessed it and so do you. It all adds up," Jeremy said eagerly. "Do you know what this means? You can come back to Atlantis! The King has to allow it since you are one of us."

"Come on." I grabbed his hand once again with a determined stride, trying not to be angry at all the lies he was saying.

"Where are we going?"

"To see my father."

CHAPTER 22

Unfinished Business

We marched into my Dad's office, ignoring his assistant's plea for my return, and threw open the double doors. His office wasn't anything special. A file cabinet in the corner, computer on the desk, fax machine, and papers scattered everywhere. Two phones sat on his desk, along with a calculator and pictures that covered his walls. A Venus flytrap sat in the other corner. Pictures of our family littered the table behind his desk and bobble heads of Mickey, Minnie, Goofy and Donald were wobbling in-between the pictures. Souvenirs from when we went to Florida eons ago. *I couldn't believe he'd kept them all.* A Chinese fighting fish watched me from his fish bowl by the window.

"Felicity, what are you doing here? You should be at school," Dad stuttered in surprise. He looked behind me as Jeremy tagged along, examining everything in sight. It had taken us a half hour longer than usual because Jeremy wanted to look at the cars, trees and everything else that crossed his path. He wasn't exactly afraid to touch anything either. If I had acted the way he was acting right now in Atlantis, I would have been dead, no doubt about it. My Dad's eyes lingered on him for a bit longer, then widened as he noticed Jeremy's mer qualities. It wasn't hard to miss - extremely handsome, golden flawless skin and crystalline eyes.

"You know what he is!" I said incredulously. One look on my Dad's face and I realized Jeremy's story was all true. I felt the room spin and started blinking my eyes, hoping it would stop.

He put his head in his hands and rested his elbows on the desk. "I always knew this day would come." He grabbed his phone and dialled his assistant. "Nancy, I'm going to need the rest of the day off. I'm not feeling very well." He nodded his head. He certainly looked sick. "Thanks, I should be in tomorrow. Bye."

"I want some answers," I said in a no-nonsense tone.

"How did this even happen?" Dad spoke quietly.

"I've been there," I said sharply.

Dad sucked in some air. "You know the location of Atlantis?" he asked in awe. "If you only knew how long I have been searching…so that explains where you've been running off to."

I shook my head. This was some kind of horrible dream. "How could you not have told me? You could have made my life so much easier if you had confided in me. Of course, it's not exactly like you've ever spent much time with me."

"I have no excuse. I haven't been there like a real father should be. You look so much like her. You always reminded me of Monique. One day she was with me and we were happy and content; the next she up and left me with nothing but a baby in our crib and a letter telling me goodbye. We…

" Dad grew silent. "We were supposed to start a family up here. She would tell me stories about Atlantis. They seemed too good to be true. I wanted to see Atlantis with my own eyes but she said I was never to go there. I never saw her again. I loved your Mom so much. She's all I ever thought about until I met April. She's on my mind and in my heart always."

"How did you two meet?" I asked, unsure if I wanted to tell him the truth about what had actually happened to her.

Dad smiled. "I was on my way home and she was walking in the middle of the street. It was the first day she had come up from Atlantis. She was the most beautiful woman I had ever seen. It was dark out. She didn't know that an oncoming car was about to hit her and I ran out and rescued her. She looked so frightened and lost I took her home. After that, we just started to click. Then she became pregnant and that was when we had some of the best days of our lives. We couldn't wait until you were born. We would stay up late into the night wondering what you would look like, thinking of a name, wondering how you would be able to grow up being half mer and half human. In the end, I guess it was too much for her to deal with. She had always dropped little hints about our relationship and how it could lead to her death but I thought if she stayed up here with me I could prevent it. I guess once you've been to Atlantis you never truly leave it."

I glanced over at Jeremy and he was looking very guilty but didn't say anything. I knew he felt bad about what the King had done to my Mom but what was he going to do? He wasn't even alive back then. I waited a couple of minutes so Dad could regroup.

"Does April know about this?"

"No and I want to keep it that way. She'd never believe it anyways. April is too practical and not very open-minded. I'm sorry I kept this a secret. I wanted you to have a normal life."

"My life has never felt normal."

"I know that - but I've tried. I thought April was the key, to have a mother to guide you. It worked for a while. For the first time in a long time, I was happy again. After a while, we were married. Then the twins came. You were just a child at that point."

"How are we still alive? Down in Atlantis this happened, years and years ago," I said, puzzled. "We should be dead by now. Did I grow up like a human or like the stages of a Mer?"

Jeremy joined the conversation. "Merpeople have a special kind of magic, especially when it comes to love. Chances are, Monique probably knew this would happen. Mer have a love pearl and a life pearl. When merpeople die, their blue pearl of life comes out of their mouth, much like the love pearl, so that it can ride the current of the sea and remain connected to the sea after death. From the stories I've heard from Sebastian and read in our history books, when the King killed Monique, he realized she was a mermaid from the smallest wisp of her blue life pearl leaving her body. Her love pearl wasn't there either. The King figured out that she gave up half of her love pearl to your Dad when they created you and the other half to you when she left you in your crib."

He turned to my Dad, who seemed lost in thought, pain clear as day on his face as he heard what had happened to his beloved after all these years of being left in the dark. "She sacrificed her whole life pearl and spread it across Lakewood to shield the world from your true identity, leaving just enough for her to return to Atlantis. It must have been mere seconds before she returned to Atlantis, because the King grabbed her immediately, but she was already dying when they killed her. No one can live without a life pearl." Jeremy was finally able to piece all the information together. He gave my father an apologetic look. "Since you both have mer in you, your life span is a lot longer than everyone's in this world. That being said, it allows you to be excluded from the haze of magic Monique put on Lakewood. How the stages work I can't tell you," he said, obviously puzzled.

"The day you turned from stage two - a child - to stage three - a teenager was the scariest moment of my life," Dad explained. "You were just sitting on the couch colouring in your book and then, all of a sudden, I had a teenager looking at me. You sprouted from a girl to a woman in a matter of seconds. Monique had explained it to me briefly but I hadn't expected it to be as much of a transformation as when you had changed from a baby to a child. April walked into the room shortly after and I thought we were done for, but she didn't even blink an eye at your rapid growth.

"As time went on, the spell Monique put on Lakewood made people think you were growing like a normal human. April would joke about my greying hair but when I looked in the mirror I saw the same me I saw all those years ago. April is around the same age as Monique so our differences aren't too apparent in my eyes for age, but she is getting older. Once I hit 80 years old, people I know will just forget about me as though I don't exist and I'll have to move to another part of Lakewood and start over.

"The spell Monique gave us will take over as soon as I leave. April will forget about me and live out the rest of her life, while I begin again. The twins will forget about me, too. They will not remember me as their father. Instead, the spell will conjure up a father who had died doing something heroic or maybe just simply of old age. It won't be me, but a stranger.

"That's the way the spell warps and twists minds. It fools everyone. Even people talking about me come to some kind of agreement about my age without even knowing it. The spell gives off an illusion of aging but illusions can only work for so long. I've had to be very careful." He leaned back, gauging my reaction as I saw an immense weight lift off his shoulders. "I shouldn't have left this conversation until now. I should have told you the moment you turned into a teenager. You had so many questions when it happened I had to take you for a drive to keep April from hearing any of them."

"You both have given up so much for me," I sighed, re-alizing how hard a life my Dad really had, never really know-ing anyone - a best friend one day, a stranger the next. "Aren't you mad at Monique for doing this to you? For making you live this life?"

Dad gave a sad smile. "If she hadn't, I wouldn't have had you and wouldn't have been able to keep you. If I had it to do again, I wouldn't change anything."

I felt my eyes water. *How could I leave him for Atlantis?* "How old are we?" I asked, looking at the floor and hiding my emotions behind my hair.

He sighed. "Too old. After a hundred years I lost count.

I've had so many close friends come and go. The only woman I ever married was April and that was 20 years ago." He leaned forward. "Now I've told you my story, how about you tell me yours? How did you come across Atlantis?"

I told him the long version, not sugar coating it. I wanted him to get the full picture of a place he had never seen, the good and the bad. I told him about my life as Crystal and all my adventures in Atlantis. Jeremy was listening, as well, since he probably wanted to know the whole story, too.

When I finished, Dad leaned back with a grin plastered on his face. "It's no wonder you don't like it up here. This whole time - I can't believe it was behind the baseball diamond. When Monique left, I never looked there. I could have saved her!" he said, remorsefully.

"They would have killed you if you had followed her with Crystal," said Jeremy sadly. "Crystal would have died, too."

"Dad, I came here to tell you that I was leaving Lakewood and going to live in Atlantis. But now, I can't possibly do that after hearing your story and everything you have done for me." He sat there very quietly as I walked over and gave him a hug. "You never have to worry. I will never leave you," I said, pained. Even though I knew it would be misery staying in Lakewood, I also knew it would be something I was willing to do, just to keep my father happy.

"You are your mother's daughter. She could never stay away from the sea and you will never be happy if you don't go back to Atlantis. I can see it in your eyes. I would rather see my daughter happy than sad. That is all I ever wanted and clearly you are not happy here. You have to return to your real home."

"Dad," my voice cracked, as I began to cry. "Thank you for understanding. There's something I want you to have, but it's back at the house," I said, trying to get my tears under control.

When we returned home, I unlocked the door and felt homesickness hit me immediately. This was going to be the last day I'd ever spend in this house. Sunlight was streaming in all the windows making the rooms cheery and bright. Jeremy and my father shuffled in behind me. Jeremy eyed the pool outside. "Go ahead. I want to be alone with my Dad anyway," I said, as he rushed towards the glass sliding doors. "BANG!" He ran right into it. I chuckled briefly as he shook his head, slid open the door and jumped into the pool. I guess he was getting a little homesick, too. I stared at Jeremy as I saw his feet transform into a tail. *How was that possible?*

I felt my Dad put his arm around my shoulder, fixated on the pool. "I haven't seen a sight like that in a very long time… " His voice trailed off, shaking his head.

"Why do Jeremy's feet turn into a tail? I never changed in the pool."

"Your Mom's always did. I suspect it's because you are only half mer and he is a full mer. Maybe you should bring him back inside. Can't have the Darnels finding out our secret."

"Good point." I ran out and dragged Jeremy out of the pool. I wrapped him in a towel and left him in the living room as I ushered my father upstairs to my bedroom.

I walked into my closet and grabbed the brandy glass. "This is yours to keep so that you will always remember me."

I handed the glass to my Dad and touched the tip. The lily peeled back slowly and colours shot out in every direction, revealing me and Tidalwave battling a wave back in Atlantis.

"That's Tidalwave, you'd like him. He's really brave and has lots of spunk. He helped me fight the Kraken." I pulled out the small dagger with the replica of Mystical Illusion. "This is my dragon, Mystical Illusion, who is snarky, just like me. He taught me how to fight and helped me destroy the darkness that surrounded the city." My voice wobbled. "So my friends are always with you just as they are always with me." I hugged him tightly and cried. "You must make sure no one finds them." I cried into his shoulder as he stroked my hair. "I…I can't leave you. Not here all by yourself. You lost Mom and now you're going to lose me, as well."

My mind raced. I wanted more than anything in the world to live in Atlantis but I couldn't leave Dad here by himself. I couldn't let him go through the pain all over again. I started to cry, "I can't leave you, and I won't… I love you Dad." I started to clutch onto his shirt. "You've cared for me all my life." An idea sprang into my mind. "What if you come with me?" I stared at him eagerly, ignoring the fact the King probably wouldn't let a human ever live down there.

He shook his head and kissed me on the brow. "I can't. My life is finally back on track. I have a wife and two kids here. I know you want to stay with me but your mother would want you in Atlantis."

"Someday, I'll come back for you!" I promised and hugged him tighter. I would not let him live out his life waiting for the right person to come along every few hundred years to start his life over again. *What was he going to do when April and his daughters died?* Someday, but not for a long time, I would come for him.

CHAPTER 23

What to do?

For the next two hours, the three of us barricaded our-selves in my room, brainstorming ways to move the puddle and where to move it. It was no easy task, especially since my sisters saw Jeremy in the house. All they wanted to do was hang out with him.

"What if the puddle was put in our backyard? That way you could still see me and I could keep it safe," Dad sug-gested for the third time. I knew it was going to be hard for him to live without me.

"We can't have it anywhere near civilization. People would find it too easily."

Dad had suggested another idea, "How about up in the mountains?"

"Nice try, Dad. What if a mountain lion wants a drink and falls in or a hiker stumbles upon it? The mountains aren't as deserted as you might think. How do you propose we carry a whole underwater city up the mountain? None of us are what I would call experienced hikers." I let out a deep breath, flus-tered. "This is impossible. There are almost seven billion people on Earth. We could hide it at the ends of the planet and it *still* wouldn't be good enough."

Jeremy said, "No matter where we put it, there will *always* be a chance of Atlantis being found, unless it is destroyed. The King wants it destroyed but a lot of Mer want to keep it. It's what gives Atlantis its allure. As much as we hate and fear humans, we are also very curious about them. It is debatable about whether or not to keep the Forbidden Area," Jeremy said, staring out the window. "It is not safe where it is now. Wherever the puddle is moved, the magic to keep it concealed goes with it." He stayed quiet for a few moments. "We will take it to the mountains."

"Jeremy, you have never climbed a mountain before. The terrain is rough and the ground is hard and full of stones. It's not smooth like our sidewalks or streets. We could sprain an ankle or trip while carrying Atlantis and spill all the water and destroy the city. It's not worth the risk."

"Is there water up on these mountains?" Jeremy asked, the gears in his head turning.

"Well, halfway up there is a clear trail that leads to Blue Creek waterfall," Dad answered.

"Kids, dinner!" Mom yelled from downstairs.

Dad touched my shoulder gently. "I'll tell her you're swamped with homework and that you won't be down. You should take that lily back to Atlantis. If someone were to find it and, through that lily, find Atlantis, I would never forgive myself. Good luck on your mission. Both of you are smart, so I know you'll figure something out. Take the truck in the garage. I'll pick it up at the foot of the mountains in the morning."

I gave him a hug. "Goodbye, Daddy. I love you." I ran to my dresser and gave him the letter I had written. "I wrote this awhile ago. I think you should have it. It'll help explain to Mom and the twins why I'm not going to be here tomorrow. Please inform Mandy and Jesse about me. I don't want them to worry, so think up something good that will help ease the sadness."

"Of course, I can do that. Now, you better get going. Even though I can't believe I'm saying this, I guess it's the last time I'll ever see you. Good luck and be safe. You can do this. Most important, I love you very much." He kissed me on my forehead and left.

I stared at the door as my throat swelled up and I started blinking back tears. I wanted to run after him and tell him to come back so that both of us could live in Atlantis. My body felt like it was being cut through the centre, wanting to go in both directions. Jeremy paced back and forth muttering to himself.

"Crystal." Jeremy stopped abruptly, grabbed my hand and stared into my eyes. The heat from his touch coursed through me, giving me courage and settling my nerves. "There's something I need to tell you about what we're doing. No matter what happens, we *cannot* spill a single drop of water while Atlantis is uprooted. The water becomes free range. If a drop spills, magic goes with it, creating another entrance into the merworld. If that happens, all of the work we have done will be for nothing."

I paled. "Thanks for the heads up. No pressure, right?"

"We will get through this together," Jeremy said. "The magic will help us. I'm sure of it."

The baseball park was empty as a swing set squeaked on its rusty chains in the gentle breeze. I turned the lights off in the truck. Crickets filled the silence. Fireflies darted in and out of the bushes. I unloaded two shovels and a wheelbarrow. We pushed it to the back of the ball diamond where Jeremy began chopping at the brush with the shovel, clearing a path. I adjusted my backpack that had food in it for a couple of days and Atlantis' mementos, including the lily Sebastian gave me wrapped safely inside. Who knew how long it would take to find this magic hocus pocus place to hide Atlantis?

Once we came to the puddle, we stared at it with a desperate longing to jump in. We stood there watching silently as the moonlight reflected across the water. The moon was full and bright. We had no need to use the four flashlights I had packed.

"I think what we need to do is go down as far as we can and hope that we don't puncture a hole while we're digging," Jeremy said, as he shook himself out of his dreamlike state.

I pushed the shovel into the hard compact soil, just wanting to get it over with and feel the rush of Atlantis all around me. I tried to forget about how I had just abandoned my father. I groaned as I lifted the first shovelful of dirt. *This was going to be a long night.*

As I dug, it didn't take long for the palms of our hands to blister. We had dug around the puddle, making Atlantis look like an island. "How do we know how far down Atlantis goes?" I asked, not wanting to dig any deeper or else the puddle wouldn't fit in the wheelbarrow. I sat down on a mound of dirt.

He leaned down and shone the flashlight around the circle

we had. He examined the dirt with his hands. "Look at this. The dirt is dry. Don't you think if Atlantis went this far down then the dirt would be wet?"

My fingers slid up from the bottom of our hole to the top until I felt wet soil. It was about 10 inches deep from The Surface. *How could all of Atlantis have fit in that?* "All this time it was this high off the ground!" I cried out, staring at the piles of dirt we had removed. *What a waste of energy.*

"Come on!" Jeremy said excitedly. "Let's throw some dirt into the wheelbarrow and get Atlantis to the mountains and to safety. I want to go home."

We filled the wheelbarrow up halfway with soil, creating a hole in the middle. We chipped away horizontally until we were balancing Atlantis in our hands, ready to lift the puddle up out of the ground and into the wheelbarrow.

"Remember, don't spill it or else we'll have to bring back a whole bushel of wheelbarrows for all the other puddles we make," Jeremy warned. "We could end up being here all night cleaning up Atlantis' puddles. By the way, I had the King announce that an earthquake might happen tonight, so the Mer would bolt down everything like statues, tables, etc."

I let out a deep breath. We had one shot. "This is crazy."

Ignoring my crazy comment, he continued. "Now, on the count of three, you knock off the last bit of dirt keeping Atlantis rooted to the ground. I can hold it up but you have to help me lift it into the wheelbarrow. We need to move slowly and steadily." He took a deep breath and we counted to three at the same time.

"One...two...three." We grunted and groaned until we had the puddle in the air. The water licked the edges, causing me to sweat with nervousness. As soon as Atlantis was no longer in the ground, the oak tree area lost its enchantment. It didn't look as magical as when I had seen it the first time. The moonlight's rays suddenly became duller, the leaves lost their lustre, flowers no longer bloomed, weeds began to sprout in various areas and the fireflies flew away. Suddenly, the hole we had dug filled in as tiny trees began to grow into the empty space and bats came out into the night. Cautiously, we set Atlantis into the wheelbarrow, filling soil underneath and around it until it sat inside snugly.

"Jeremy, look at it! There is *no way* we will be able to lift the wheelbarrow into the back of the truck and not spill the water, not even if I drive at a snail's pace. Look how close we came to spilling it just by putting it into the wheelbarrow," I cried. "This is impossible!" I wanted to kick the wheelbarrow. "What we need is some kind of plastic barrier to keep the water in and a smaller container. Come with me. We need more supplies. Let's hide our stuff and we'll be back in half an hour, 40 minutes tops," I said, thinking about a nearby house that had a lot of junk lying around the backyard.

"You want us to leave Atlantis just sitting here in a wheelbarrow for anyone to come and take?"

"Jeremy, I know you don't want to leave Atlantis here where it's vulnerable, but what choice do we have? You and I both know it's not going to make it up the mountain if we can't keep the puddle from spilling. I need your help."

"I'm sorry, but I can't just leave my whole world lying in a filthy contraption with one wheel among humans," he said with cheek. "There must be another way."

"None that I can think of," I said uneasily.

"I'm not leaving," he stated firmly.

I threw my hands up in the air. There was just no pleasing this merman. "Fine, I'll do it myself." I marched off towards the lights in the distance, leaving Jeremy in the small grouping of trees. *A wheelbarrow! What was I thinking? You couldn't even roll it without spilling water.*

Green floodlights filled the Wilson's backyard, making the area extremely creepy. Mr. Wilson was a mechanic who worked out of his garage in the backyard. He was also a notorious hoarder. Old cars and mountains of car parts surrounded the area. I looked around searching for his German Sheppard, Spike, but didn't see him anywhere. He was a mean looking thing that guarded their property. I realized if a cop drove by I could be charged for trespassing, but went ahead anyway, opening their gate and sliding into the backyard. A branch snapped under my foot and a squirrel that had been sleeping on a branch right above my head stared at me with his beady eyes causing me to jump. *Fiddlesticks!* I let out a breath of relief. *Pull it together, Felicity.* There was a lot of metal in the yard, but not any plastic. Not seeing anything, I lifted his doormat to find a key and unlocked his garage. The days of my short-lived babysitting career when I was in grade 9 paid off.

As I shined a flashlight into the garage, I could see tons of crap lying everywhere. I didn't see how I was going to be able to find what I was looking for in there. That's when I spotted it. A large bucket was flipped over in the corner, about as round and deep as the puddle, a perfect fit, hopefully. Handles occupied each end, making it easy for two people to carry. I found a piece of plastic that was long, flat and mouldable. I could wrap it around the bucket after the puddle was placed in it to keep the water from spilling over the edges when it was moved, locking the water in. I grabbed the duct tape that was sitting on the lawn mower and knew it would keep the plastic that was wrapped around the bucket from sliding off.

I squeezed through the door of the garage, carrying my treasures careful not to make any noise as I locked up. *If this bucket was the right size, it would make our job a lot easier.* Sunrise would soon be here and I was starting to panic. I didn't want to leave Jeremy alone much longer. I heard a noise by the back door. A blackish brown German Shepard was snarling at me. His doggy door was swinging wildly as I was confronted with the demon dog. Drool dripped from his mouth, slopping onto the deck.

"Crap!" I stared at the snarling little pest and clutched my items tightly in preparation to run. "Nice doggy," I said in a calm voice. "Good doggy." I edged my way slowly towards the front gate. He sprinted towards me, barking ferociously. Lights went on in the house as I ran towards the gate, fumbling with the latch to get out. I felt his teeth sink into my pant leg, just missing my calf. I kicked out, sending him flying, as my heart pumped rapidly, just barely making it out before I slammed the door in Spike's face and took off into the night.

I ran to the puddle and there was Jeremy. "Are you okay?" He cupped his hands around my face and I pulled my face out of his hands. Just because he was here didn't mean I wasn't apprehensive of him. This could all be some ploy to get the puddle moved and then stop caring about me. I still didn't forget how he had treated me on my final days.

I huffed as I caught my breath. "Just peachy," I winced, thinking that my torn pant leg could have been my calf.

"What happened?" Jeremy inquired.

"Damn dog tried to kill me."

Jeremy started to laugh. "Those tiny things that humans walk? You're scared of them? You fought the Kraken!"

"Yeah, well, you would have been scared, too," I said defensively. I walked towards the wheelbarrow. "Any bogey monsters sneaking about, officer?" I joked.

Jeremy was strangely silent and had a serious look on his face. "I'm sorry I left you in Atlantis. I heard you and your father talking about Jesse and how he was going to tell him that you two were no longer an item."

"Jesse," I said sadly, knowing I had taken the coward's way out by getting my father to do my dirty work. "He was a very close friend of mine. After everyone banished me from Atlantis, I thought I'd never see you again. You hated me. Then he kissed me and I felt something. A very tiny something and I thought that if I stayed with him maybe it would get stronger. It didn't." I sensed that a lot of questions were running through his mind about Jesse, but he stayed silent. "Come on, we can talk about this later. This isn't the right time or place."

We looked at the puddle and measured using our hands to see if it would fit the bucket. We removed the dirt shakily from around the wheelbarrow, using our fingertips to set the puddle into the bucket gently. It was a perfect fit. I wrapped the plastic around the edge of the bucket to protect the water from spilling out and we finished taping the edges with duct tape. We each grabbed a handle and slowly carried it to the truck.

"Don't put it in the back of the truck. I don't want to take any chances of spilling it. Let's put in on the floor between my legs to keep it from moving around. The bucket isn't that big."

"Sounds good to me," I commented, wishing I had thought of that. We set the puddle down and Jeremy opened the truck's passenger door as I shifted the seat back as far as it could go. He got him and the puddle situated, then I ran to the bed of the truck and threw in the wheelbarrow and shovels.

I started the truck and backed out slowly, glancing nervously at the water swishing around in the bucket, glad the duct tape was holding up. Jeremy had the bucket on the floor and started to fiddle with the radio.

"What does this do?" That's when Jeremy found the volume button and cranked it. Out came ear-shattering country tunes. I punched the FM station to something else. The truck stopped shaking from the vibrations of the music as I lowered the volume.

I noticed for the first time that we were caked with dirt - all over our faces, arms and even in our hair - and I laughed. "We look like we just popped out of the ground," I said. I merged onto a country road, making sure my stops were smooth and slow so no water would spill. I realized we were actually doing this and could be successful. For the first time that night, I relaxed. The mountains were just outside of town. It would take us about a half-hour, since I was going well under the speed limit. I wasn't taking any chances of hitting a deer with the truck or having a tire hit a hole and causing Atlantis to spill. Jeremy was talking to me non-stop about everything in this world that he found interesting, keeping me awake as I felt my eyelids turn to lead.

"Jeremy, it's great that you want to know more about Earth. When I was in Atlantis, I never got to ask any questions or else I would have been exposed as a human in an instant." I had to admit I did love seeing his eyes light up whenever he saw something new and different. "If I had asked questions and done all the things you're doing here when I was back in Atlantis, I would have been spotted a mile away."

"But that's why I have you here, to keep me from doing stupid things. And your trees are so much different than my trees. The textures are different, the leaves change colour and they fall to the ground. That's what your Dad told me. Ours just look like green puffballs with starfish in them. Good to eat but not much fun to pick, stubborn things. Thanks to you, the dome is down and, by destroying the darkness, we can now have orchards again full of trees. The pickers get paid a lot of sand dollars. Are those the mountains?" Jeremy asked.

"Yep. That's them, alright."

"They're huge. It's going to take us forever to get up there."

"Not if I have anything to say about it." I put the truck in four-wheel drive and sped up. "If you went to The Surface when you were in Atlantis, you would have seen underwater mountains just as high."

"You visited The Surface?" he asked, shocked.

"Er…yeah," I said. "With Sebastian," I added. "Wait until

the mer know that you entered the human realm. The Surface won't compare to what you've seen on land."

He stared out the window bitterly. "I'm forbidden to say anything. It's going to be hard to keep quiet. Only the King and you will be able to hear my stories. This was a mission between the King and me. If the merpeople knew about it then more and more of them would want to see this place. We can't have our kind just popping up out of the mountains. It would draw too much attention. You saw how the humans reacted with just me in their midst. The King gave me something to help conceal Atlantis."

"Wait, what mission?"

"To save Atlantis," he stated matter of factly.

I resisted the urge to slam on the brakes. "Did you come for me or did you come to save Atlantis? Was I just a detour that seemed to work in the King's favour?" I asked, my mind thinking back to Jesse and how I might have made a big mistake.

He looked at me, surprised. "Tidalwave told me everything and then I went to the King. There wasn't much I could do, Crystal. He has the Forbidden Area monitored by six guards. After the war, the King promoted me to be one of his guards. I couldn't go against his orders, even if I wanted to. I'm the youngest mer soldier in Atlantis history! I was the first one to volunteer when the decision was made to save Atlantis. Sebastian and I had to fight it out to decide who went. He discovered the truth about your past, but I had your whole love pearl inside me. Plus, I knew more about humans than he did. I came to find you and save Atlantis. I've missed you. I was angry, confused and even frightened when I had to escort you to the chopping stone. I've never had my heart pulled in so many directions at one time. Then you were saved. Tidalwave came and told me everything. Now I'm glad the King didn't have you killed. Half-mer or not, I *do* care about you."

I calmed down once I heard the truth. There would be time to sort through my feelings later. Why did Jeremy have to be so bound by duty all the time? I pressed on the gas, trying to stay focused. "As I recall you were pretty excited to see my body without a head attached to it." I spoke quietly remembering the pain the comment had brought. "And now you suddenly care about me."

He sat their silently. "I'm sorry. My feelings are so mixed up."

"Bull! It has nothing to do with feelings, it's a matter of right and wrong. Now that I'm half mer everything is suppose to be perfect now?" I questioned.

"What do you want me to say Crystal? That I'm an idiot and I was a big jerk. That I regret every day the way that I treated you. That from here on out I'm going to try and be better even if you are half human."

"Yeah maybe something around those lines is a good starter." I said harshly. "Not everyday your friend wishes for your death." The mountain came into view and I heaved a sigh of relief. "About bloody time," I mumbled, as I stopped the truck gently at the bottom of the mountain. Traffic would soon be coming out onto the roads and, worse, there would be cops hanging around, looking for speeders going to work.

I pulled into a parking lot designated for hikers. "You ready?" Jeremy asked, as his vigor returned.

"It's now or never." As we both forgot about our previous conversation at the prospect of going home.

He hopped out of the truck, careful to avoid knocking the bucket over, and we both reached in and grabbed a handle. We took the hikers' path because it was the easiest. We listened to see if we could hear anyone or anything on the path, but all was quiet. "Are we close to the Blue Creek waterfall yet?" he asked.

"Soon," I said. "I can hear it faintly from here." We continued on as bright blue and purple flowers sprouted up from the ground, glowing in the sunrise as they created a path into the forest. It was as though the flowers were directing us.

"Come on!" He smiled, trying to stay calm so he wouldn't toss the water around. I smiled back as we left the path. After we passed each flower, it disappeared into a wisp of smoke and the vegetation that had been disturbed reappeared. The flowers ended at a cave. Trees and shrubs concealed the opening and a stream ran nearby. The cave tunnelled deep into the ground, giving me the creeps, but Jeremy went down to the bottom, unafraid to check it out with a flashlight. He came back to the opening and tugged slightly on the bucket, causing me to follow until we hit the bottom.

"So, what do we do? Plop it on the ground and that's that?" I asked.

"Yup, pretty much." He summed it up by setting the bucket down on the spot he liked. We both realized it was one of the last steps until we were back in our golden city of glory.

"But, there's no soil," I said sceptically.

"Let the magic do the work. Here, help me lift it." We

picked up Atlantis carefully and set it on the hard ground. Miraculously, the bucket split in two and a hole appeared, making a perfect fit. The cave started to glow brightly. As the water's reflection leapt across the walls of the cave, a strong burst of wind passed through, clearing the area of dirt, grime and cobwebs, along with the bucket and duct tape. The opening of the cave began to knit itself shut, making the entrance impossible to find. "This will have to do until I talk to the King about it. Then we should be able to devise a better plan."

"I will not be left out of the decisions when it comes to the puddle. Now that I belong, I want to be treated like everyone else. I should have equal rights."

"Okay, okay. I didn't think it mattered."

"Didn't think it mattered? I left my Dad to help save this place. You have no idea how hard that was. I wanted to bring him but I knew the King wouldn't let me - and he wouldn't leave his new family. So, don't tell me this doesn't matter to me!" I started to realize that, once I did this, I wouldn't see my Dad for a long, long time. "Listen, sorry about that. I just…"

"It's okay. You don't have to explain. I can't imagine the pain you're going through right now. It was a stupid thing for me to say."

"No, no - I'm going to have to get used to it. All Dad wanted was for me to be happy. We stood back and admired our handiwork. The puddle looked like it was never moved. "Not one single drop," I said proudly, satisfied with our accomplishment. "You first, Jeremy." He gave me one of his looks.

"Don't worry, I'll be right in after you."

He smiled and reached to give me a hug but then thought better of it. "Thanks for saving Atlantis a third time. Many Merpeople will not know what you have done for this city, but I will - and so will the King." He pencil-dived into the puddle and down he went.

I realized that if something happened, if Atlantis ever had to surface, the merpeople would need money to survive in this world. I took out the jewels and shells Sebastian had given me and placed them in some of the crevasses in the walls. The place was all glittery and flashy when I was done. I took the lily out and set it in the puddle's water. If Dad ever found this cave, he would see the lily and know. I also set the four flashlights down right beside the puddle. I smiled to myself and jumped into the water.

I landed in the vortex. Jeremy was there waiting for me, along with the King's closest guards who, apparently, already knew about the mission. The King was absent and Jeremy informed me Sebastian had spread the word about my half-mer background across the city. "What took you so long?"

"Just, you know, taking one last look around." I slung the backpack onto my shoulder and swam towards him. My tail hit something. I swished away some of the sand and picked it up. I smiled at the baseball in my hand. Good ol' Dad must have snuck out and tossed it in the puddle before we dug up Atlantis. I held it to my chest lovingly. I would always remember playing baseball as one of the best memories I had growing up with my father. Tossing the ball in the air, I thought about what my future would hold in Atlantis, all the adventures I'd have. And, with a twinkle in my eye, I pictured myself teaching these merpeople a thing or two about how to play one of the best games in the world.

Epilogue

2 weeks later…

I sat on top of Tidalwave, watching in horror as a competitor was tossed out of the black hole. So far, only 25 of the 50 participants had completed the obstacle course. *What had I gotten myself into?*

"*Crystal, Crystal…let go! You're hurting me.*"

"Whoops, sorry." I lifted my hands off Tidalwave's skin and saw ten half-moon imprints from my nails. "I think I'm a little nervous."

"*Just a little? Trust me, you have nothing to worry about. You've dealt with worse.*"

I stared off into the distance at the obstacle course they called the Swirling Deathtrap of Doom. It didn't take a genius to figure out why they decided to call it that. There were five obstacles we had to complete and it had already been a long day of competition. I stared at the five water tornados in a row, reminding me of the vortex trap in the Forbidden Area. I swallowed. The rapids were the second obstacle and they looked like massive ripples in the ocean, as if there was a storm. Then the two hardest were left until the end, the slingshot and the black hole. I shuddered just looking at them. I saw someone shoot out the side of the black hole. Contestant number 49 and his dolphin went spiralling off course, unable to make it past the finish line.

The announcer blared, "And competitor number 49 is disqualified for not completing the course. Better luck next time. Up next is Crystal Clearwater."

I glanced at the crowd as they cheered me on, suddenly a hero instead of an enemy since my return. Hard to believe that, just a few weeks ago, they were screaming for my death. Most of the merpeople's views on my human heritage had changed drastically since they discovered my Mom was a mermaid, but there were still a select few who would probably never accept me. Nonetheless, I had already settled nicely into my new home, making lots of friends and teaching a class at the school on humans.

I felt Tidalwave's anxiousness to start the race as I hopped on and got into standard dolphin rider position.

"This is going to be fun," Tidalwave said. *"Think we will be able to beat Jeremy and Shell's scores?"*

I smiled as I felt my natural competitiveness creep into my system. Jeremy was in tenth place and Shell was in fourth. "Well, we can always try." I patted him on the head as I felt my heart speed up at the mere mention of his name. Jeremy and I weren't together, but it didn't mean we couldn't have feelings for one another. He was no longer dating Shell, which gave me hope but, for now, I was glad to have him as a friend. He needed time and space to sort through his feelings for me, and I needed to try and put the past behind me. After what we had been through, just being near him was enough to keep me happy.

"Here comes Crystal Clearwater, riding Tidalwave the Magnificent!" blared the announcer.

I smiled to myself, thinking back to my dream of becoming a professional baseball player and hearing those words from an announcer in front of a huge crowd. I held my head high at everything I had accomplished in my short life and took a deep breath. This was my favourite part. I loved the anticipation and the unknown outcome of a game. We swam towards the five tornados in a row. Speed was the key for this competition, as well as skill. There was a time limit of no more than fifteen minutes to complete the whole course.

Water was swirling and flinging sand in my eyes. Immediately, I dropped down and grabbed both of Tidalwave's pectoral fins as we leaped into the first tornado. I felt us go around in circles like a corkscrew and my mind turn to mush as my head began to throb. Tidalwave searched for a weak break in the tornado to jump into the second one. Around and around we went as we were twirled into oblivion. Each tornado increased in speed. I realized this competition was not for beginners. I felt my stomach start to heave as Tidalwave jumped out of the last tornado, almost causing me to lose my grip as we tried to regain our balance.

That was the tricky part of the course. A merperson and dolphin could spend the whole fifteen minutes trying to find the weak spot in the tornados. If they went too soon, they'd risk being thrown in the wrong direction. Wait too long and you'd be too dizzy to know what was up or what was down. I estimated that we had only spent five minutes. The rapids needed at least four minutes; it was where the most points were collected. The slingshot wouldn't take long and the rest of the time could be used up in the black hole. We should be able to make it in time if we hurried.

Everything was a blur when Tidalwave powered towards the rapids, giving me time to settle my spinning head. Moby Dick and Rhinestone were waving both their tails, causing massive waves in the water. *Great!* Seeing this brought to mind how humans surfed on the waves. If the two whales provided some good waves, we might be able to find that one perfect one that would give us our big clincher. This sport required precision, patience and timing - three traits I had never excelled in. I stood up on Tidalwave as we dipped and dodged a few big waves, riding the currents, doing spins and slides, and managing to sneak in a quick back flip as we flipped in sync with one another. A big wave came upon us and I rebalanced. It was a huge one, large enough to send us straight towards the slingshot, which is what the judges were looking for. We flew towards the slingshot bubbles and waves pushing against our backs. It looked just like calm water ahead, but I knew from watching other contestants it was anything but. Once you hit that wall, the whole thing bent inwards like a rubber band. The problem was you never knew when you were about to hit the wall. There was a slight jolt as I felt the pull like an undertow. I knew we had to make this shot count. It had to give us enough power for us to get to the black hole. The water coiled. We were pulled downward on an angle. Right when I thought it was going to swallow us, it spit us out like a bad seed, hardly giving me time to grab hold of Tidalwave's dorsal fin. I felt like I was hanging onto a rocket as we headed in the direction of the final obstacle.

The black hole was tiny. Aiming for the centre of this dark dot in the water was going to be tricky at the rate we were going. It was a mesmerizing sight as the black water slowly churned. Feeling the pace slacken a little as we got farther away from the slingshot, I stood up carefully. We had come so close, I didn't want to botch it now and get disqualified like the last contestant, all because I had lost my balance.

While you're in the black hole, the whole time you spin around and then, suddenly, the merperson gets sucked up into nowhere while your dolphin waits for you, continually circling the hole. While he waits, your job is to find your way out of the hole, knowing that your dolphin was close by which should in turn prevent panic. This part was to test the bond of you and your dolphin. So far they had fetched ten merpeople out of the black hole who could not find there way out.

We entered the dark opening. Around and around we went, knowing this would be tricky. Each full circle that I completed while not grabbing hold of Tidalwave's fin was a bonus. As well, each round the hole decreased in size, getting smaller and smaller as we completed a ring. I felt myself snapped up and off Tidalwave. The crowd disappeared and quiet took over as darkness surrounded me. It was not a feeling I liked and, having seen the darkness, it was something I no longer wanted to be a part of. I had destroyed the darkness in Atlantis where no red eyes could lurk and now it was a much better place.

The King had also decided to leave the puddle in the cave, which gave me a small hope that, maybe in time, I could convince him to let my father come and live with me or let me go and visit him. Once April and the twins passed away, there would be nothing to keep him in the human world. I would talk to the King, but that would not be for many years to come. I closed my eyes and took a deep breath as I felt myself stripping away precious time. That's when I saw it - a tiny pinhole of light. As I swam towards it, the hole became bigger and bigger, allowing me to see Tidalwave doing his laps and searching the water for me frantically. The black hole didn't allow us to echolocate, but somehow I felt like we were still communicating. I waited until he came closer and pushed off with my tail, using all my might to grab onto his fin, hoping my impact wouldn't steer him off-course.

I whooped in success as we flew up and out of the black hole's dark, churning waters and executed three front flips high above the crowd. The audience cheered as I grabbed back on and headed to the finish line. This was what it must feel like to fly. I had finally found a sport that was like no other. Dare I say better than football and even baseball?

"And in fifth place is Crystal Clearwater and Tidalwave the Magnificent!" The crowd went wild over the announcement.

"Fifth place. Not bad for our first time," I grinned at Tidalwave, thinking of how proud my father would have been. I wished he was here to see me and meet Tidalwave and all my friends. It was a moment I'd never forget. If only my Dad had been there to share it with me. To me, this is my "Neverland." Finally, I belong somewhere. I'm home.

Never Stop Believing...

Author's Note

This was my very first novel, which I wrote back in Grade 9 - and it all started from a dream. That is mainly why I wanted the opening chapter to begin the way it did, to represent how it all began.

I had been watching Peter Pan, the non-animated version, and that night I had an amazing dream but didn't remember it. I only knew four things: a puddle, a mermaid's tail, Jeremy Sumpter (the actor) and a streak of gold across water. A story started to form and the only way to get it out of my head and ease my pain was to write it down. It became much more than I had ever imagined it to be. It is how I became an author.

Peter Pan has always been a big influence on me because no one wants to grow up and I've always had a hard time accepting the fact that I can't be a kid forever. I still do. Wendy has to make a choice about which life she wants to lead: stay a child or grow up. It's a struggle many of us face, but in different ways.

The key to a good story can come from anywhere. I created mine from four things. With some imagination and determination, just think what you can do. I hope you all enjoyed reading the first novel I wrote, all those years ago.

www.ingramcontent.com/pod-product-compliance
Lightning Source LLC
Chambersburg PA
CBHW071855020726
47502CB00003B/757